NEVER DOUBT ME

S.R. GREY

This is a work of fiction. Names, characters, places, and incidents are products of the author's imagination or are used fictitiously and are not considered to be real. Any resemblance to actual events, locales, organizations, or persons, living or dead, is entirely coincidental.

Never Doubt Me (Judge Me Not #2)
Copyright © 2014 by S.R. Grey

Copy Editing: Ashley
Cover Design: Damonza
Print and E-book formatting: Benjamin at Awesome Book Layouts

ISBN-10: 0615964079
ISBN-13: 978-0615964072

S.R. GREY NOVELS

A Harbour Falls Mystery trilogy:

Harbour Falls

Willow Point

Wickingham Way

Judge Me Not series:

I Stand Before You

Never Doubt Me

CHAPTER ONE
CHASE

I hesitate, glancing from my fifteen-year-old runaway brother, Will, to his waiflike girlfriend, Cassie. But it's the woman who helps me keep my shit together, in situations as fucked up as the one I'm in tonight, who garners my full attention.

Kay Stanton. As my eyes linger on her, she sends the sweetest smile my way. I can't help but smile back.

Shit, I sometimes can't believe this demure beauty who works at the church down the road is the love of my life. I mean, damn, who would have ever expected someone like me—an ex-con with a drug-soaked past—to find love in the first place?

Certainly not me… But I did find love, and now I can't imagine life without her.

Kay has learned me well enough to know I'm stalling by focusing on her. She nods encouragingly at Will and Cassie while flipping her long chestnut-brown hair over her shoulder.

"Okay, okay," I mumble under my breath, smiling.

Knowing I have Kay's support no matter what strengthens my resolve, but, damn, I wish I could read her thoughts. Then I'd know exactly what her take is on this crazy situa-

Never Doubt Me

tion, which would be helpful before I open my mouth and say the wrong thing.

But is there really a choice here?

Not that I can see.

As it stands, I am still coming to grips with the fact that dear little bro ran away from home. He traveled thousands of miles from Nevada to Ohio with his sixteen-year-old girl-friend in tow, and they showed up on the doorstep of my farmhouse, like, ten minutes ago. So here he is. My brother is in Harmony Creek, standing next to Cassie, while her corn-silk hair blows gently in the nighttime summer breeze. The old yellow porch light bathes Will and Cassie's faces in a warm kind of glow, making them look even younger than they are.

Will, catching me red-handed as I stare at him and his girlfriend, says, "So, what's it gonna be, Chase? Can we crash here for a few weeks or not?"

I sigh, thinking, *Christ, how did we all end up here?* My brother and his girl should be out having fun, not on the run. My eyes slide briefly to Cassie. She's the real reason they're here in Harmony Creek...instead of back in Las Vegas where they belong.

Okay, everyone has waited long enough.

I take a deep breath and announce my decision. "This is what's going to happen." I point to Will and Cassie. "You two can't stay here. You're runaways and you're both under eighteen. I am not going back to prison for illegally harbor-ing your teenage asses." I say to Will specifically, "Sorry, bro, but you have to go home."

Will curses and grumbles under his breath, "This is such bullshit."

Conversely, Cassie's shoulders relax. If I were to guess, I'd venture that she's mostly relieved, confirming what I've been thinking all along—this cross-country escapade was my brother's harebrained scheme from the start. I have no doubt this "running away" is just part one of his big plan to "save" his girlfriend from her sleazy stepfather's inappropriate advances.

Will's intentions are honorable, true, but his execution—running away—is for shit.

Before Will can argue my decision, I tell him he needs to call our mother. "She's worried sick about you, kid."

Will shrugs his shoulders and shoots me a fuck-you expression. "I can't call Mom," he retorts. "My phone died hours ago. And we didn't have a charger that worked in Cassie's car."

"Not a problem," I shoot back, complete with a smirk to rival the one plastered on little bro's smug face.

"Oh yeah, how's that not a problem? You got a charger up your ass?"

I bite my tongue, hold my cell phone out to him. "I was talking with Mom before you got here. Now, quit being such a smart-ass and call your mother."

Will hesitates, so I jiggle the phone in front of his face. "Take it, Will." My tone is deadly serious. "Mom needs to know you're safe. She can book a couple of flights for tomorrow for you and Cassie. You two can spend the night here. I'll call off work and drive you to the airport in the morning."

My brother's eyes burn hot, fiery green, just like our mother's do when she's pissed.

"What about Cassie's car?" My brother gestures wildly

3

to the sporty, too-fucking-nice-for-a-kid car parked in my gravel driveway. "We can't just leave it here, like, forever."

Will is stalling. He knows when he makes that call to Mom, his reckless runaway days are done.

"We'll figure that shit out later." I sigh and rake my fingers through my hair, pulling on the ends for good measure. This kid is going to be the death of me. "Just make the call before I run out of patience."

Suddenly, Will hurls the phone in my direction, yelling, "Fuck you, Chase. I'm not calling anyone."

Unfortunately for Will, his outburst lacks effect. My reflexes are too sharp, and I catch the cell, no problem. If the phone had hit me and fallen to the solid-wood slats that make up the porch floor, it surely would have shattered into a million pieces.

No doubt that was Will's intent, prompting me to mumble, "Little shit," under my breath.

Will hears my comment and starts to go off on how this house shouldn't even belong to my ungrateful, undeserving ass. "I have as much right to this house as you do"— he shakes his head, disgusted, and adds a sarcastic—"*big brother.*"

"Whatever, Will."

"It's not right," he persists as he gets right up in my face.

Well, he tries to get all up in my grill. But little brother has to stand on his toes to reach eye level with me. He's not quite six foot two.

I press my lips together and shake my head. "Better turn it down a notch, baby brother," I warn.

"Or what?" Will snaps.

Despite the fact he's brave enough to give me this much

grief, I notice he does indeed take a step back, maybe even two.

But he's not done yapping, not yet. "Dad would have wanted us to share what was left when Gram died," he continues, gesturing wildly to the surrounding property, even though the moon is hidden and you can't see much more beyond the house and the driveway. "She had no right to give all of this to just you."

"Actually, she did, Will. This was *her* farmhouse, *her* property. None of this belonged to Dad. Let's not forget her dear Jack—our fucking father—offed his ass before anyone could ever give him anything."

Will screams that I'm an asshole, and Kay, who's moved so close to me that I feel her warmth, touches my arm. "Chase," she murmurs, clearly disappointed I've chosen to go *there*.

Shit, maybe Kay is right. I probably shouldn't bring Dad into this clusterfuck of a conversation. Then again, how can I not? As I see it, none of this shit would be happening if my father hadn't killed himself seven years ago. Will probably wouldn't be a runaway, and I wouldn't be the guy always trying to fill the void my father left in his wake.

Like I'm fucking capable of shit like that. Hell, I'm only three months out of prison, another indirect consequence of Dad's selfish act. I have no doubt if my father hadn't taken the easy way out, this family would have remained solid. Jack Gartner's suicide broke the wills and hearts of those who loved him most.

Life binds. Death shatters.

My mom tried to pick up her broken pieces with gambling and men, while I filled the gaping hole that had been

punched in my heart with drugs, fighting, and loose wom-
en. And Will, though he exhibited outward signs of depres-
sion for a while, mostly chose to keep his shit internalized.

He never really acted out. Well, until recently.

Will's eyes narrow. "I don't need to listen to this shit,"
he spits, before he spins around and thunders down the
porch steps.

"Hey, wait." My tone has softened, since I'm beginning
to feel like a tool.

I'm trying here, I am, but Will's feet keep moving. When
he reaches the base of the steps, he suddenly stops. Slowly,
he turns to face me, like maybe he's forgotten something.

Apparently, he has. He has more crap to spew.

"You know, Chase," he begins, "you can bring Dad into
this all-l-l-l you want. But the fact remains that your fuck-
ups are no one's fault but your own. You made your own
decisions. No one shoved that shit you used to love so much
up your nose. No one made you run from the police the
night you got busted. That was all you, bro." He points at
me, shakes his head, disgusted. "And forty hits of E? Really,
man, how dumb could you have been?"

Will is challenging me, pushing my buttons. And it's
working. My fists clench at my sides, despite Kay running
her hand up and down my arm, trying in vain to calm me.

"You can hide out here in the country," Will continues,
"live in Gram's old farmhouse, work for the church down
the street"—he points in the direction of town and then to
Kay—"date the prettiest girl in town. But you're not fooling
anyone. You're still that guy, Chase, that guy who used to
fill his nose with blow. That guy who—"

Will doesn't get any further with his colorful diatribe. I

am down the steps and in his face in a heartbeat. "Care to go on?" I snap, eyes blazing.

Will shuts the fuck up. In fact, everything quiets. Or maybe it's just my imagination. Most likely, my boiling blood has distorting my hearing. But I swear even the crickets that were chirping in the background seconds ago have fallen silent, like they're transfixed by this family drama.

Will presses his lips together, puffs up a little. He tries to look tough, but, really, he's shaking in his scuffed black Chucks.

Kay has thankfully remained up on the porch with Cassie. Thank fuck she didn't follow me down the steps. I don't like her seeing this side of me, certainly not close up.

But when Will's girlfriend gasps and cries out, "Kay, please make them stop," I worry both girls will soon be in the fray.

I guess I've underestimated Kay, though. She apparently knows me well enough to realize I'd never actually hurt my brother.

Calmly, she says to Cassie, "Will and Chase are fine, sweetie." After a pause, she murmurs, more to herself than to Cassie, "They need this."

Oh, we do, Kay, we so very much do. It's been a long time coming.

While Kay and Cassie remain on the porch, Will takes one huge step away from me. But when I take two steps forward, my brother and I are once again inches apart.

I assess my brother. He's changed in so many ways. Will has filled out a lot; he's not the gangly kid he used to be. His shoulders are wide, and the muscles in his arms are corded and tight. He's still pretty lean, though, and I can tell he'd come out on the other end of a fight pretty much fucked up. Not that he'll be getting any fight from me tonight. My goal is to intimidate him a bit, make him start showing me some goddamn respect.

Will tries one final time, like a last stand, to stare me down. "Hit me," he urges with a cocky up-tilt of his chin.

I shake my head and resist the urge to laugh. "Not gonna happen. But I give you props for having some big-ass balls, baby brother."

"Quit calling me that," Will hisses.

I hold my ground and he, no surprise, capitulates.

But he tosses out this last, "Shit, I've got nothing more to say to you anyway. In fact, we're out of here." He turns his back on me and beckons to his girlfriend. "Come on, Cass."

Will doesn't know it, but he's not going anywhere. I grab the back of his T-shirt and spin him around roughly.

And that's when he takes a swing at me.

Easily, I lean out of the arc of Will's fist and he misses me by a mile. Stumbling a little, he winces, making him look more like ten than fifteen.

"Will," I whisper.

Despite the fact he just tried to hit me, all I feel is compassion, regret, sadness. Like flash cards flipping in my head, a barrage of memories starring cute little-kid Will, small and uncoordinated, block out everything else. My little brother may be growing up, but in so many ways, he'll always be the little boy who tried like crazy—but continually failed—to keep up with me.

I'm still feeling bad for him when he takes a second swing.

Doesn't matter, since, once again, I am much too quick

for him. I catch my brother's fist, long before he makes contact with his intended target, my jaw.

I guess Will's second attempt to punch me is enough for Kay. She screams out my name, and out of the corner of my eye, I catch her starting down the porch steps. Her action, however, prompts Cassie to follow, and Kay has no choice but to stop on the second to the last step in order to stop Will's girlfriend from racing to him.

With Kay and Cassie occupied, I turn my attention back to Will.

Shit, there's real fear in his eyes. He must think I'm about to lay him out. "Not really the plan," I mutter under my breath.

I take a step back, and it's then that I realize Will's hand is still in my grasp and I'm crushing four of his five fingers.

"Sorry," I mumble as I let go.

My brother stumbles back and rubs his no doubt aching appendages. "You're such a dick," he croaks. "I fucking hate you."

"Well, I fucking love you," I retort, "you dumb little shit."

Will's rendered speechless. But he shouldn't be. He can deny it all he wants, but he knows in his heart that I love him right now, today, as much as I ever have. Probably more. Just because we're not getting along at the moment doesn't mean I don't care for him. And just because I was locked up in prison and missed four years of his life sure as shit doesn't mean my love for him just up and faded.

Just like in the past, I'd do anything for my brother. Despite my big proclamation when he first arrived that I wasn't going back to prison as a result of his runaway antics, in all truthfulness, I would. In a heartbeat.

Hell, my criminal career began with me attempting to help Will.

When I was seventeen, our fractured family found an apartment near the Vegas Strip, and with Dad gone, Mom took to disappearing for days at a time. Money ran out quickly during her absences, and Will and I often went hungry. Luckily, there was a convenience store around the corner from our hovel. So when the choice I faced was let my brother starve…or steal…

Well, let's just say I wasn't about to let my brother suffer.

I'd hustle over to the convenience store and stuff my backpack with junk food while the store clerk's head was turned. Then, back at the apartment, I'd dump my loot out on the two twin beds in the tiny room we shared. Will and I would kick back and feast on all the chips and candy I'd lifted. Since it was always fucking hot as hell in our room (the air conditioner in the living room never quite reached the back of the apartment), I'd open the one lone window to let in some air.

Will and I would sit on the floor, crunch away in relative silence, and wait for that one small breeze. Our eyes would remain glued to the one thing decorating the otherwise blank walls—a sketch of a tree house I'd drawn for my brother when he was five. That sketch was our indicator of better things to come. We'd wait and wait for the sketch to start flittering. When the piece of paper would move at last, even just a flutter, Will and I would whoop and high-five, like we'd just won the fucking lottery or something.

Trust me, it was like we *had* hit the jackpot. When you're

in hell, it's the little things everyone takes for granted that mean the most.

"Hey." I kick at one of Will's shoes, adding another dusty scuff mark. "Remember that tree house sketch? The one I drew for you way back when, the one you taped to the wall in that shit apartment we had."

Will's green eyes slowly meet mine. He purses his lips and nods.

Encouraged, I continue, "Remember how we used to watch for the sketch to move to see if we were going to get lucky and catch a breeze?"

"Yeah, I remember," my brother responds softly.

But when I add, "You used to say that sketch gave you hope," he quickly looks away.

"You still got it?" I press.

"Shit, Chase, enough with the trip down memory lane." Will puffs up his chest and tries to act nonchalant. "That stupid sketch is long gone."

If that's true, then it saddens me that my brother didn't hang on to his hope. And maybe that thought makes Will a little sad, too, since I see tears brimming in his eyes.

I sigh, deflated. "Look, I don't want to fight."

Will swipes at his cheeks. "Me neither, Chase."

"What do you want to do?" I ask. "How are we going to fix this?"

Will jerks his chin toward the cell in my hand. "Give me the phone." He sighs. "I'll call Mom."

I pass the phone to Will while he brushes wayward strands of dark blond hair, the exact same shade as our mother's, away from his forehead. He then calls the parent he took after the most. I immediately hear our mother on the other end, giving him hell. I turn around to give Will a modicum of privacy, and just as I do, Cassie runs the rest of the way down the steps.

The girl is so focused on getting to Will that she practically slams right into me.

"Whoa, hold up there," I say, steadying her with my hands on her slumped shoulders.

"Sorry," she mumbles, and then she glances up at me with sorrowful blue eyes.

"No need to apologize," I say gently. "You may as well stay right where you are, though. You're calling *your* mom next."

"Okay," she squeaks out.

Cassie lowers her head and stares down at her sandal-covered feet, while her long hair frames her ethereal features like a champagne-blond veil. She strikes me as vulnerable, fragile. Just tonight, I've seen enough interaction between her and my brother that it's clear Will has the upper hand in their relationship.

And that makes me want to check on something.

I jerk my head back to where Will is preoccupied on the phone. And then I ask Cassie, "My brother treats you right, yeah?"

"Of course," she says, like it's ridiculous to even pose such a question.

"Okay, okay"—I hold up my hands—"I was just checking."

Hell, I'm just relieved none of Will's recent acting out has manifested in his behavior towards Cassie. My brother can be pretty damn disrespectful when it comes to Mom, and it would kill me to hear he's started treating the other women in his life in the same shitty way.

While I'm thinking all of this, Kay walks over to where we're standing. She positions her body slightly in front of Cassie, so Cassie can't see when Kay frowns at me and mouths, "Go easy on her."

"I am," I mumble.

Kay obviously missed me checking with Cassie to make sure my brother is treating her right.

Oh well. I'll get Kay up to speed later. Right now I'm glancing over at Will to see if he's done talking with Mom.

He nods my way and wraps up with our mom. He steps back over to where we're all standing and hands me the phone. I pass it straight to Cassie. She takes the cell, presses a few keys, and then walks far enough away that she's out of hearing range.

I throw a parting glance to her turned back, shake my head, and then redirect my attention to Will. "What did Mom say?"

Kay steps forward, until she's next to me.

"We have to go back to Vegas, of course," Will says.

My brother lowers his gaze and kicks at the bottom step. He's retreated back into himself. I remind myself he's a mixed-up kid who's confused, moody, and frustrated. This running away has more to do with Cassie longing to escape a bad home situation than anything else. I'm pretty sure Will didn't really *want* to leave home. Things aren't perfect for him with Mom and her relatively new husband, Greg, but I know things are far better than they've been in ages. As for the Cassie situation, my brother won't tell me everything, but he's said enough throughout the past few weeks that it's clear Cassie's stepfather—some scumbag named Paul who her mother married not all that long ago—has been making her feel uncomfortable in her own home. And by uncomfortable, I mean the prick is hitting on her.

Will's mentioned, more than once, that Paul spouts off inappropriate remarks to Cassie, but only when her mother isn't around. Problem is, Cassie's mom has some high-flying career and works all the time. Cassie's biological father can't help—he died a few years back. In fact, it's that loss that helps bind Will and Cassie. They've both lost fathers, and from what Will's intimated, they find solace in their shared grief when they're together.

"Everything's going to be okay," I say to Will, feeling empathy for what he's ultimately trying to do—save Cassie from harm.

My brother grunts and kicks at the step again. "Sure, bro, whatever you say."

Cassie finishes her call and returns to where we're standing.

She hands me the phone, states resolutely, "My mom doesn't want the car staying here indefinitely. But she also doesn't want me and Will driving all the way back across the country alone."

"Why?" Will asks, turning to his girlfriend. "We did just fine getting here."

"What's this 'we' shit?" I interject, eyeing Will suspiciously.

Up to this point, I guess I just assumed Cassie drove the whole way since she's sixteen and has a driver's license—unlike Will.

I raise a questioning eyebrow when neither kid responds.

Cassie quickly glances away, but Will looks nothing short of fucking jubilant. Oh great, defiant-Will is back.

"What about it?" he challenges. "You got a problem with that?"

"You bet I do. You don't even have a driver's license, Will. You're only fifteen fucking years old."

Will has the nerve to find my comments amusing. At least, I assume he does, since he laughs and says, "Hate to break it to you, Chase, but I've known how to drive for a while now. Mom taught me last year. She took me out to the desert to practice, said it was like insurance, in case something, you know, happened and she couldn't drive."

Jesus. What am I supposed to do with that? I have no idea, so I just let it go.

Cassie leans into Will. "Hey," she whispers. "My mom's flying out of Vegas tonight. She has some business-thing in New York City. Her meetings run through Thursday, but she can come get us on Friday. She's going to fly into Pittsburgh and take a taxi here. Then she'll drive us back to Vegas in my car."

"Whoa, wait," I chime in. Pointing to Will, I say, "Mom expects you home tomorrow, right? Friday is four days away. And counting the drive time back, you won't get home till sometime next week."

Will and Cassie exchange a look. *These two,* I think, shaking my head.

"Mom won't care," Will insists, looking nothing short of bothered by my commentary. "As long as she knows I'm definitely coming home. And if Mrs. Sutter is driving, Mom

15

will like that even more. Cassie's mom offers, like, parental supervision or some stupid shit that you know Mom will be all over."

I shake my head, but I can't really argue. With the car situation, Cassie's mom's plan does make more sense. Our mom will like that plan better too, for the exact reasons Will mentioned.

"Where are you supposed to stay, honey, if you're not leaving until Friday?" I overhear Kay asking Cassie.

Shit, I hadn't even considered that not-so-minor detail.

"Um, my mom said I can use my credit card to book us hotel rooms. She said to get two, but one should be enough. Will can just stay with me in my room." Cassie slips a sly little smile to my brother, who actually has the balls to wink at her.

"Uh, I don't think so," I interrupt, quickly putting the kibosh on what would surely be a teenage sex-soaked few days.

Shit, you'd think these two would be sexed out. I'm sure they got it on all the time throughout their cross-country trip. But then I remember my brother is a Gartner, and well, that goes without saying…

Both kids give me a look like I'm the biggest buzzkill. Too fucking bad. I accept that my brother and his girlfriend have sex, but that doesn't mean I'm on board with the running-off-to-stay-in-a-hotel-alone scenario. Not when they can stay in my house, under my supervision. Will claims he and Cassie diligently use protection, but my brother has a tendency to twist the truth. And frankly I don't care to become an uncle anytime soon. So, yeah…

Will groans, aggravated, but I am not budging on this one.

"You two can stay here." I hand Will the phone again. "Call Mom and tell her what's going on. Catch her before she books your flights to Vegas."

My brother starts to grab the phone, but I hold it just out of his grasp.

"What now?" he huffs.

"Just…no funny stuff, okay?" My eyes meet his. "No rearranging the plan, Will. You're staying here. I mean it. No hotel." I don't trust what my brother might tell our mom.

Will rolls his eyes and grabs again for the phone. I let him have it this time. He walks away, out of hearing range, just like his girlfriend did when she made her phone call. Again, I'm reminded that I really need to keep an eye on these two this week.

When I divert my attention away from my brother's turned back, I hear Cassie asking Kay where she lives. Kay points to the small building across the driveway. "I live above the garage. There's an apartment up there."

Cassie makes a face, and Kay laughs. "Hey, it's actually very nice."

"Really?" Cassie's expression conveys her doubt.

"Yes, really."

Cassie ponders for a few seconds, then says to Kay, "Um, since it looks the hotel thing is a no-go, can I stay with you this week?"

Kay's caramel-brown eyes slide to mine, her gaze questioning.

I nod an assent, and Kay says to Cassie, "Sure, you can stay with me."

It's actually ideal. There's much less likelihood of my brother and his girlfriend trying to sneak off to hook up if he stays in the main house with me and Cassie is next door with Kay. Of course, that means I won't be sleeping with Kay, like we do every fucking night. It looks like this Gartner won't be getting any sex, either. But, hey, I can deal.

I think.

Maybe Kay and I can find some alone-time once Will and Cassie drift off to sleep. I doubt I can make it four whole days without touching my girl. Now that it's promising to be somewhat of a challenge, a slew of dirty thoughts begin to race through my mind, thoughts of how Kay and I just might be able to make a sneaking-around thing work to our advantage.

I like the possibilities. In fact, the thought of dirty, nasty sex that's not supposed to be happening makes my cock twitch in my jeans. I try to think of something else, anything, but there's no use. Consequently, my gaze is pretty much smoldering when Kay glances my way.

Her eyes hold mine, and she starts to smile. Poor Cassie is chatting away to Kay—they seem to be really hitting it off—but Kay's attention is wavering because of me. Still, I can't help but distract her further. I smile back at her, the kind of crooked smile I know she fucking loves.

Kay blushes, her cheeks turning pink, the kind of reaction *I* fucking love.

So much for ever clearing my head of dirty thoughts— but I'm sure Kay's right there with me. She can be as filthy as I am when it comes to sex. And that's saying a lot.

Shit, now all I can think of is how soon I can get Kay

naked and spread out before me. When I do, I plan to love her long and hard.

Hopefully, we can work something out for later tonight. Sneaking around, getting down and dirty, all while trying not to get caught, promises to be a lot of fun.

Yeah, I am most definitely reassessing. Maybe my brother's unexpected arrival will result in me reaping some well-deserved benefits, benefits I can't wait to cash in on.

CHAPTER TWO

KAY

Cassie is going on and on about something, details about her trip with Will. I think. I am striving to pay attention, I swear I am, but Chase keeps distracting me. Trust me, he'd distract you too. And not just because he's stunning, though there is definitely that. But it's his eyes, pale and blue, that don't allow me to focus. And when one side of his mouth curves up into the kind of grin he knows I love, he's hooked me completely. That half smile, full of sex and promise, is my favorite Chase Gartner smile.

"Stop," I mouth.

Chase rakes his fingers through his light-brown hair, pushing it into a messier-than-usual state. *So sexy.*

He mouths back to me, "Later."

Cassie quiets when Will, who's apparently finished with his phone call to his mom, walks back over to his brother and hands him the phone. Chase gives me a quick wink and then motions for Will to follow him back up the porch steps. I can't help but check out Chase's incredibly fine ass while he's walking away.

Sighing, I wonder: *How did I get so lucky?*

Chase is hot as hell, sexy, great in bed, and beyond gorgeous. Truly, he's beautiful in a way that makes heads turn and knees weaken. He's tall, muscular, and swoon-worthy strong. Chase's strength never ceases to amaze me. Under the jeans and tees he's usually wearing, Chase is solid, hard, and cut from years of working out—and fighting—in prison. And though his body is hard, his heart isn't. Chase is good and kind, thoughtful and sensitive, the kind of guy who brings Paris to you on a summer evening, then wows you with a rooftop picnic at sunset.

I hear Chase laugh, a really happy laugh, loud and from the heart. Will has just made him crack up about something.

Cassie and I glance at one another, our eyes meeting meaningfully. "Finally," I mutter on a relieved sigh.

"I know, right?" Cassie grins.

I'm relieved and happy these brothers, who I know love one another so damn much, are finally getting along. The heavy tension permeating the air following Will and Cassie's surprise arrival had me worried. I know Chase would never hurt his brother, but concern overtook me when Will tried to hit him. I'm glad that situation diffused quickly.

Cassie glances around the property, which is a little more visible now that the bright summer moon has come out from behind a cloud. "Wow," she says. "This is like a real farm, isn't it?"

"Well, it was at one time," I tell her. "But there aren't any animals here, and Chase doesn't grow crops or anything."

"Not even corn?" Cassie asks, as though this is surprising.

"Not a single stalk," I reply, laughing.

Cassie appears mostly thoughtful. "Huh," she says, "okay. I sure saw a lot of corn on the way here, though. Like, everywhere." She pauses, then adds, "This part of the country is so different from home. Everything is so green, even at night. It's just…strange."

I nod. "Yeah, I'd imagine so." I suppose from her perspective—she's lived in the desert all her life—things would certainly seem different.

While Cassie continues to glance around the property, I assess this young girl who's captured Chase's brother's heart. The first thing I notice is how blue Cassie's eyes are. They're very pretty, similar to Chase's, but darker and with no flecks of gray. Chase's blues are what I long-ago termed gunmetal blue, whereas Cassie's eyes are more of a cornflower blue shade.

I also take note of Will's girlfriend's cute vintage-style outfit—wide-bottomed jeans and a gauzy bohemian-style top. They're adorable clothes, suited to Cassie, for sure. I can see how Will would feel compelled to protect her. Everything about Cassie screams young, vulnerable girl. So different from Chase's brother, who is more cocksure than I ever would have imagined. I guess I've heard too many little-boy Will stories, like the tale of a kid who couldn't catch lizards.

Well, Will might have been clumsy and uncoordinated in the past, but he seems rather sure of himself nowadays. Not completely, of course. He is just a kid. But his swagger is far beyond what you'd expect at fifteen.

Will is a lot like Chase. And just like with Chase, under all that bravado, there's a guy who has been through some tough times. Jack Gartner's suicide, losing the family home, living in a car for a period of time, those things have shaped the Gartner boys.

Cassie shifts uncomfortably and starts bouncing on her

toes. She asks if she can use the bathroom. "We haven't stopped for a really long time," she adds apologetically.

"Oh, of course, honey," I say. "You should have said something sooner." I gesture to my apartment above the garage. "Here, follow me."

I lead Cassie over to my place. It's a little farther than if we just went into the main house, but I figure this way Cassie can get a glimpse of where she'll be staying for the next few days. Plus, the extra time it takes to walk back and forth will give Chase and his brother more time to reconnect.

When we walk into my apartment, I show Cassie where the bathroom is, then wait for her in the living room. When she comes out, she surveys the small, but nicely decorated rooms and says, "You were right. Your place *is* really nice. It's...cute."

"Thank you," I reply, smiling.

We head back over to the house, but as we near the main house, Cassie slows to a stop. She starts to giggle, and I ask, "What? What's so funny?"

She gestures to our guys, who are still standing on the porch, laughing and talking. "It's just funny that neither one of them had any idea what the other was wearing today, yet, check it out, they're dressed almost exactly alike."

Now I'm chuckling, too, since what Cassie is saying is so true. Both Chase and Will are wearing dark T-shirts and low-riding jeans, only Will's T-shirt is dark blue and Chase's is black. Oh, and Will's jeans hang *way* low, lower than Chase's, leaving the top part of Will's boxers exposed.

"Nice white boxers," I mutter to Cassie, teasingly, since

I'm hoping to keep things light like this. There was enough drama earlier.

Cassie plays right along. "I can see the top edge of Chase's underwear, too, you know. They're black and look like boxer briefs."

I start laughing. Cassie just called it, right on the nose.

"They are boxer briefs," I confirm. I then nudge her arm and nod over to the boys. "Hey, you should yell over to Chase to pull up his pants. Tell him you can see his underwear."

Her eyes widen. "God," she gasps, "no way!"

"I'm just kidding," I assure her.

While we laugh, Chase and Will have no idea we're discussing their underwear. The brothers appear far too busy catching up.

Cassie and I glance over at each other and just lose it for no particular reason. It's been a stressful night and laughing feels good. Chase glances our way, but otherwise doesn't pay us much heed. "Typical man," I say when he resumes talking to his brother.

Cassie giggles, then says, "I like you, Kay. You're pretty cool."

I'm flattered Will's girlfriend has decided I'm "cool."

We start walking again, and Cassie wants to know, "What's Chase like?"

"Oh, that's easy," I reply. "He's basically incredible."

"Yeah..." She smiles as she eyes Will. "I believe it. Will is pretty much great, too."

"They're probably a lot alike," I muse, giving my guy a wistful once-over, as well.

Cassie sighs and slows, since we're almost within earshot. "Can I ask you something, Kay?" she quietly murmurs.

"Sure."

"Is Chase really pissed Will drove without a license?"

I shake my head. "I don't know, Cassie, probably not. I think he just doesn't want to see Will get into any trouble."

"That makes sense," she replies, nodding. "But, seriously, Will was the logical choice. He's actually a much better driver than me, especially on the interstates. The trucks get so close when they pass." She shudders. "Ugh, they freak me out."

"I completely understand," I tell her, since I do. "Trucks make me nervous, too."

Cassie quiets, perhaps reflecting, and then she says in a low, low voice, "Will was so cute, Kay. Like the whole way here, he kept doing the sweetest things."

I sense she wants to share, so I ask, "Like what?"

"Well, for starters, he made sure we stopped for meals at what he termed 'regular intervals.'" She pauses and smiles. "And even though we ate mostly fast food, Will always made sure all the food groups were covered."

"That is sweet," I agree.

And it is. Will's obviously a thoughtful kid. And Cassie is sweet, too. I can't help but smile as she continues to share, quietly but excitedly.

"Another thing Will insisted on doing was guarding all the ladies' rooms I went into, especially when I'd stop in to freshen up." With downcast eyes, Cassie softly adds, "Will told me he was guarding to make sure no perverts snuck in with me."

A funny look crosses Cassie's face when the word "pervert" passes her lips. Chase has told me about her stepdad, some guy named Paul. He's much younger than Cassie's mom—closer to Cassie's age, in fact. He's supposedly around the house a lot. Used to work in some casino, but he got fired. This is just what Chase has related to me. Will doesn't share much with him in the way of details, but it's been made clear Paul spends a lot of his free time basically hitting on Cassie.

Chase and I worry things will escalate if she doesn't tell her mother what's been going on. It's too much of a burden for Will and Cassie to carry alone. Case in point, running away sure wasn't the answer.

I blow out a breath and come up with an idea. Since Cassie seems to like me, maybe I can get her to open up this week. If I can find out more of what exactly goes on in Vegas, perhaps I can convince Cassie to speak with her mom. Will has good intentions, but he's a guy and can never understand that feeling of powerlessness only women are privy to sometimes.

I think about my experience with the junkie, the night I was assaulted in the parking lot of my old apartment. I was lucky my assailant was scared away by passing cop cars. I shudder at the thought of what all *could* have happened that night.

Cassie, noticing when I cross my arms and shudder again, places her hand on my elbow. "Are you okay?"

"Yeah." I nod once. "It's just kind of chilly. We should go inside the house."

Cassie and I walk up the porch steps, and in keeping with my assertion that I'm cold, I suggest to the guys that we all go into the house.

Chase agrees, and once we're inside the front hall, he stops and turns to his brother and Cassie. He proceeds to lay out some ground rules. "Like no sneaking off to do God-knows-what," he says.

Will and Cassie nod in unison, and Chase adds, "If you're hungry, there's grub in the kitchen. Kay and I will wait in the living room so you two can have some alone time before bed."

"That was very nice of you," I say once Cassie and Will are out of hearing range.

"Yeah, that's me"—Chase rolls his eyes—"Mr. Nice Guy. We'll see how long that lasts."

Chase is always expecting to screw things up somehow.

"You're too hard on yourself," I tell him, since it's unfortunately true.

Chase shrugs his wide shoulders and mumbles, "Whatever, babe."

From the kitchen, noises begin to drift out to the hall, Cabinets opening, plates and cups rattling. Someone opens the refrigerator door, and Cassie laughs as she and Will playfully argue over what kind of sandwiches to make.

"Sounds like they're having fun," I say, nudging Chase.

He smiles and drapes his arm around my shoulder. "Yeah, it does."

He leads me into the living room, and once we're seated on the sofa, Chase draws me into an all-encompassing hug. Now that things are calming, I feel him letting go. Tension in his shoulders and back begins to ease up. I know Chase needs me the most when he holds me like this.

"You always feel so good," he murmurs into my hair.

"Chase..." I release a breath and squeeze him a little tighter.

After a few minutes, he leans back slightly, says, "Jesus... What a fucking night, yeah?"

"You're not kidding," I agree. "It was a little crazy there for a while."

Our arms remain around each another, and our eyes meet. Holding his gaze, I slowly lift the back of his T-shirt. Touching skin to skin always soothes us both, so I continue to touch, trailing my hands along Chase's heavily muscled back.

He sighs and closes his eyes.

"I love how your skin feels," I whisper.

His back is warm and smooth, but the texture of his skin differs slightly where his tattoos lie. Chase has several tattoos, all of which I love. From the scroll of words on his left bicep that reads, *As I stand before you, judge me not,* to the numeral *72* inked on his right bicep.

All of Chase's ink is beyond stunning. But my favorite, hands down, is the tattoo on his back.

With care, I slowly trail my fingertips over the inked wings spanning his shoulders...then skim down to the angel kneeling underneath. I linger when I reach a feather that rains down past the angel. Several more feathers fall nearby. I now touch each one, all the way down to the base of Chase's back. I've learned this ink so well that I don't need to see his tattoos to know where each one is inked.

When I reach the feather near the sexy indentation above his left ass cheek, Chase shivers. "Babe, you better stop," he warns. "You're making me hard."

"So," I coyly reply, "if that's the case, does that mean I should sneak back over in a little while?"

Chase groans and runs his hand up my thigh. He reaches the edge of my shorts, and says, "I like the way you're thinking, sexy girl."

I start to respond, but quickly and without warning, Chase pulls me onto his lap. I giggle and adjust my legs around him.

When he lifts his hips and presses his arousal into me, I let out on a surprised gasp. Chase wasn't kidding, he's hard as steel.

I circle my hips, creating a little friction that quickens our breaths.

"Mmm, maybe there's something to be said for this sneaking-around thing," I murmur.

Chase kisses along the shell of my ear and whispers, "You took the words right out of my mouth, baby."

"When should I come back over?"

Chase's lips move to my mouth, and he kisses me deeply before responding.

When he gets around to replying, after phenomenal kisses that leave me breathless, he says, "I'm betting my brother will be asleep five minutes after his head hits the pillow. If he's anything like how he used to be, he'll be out till morning."

I lean my head back slightly. "Hmm… I bet Cassie will sleep just as soundly. From what she told me, they pretty much drove straight through. They have to be exhausted."

After a few more kisses, we finalize our plan.

"I won't spend the whole night," I say, "but I'll stay for a while. Definitely long enough to get you off"—I resume showering Chase with kisses along his jaw—"at least twice."

"Once is good enough for me, babe," Chase replies, chuckling.

I lean back and give him a questioning look. "You sure?" I ask. "You do realize you're turning down an extra orgasm?"

Chase laughs, tells me, "Tonight is all about you, Kay." He cups my ass while he presses his now unbelievably hard cock up into me. "You feel that?"

I nod enthusiastically.

"Good, 'cause I plan to use every inch to make sure *you* come at least half a dozen times."

Damn, how can you argue with that?

Once Cassie and I are over in my apartment, I help her get settled. And after I let her know she can have my bed, I take a sheet and a blanket out to the living room and make up a bed for myself.

I fluff up a throw pillow, and then lie down on the sofa. But there's no relaxing for me. Not when I know I'll be leaving the apartment soon, and not when I'm too wound up to stop thinking about Chase. Still, I try to rest since I am hoping Cassie is asleep by the time I slip out.

All I end up doing, though, is tossing and turning. The sheet and blanket get tangled with the peach-colored sleep shorts and matching tee I'm wearing, until I mutter, "Oh hell," and toss the blanket to the floor.

Even though I've given up on sleeping, Cassie is out. Or so I assume, as there's a light snore coming from my room.

But I want to be certain, so I get up from the sofa and go check on her.

She is sleeping soundly, with one hand under the pillow and the other resting against the iron bars of the antique headboard at the top of my bed. Tiptoeing silently back to the front of the apartment, I slip on a pair of flip-flops, and then hurry over to the main house.

When I reach the front door, I find it unlocked, as per my plan with Chase. Quietly, I let myself in. It's dark in the hall, and it takes a few seconds for my eyes to adjust, but when I can at least make out shadows and such, I kick off my flip-flops and head upstairs.

Since I have no idea which bedroom Chase gave to Will, I'm careful walking by all the closed doors. When I reach Chase's bedroom at the end of the hall, I give the door a light, silent push, allowing enough space for me to slip inside.

I've been fairly quiet up to this point, but Chase wakes immediately when he hears me step into his room.

Propping himself up on his elbows in his full-size bed, which incidentally makes all the muscles in his arms and shoulders bunch up enticingly, he whispers a sleep-thick, "Hey."

He rubs at his eyes, and the sheet slips down far enough for me to see he's naked—and already hard, if the tented cotton is any indication.

My pulse races in anticipation as I pause, just a few feet inside the doorway. Chase smiles at me. It never fails to amaze me how unaware he is of how absolutely breathtaking he can be. Like now, tonight, in this moment. I take in his smooth chest, wide and strong, and how his biceps flex when he flips back the sheet to make room for me. I sigh. The man is just perfection.

"Kay," he chuckles, the tone of his voice lowering. "Come to me."

That's all I need to hear. I go to him without hesitation.

I know we don't have a lot of time, but it doesn't matter. I'm wet and ready for Chase, like always. He has that effect on me. And my arousal heightens further still as I'm discarding my shirt, shorts, and underwear along the hasty path I blaze to the bed.

But before I can lie down next to him, Chase reaches up, halting my progress by gently placing his hand on my hip. "Wait," he says.

He skims his hand up my side, eliciting a shiver. When he reaches my left breast, he traces little circles around the nipple.

I lean my head back. "Mmm…"

With his fingers slowly trailing down my stomach, with the promise of traveling lower, he says, "You're so beautiful, Kay, standing before me like this, naked, vulnerable— *mine*."

"I am yours," I murmur.

Chase's words stir me. Not just my body, but my heart as well. There is something so raw, so sincere, in the way he speaks. And when it finally gets through to me that this man actually finds me beautiful, a lump forms in my throat. "Chase," I whisper, my voice cracking, "I don't deserve you."

"Aww, sweet girl, you've got that all mixed up." He pulls me down to him, until my naked body covers his.

Wrapping his arms around me, he softly caresses my back and whispers, "I'm the one who doesn't deserve you."

Before I can respond, to argue the point, his fingers find my core, effectively silencing me. Chase is so adept, so freaking skilled, that I can no longer think of anything but what he's doing to me.

"You're so wet," he whispers, shifting beneath me. "It turns me on, Kay, knowing you get this for me, only me."

"Only you," I confirm.

"Damn straight," he growls.

There's urgency in Chase's voice, and determination in the way he moves his fingers, circling and plying my clit, moving faster, a little rougher. Chase is suddenly feeling possessive and I like it, *a lot*. I like it so much that when he slides two fingers into me, his thumb vigorously working my nub, I come apart completely.

While I'm still climaxing, Chase pulls me roughly to his mouth, as though he has to kiss me. But God, I need to kiss him too. So very, very much.

Our tongues touch, tasting and exploring. Until, slowly and carefully, Chase rolls me over until I am beneath him. He hovers above me, the way I like, his arms caging me in. The tip of his penis presses at my core. And, God, I'm even wetter than before. With a subtle shift of my hips, he slips right in.

A moan escapes me, while Chase groans, "Fuck."

He lowers his body to me, pressing into mine, giving me more of what I never tire of—more of his weight, more of his cock. As I am stretched and filled by him, he kisses up my neck, over my chin, and to my mouth. With our breaths intermingled, we both still, and he tells me, "I love you."

Chase Gartner then gets down to what he does best, fucking.

I rise to meet his hard thrusts—thrusts that make me cry out his name.

He pulls out almost all the way at one point, and asks, "Do you love me, Kay?"

How could I not?

"Yes," I pant, writhing. "God, I love you so much, Chase. There aren't enough words to express how much."

And that is when, with one particularly piercing thrust, he fills me again completely.

I gasp, prompting him to hoist my legs up over his shoulders. He presses his body down to mine, my knees now on either side of my head, and drives into me relentlessly. He makes me say his name again and again, each time more forcefully.

Soon, I am screaming out, "Chase, yes, Chase," (among other things) way louder than intended.

He chuckles, smug that he affects me like this. His hand covers my mouth, and he pumps up into me—once, twice—as he rasps, "My brother may be a sound sleeper, baby girl, but he's not deaf."

He starts to move his hand away from my mouth, but I shake my head, urging him to keep his hand where it is. I like his hand over my mouth, keeping me quiet while he fucks me as only he can do, with power, with finesse.

He lowers my legs and flattens me to the mattress, his weight pinning me, my already-stimulated nipples tingling as his chest brushes against the hardened peaks. "You like it like this, don't you?" he asks.

I nod.

I am so close, so damn close to coming undone for the second time this night. Chase feels me tensing and picks up the pace. When he lowers his hand to my clit, touching me in the way I like best, I am gone, exploding, my sex milking his cock. Chase releases into me while I ride out my second orgasm of the night.

While I'm recovering, dizzy and satiated beyond belief, Chase whispers in my ear, "I'm not done with you yet. By my calculations, I owe you four more orgasms."

"Fine by me," I respond.

Determined man that he is, Chase gets right back to the business of pleasing me. I close my eyes and savor the feel of his soft, full lips as he kisses his way down my body. And true to his word, throughout the next couple of hours, Chase brings me to orgasm after orgasm, with his mouth, his fingers, and a cock that never seems to tire. Lucky me. Eventually, though, we become too exhausted to move.

I nod off to sleep, but awaken a while later. Slowly, I reluctantly make myself get out of the toasty warm bed. I try to stay quiet, but as I search for the clothes I discarded when I first entered the room, my movement rouses Chase.

Sitting up, he says in a sleepy voice, "Stay."

"I can't," I remind him. "If Cassie wakes up and finds me gone, she'll wonder where I snuck off to in the middle of the night. I don't want her to worry or panic the first night she's here."

Chase swings his long legs over the edge of the bed and rubs the back of his neck. "Okay, but don't go yet. Give me a minute to throw on some shorts and I'll walk you back over."

"I'm good," I say, laughing. "I think I can make it back across the driveway safely."

Chase stands and grabs a pair of discarded basketball shorts from the floor. "Nah." He pulls the nylon fabric up and adjusts himself. "I'm going with you."

"You're sweet when you're overprotective," I tell him on the way back over to my apartment.

"Maybe I just wanted a few more minutes alone with you," he replies, leaning into me.

"And that"—I bump my hip to his leg—"is why I love you so much."

"And here I thought you were just using me for sex."

"There is that too," I shoot back, smiling.

"You're turning into a bigger smart-ass than me," he quips.

"I had a good teacher," I tell him.

Our banter continues until we reach the door to my apartment. We quiet as Chase comes in with me. Together, we check in on Cassie. She's still sleeping soundly, oblivious to my little excursion next door.

Chase, attentive man that he is, insists on tucking me in on the sofa before he leaves. He kisses me silly, too, until I'm too sleepy to move my lips with his.

"Good night, Kay," he whispers in my ear. "Sweet dreams."

I mumble something incoherent and hold on to the comfort of feeling so loved and contented, and then I drift off to sleep.

I wake up disoriented without Chase by my side. We sleep

together every night, and this change in routine has me all thrown off.

I get back on track quickly, though, especially when I stretch and think about last night, the time spent in Chase's bed. I can't help but giggle and curl my toes. But then I suddenly remember it's a weekday and I have to go to work, so my euphoria subsides.

"Ugh," I mumble, before I reluctantly get up.

Before I do anything, I check in on Cassie. She's still fast asleep.

Quietly as I can, I shower and dress. I then toast a bagel to eat on the way to the church. A half hour later, I'm at my desk in the rectory, fulfilling my duties as temporary secretary at Holy Trinity.

Any other day, I'd be counting the hours until lunch, anxiously awaiting noon so I could go grab a bite to eat down at the local diner with Chase. But Chase called as I was driving in to work and told me he talked with Father Maridale, and considering what's going on with Will and Cassie, the priest who's in charge of things around here gave Chase the day off.

Chase also works for Holy Trinity, fixing things up around the church grounds, including at the grade school next door. I work at the school as a first grade teacher during the school year. The secretary gig is just for the summer, which I can't believe is more than halfway over.

Suddenly, my cell buzzes. It's Chase.

"I miss you" is the first thing out of his mouth.

"You're too cute,"

"Cute?" he says sourly, his tone mock-offended. "Shit, babe, I must have done something wrong last night if *cute* is the first thing that comes to your mind when you think of me."

He does have a point; his actions last night were definitely not definable as "cute."

With that in mind, I quickly amend, "Hmm, okay... How 'bout we go with sexy, strong, take-charge, orgasm-inducing—"

"Okay, okay." He chuckles. "So, I was thinking—"

"That could be dangerous," I interrupt, teasing.

"Ha-ha. You sure are in a good mood today."

"Uh, I wonder why."

I hope he detects the still-satisfied-from-last-night smile in my voice. I suppose he does, when, a second later, in a low voice, he rasps, "I wish you were here right now, and not stuck at work."

I start to whisper back a sexy response, but then I hear Will and Cassie in the background on Chase's end of the line.

"Ugh," I groan. "Do we need to put this discussion on hold?"

"Yeah, I think so," he replies, sighing.

I smoothly change the subject. "So how are things going today?"

Chase informs me everyone is getting along, and then he says, "So, back to my idea. I was thinking maybe we could take Will and Cassie to the drive-in out on Route 7 tonight. What do you think?"

"I think it's a great idea."

"Yeah," Chase says, "It should work out well. That big action blockbuster we were planning to take Will to is still playing."

"Perfect," I reply.

We intended to take Will to see that particular movie, before the original plan of him coming to Ohio went awry.

"Hey," I say hesitantly, "I kind of wanted to run something by you."

I'm quiet, and Chase prompts, "What is it, babe?"

I take a deep breath, exhale slowly. "Chase, I know I should stay out of it, but I can't stop thinking about the situation with Cassie and her stepdad."

"Hey, I hear ya," he scoffs. "It's a fucked up mess, no doubt about it."

"Well," I continue, "I was thinking maybe I could try to talk to Cassie about it. She seems to like me. Maybe she'll open up some." I sigh. "Anyway, it's worth a shot. If she starts by talking to me, then maybe she'll eventually feel comfortable enough to tell her mom what's been happening back in Vegas. Mrs. Sutter needs to know why her daughter ran away."

"You're right," Chase agrees. "Your idea is a good one, Kay. Hell, if anyone can get her to open up, it's you. In fact, I'd put money on it."

"Thanks for the vote of confidence," I say, pleased that Chase believes in me so much.

I hear a noise outside the double doors leading into the office. When I glance that way, I see Father Maridale is about to come in. His white hair and black frock stand out in stark contrast through the tinted glass.

"I have to go," I whisper to Chase.

Father Maridale steps into the office just as I press *End*.

He's a nice guy, and he smiles kindly as he walks over

to my desk. Nodding to my mostly clear desktop, he says, "Not much going on today, huh?"

"No, not really. Just some calls for you." I hand him a few slips of paper containing the details of the messages I took down for him.

"You can leave early today, if you'd like," he says distractedly while he flips through the slips of paper.

I am up for that, so I thank him and start to gather my stuff. Father remains next to my desk, though, so I know he has something more to say.

He sets down his messages and inquires, "Chase getting along okay with his brother? He sounded a little stressed out when I spoke to him this morning."

I lean back in my chair and confess to him that things were a little rough when Will and Cassie first arrived.

"Chase and Will had it out," I admit. "But they're getting along great now."

Father Maridale nods, seemingly deep in thought. He knows all about Chase's past, and he's fully aware of how important it is to Chase to rebuild his relationship with his brother, a relationship that was shattered four years ago.

Will refused to speak to Chase the entire time he was in prison. Will was angry, just like everyone else. Too many people gave up on Chase Gartner. But not Father Maridale. He always believed in him. He was one of only two people in this town willing to give Chase a second chance. I was the other, but not at first. Not until I met Chase—through a chance run-in, quite literally. It was at that moment, when I saw truth in his eyes, that I realized giving Chase a second chance was the right thing to do. Before that day, I had made the same assumptions and cast the same judgments as everyone else.

Since then, though, I've since learned a lot about forgiveness and starting over.

Sometimes you have to give others a chance to redeem themselves, like how I'm striving to do with my mom. I'm hoping to find some middle ground with the woman who disowned me four years ago. I have to admit, however, it's not easy.

I sigh loudly, and as though Father Maridale can read my mind, he asks, "Is your mother still keeping up with you like she promised?"

"Yes."

It's the truth. She's been calling and keeping in touch, to nobody's bigger surprise than my own. See, my mother blamed me for my little sister's death until just recently. It's ironic that a couple of days after Sarah's funeral, my mother cast me out of her home...and her heart. But almost four years later to the day, she allowed me back in. Last Friday, she sought me out at the little cemetery behind the church where Sarah is buried.

My mother wants to start anew, rebuild our relationship. But after all she has taken, I only have so much to give. She tells me she wants to learn about my life. But there are so many things she's already missed—my graduation from college, my first day as a teacher, all the highs and lows I've experienced. She's missed all that and more, and it's not so easy to dig back in time and resurrect the past.

"But I'm trying," I say to Father Maridale, answering my own question to myself, not one he has posed.

Father's pale-brown eyes fill with compassion. He

knows me as well as he knows Chase, and that means he's aware of all my good and all my bad.

He places his hand on mine. "Forgiveness may come in time, Kay, or it may not. I can counsel you in one direction, but only you can decide on your path."

"Sometimes I feel like I don't know what I'm doing," I admit. "It scares me. I don't even know how to take the first step with my mother."

"You've already taken it," he assures me. "Just the fact you've allowed her back into your life—albeit limitedly—proves your heart wants to forgive."

"Maybe that's true," I say, "but what's the next step?"

"Give your mother an opportunity to earn your forgiveness."

I nod, contemplating his words, and he adds, "Do you find her overtures thus far to be sincere?"

I think it over. "Yeah, I think so." I pause, and then I admit what's really bothering me. "It's just, she's missed *so* much, Father. And I don't know how to let it all go..."

As I trail off, he sighs. "We can't move forward, Kay, when we're staring back at the past. Try focusing on the here and now. Build for a possible future with your mother. Give her a chance to be there when you need her most. Who knows, maybe she'll come through."

"Yeah," I say slowly, "I guess."

I hope he's right, and I thank Father Maridale for his wise words, then I say, "You always know what to say to make me feel better."

He pats my hand reassuringly. "That's why I'm here, my child."

Father Maridale then leaves me to my thoughts. And

what I'm thinking is that maybe I've been making this far more complicated than it has to be.

The past cannot be changed; that is a fact.

So do I keep staring back at it? Do I allow myself to be held captive by what's behind me, like I've done in the past?

Or do I try to do as Father Maridale has counseled—focus on moving forward?

I've already taken the first step, right?

I gather up my things and decide to look to the future, which requires opening my heart…to my mother.

CHAPTER THREE
CHASE

The old drive-in out on Route 7 is packed. But we luck out and find a spot smack dab in the center of the front row.

I back my truck into the narrow space and shut down the ignition. "Okay," I say, "let's get set up in the back."

Kay, who's next to me, and Will and Cassie, back in the extended cab area, reply a chorus of "okay" and "cool." Minutes later we are standing by the bed of the truck.

I place my hand on a stout pole with an old-time speaker that appears clunky and outdated, leading me to conclude it probably barely works.

"We won't need it," Kay says when she catches me frowning at the antiquated sound system. "I grabbed a portable radio from your gram's old bedroom. We'll use that."

"Good thinking." I lean over and kiss Kay's cheek.

She smiles and passes the radio up to Will, who is standing in the bed of the truck, taking in the parked-up lot. "Sure is busy here tonight," he comments.

"True that," Cassie says as she jumps up to stand next to him. She starts unfolding one of three big blankets we packed for the evening.

I remind Will about the radio. He crouches down, sets

the radio up, then gets to work on tuning in the correct station. "There," he says after a few seconds, "all set."

Cassie is still messing with laying out the blankets, so I say to Will, "Hey, you want to come with me to the concession stand, grab some popcorn and drinks?"

"Yeah, sure." Will hops down from the bed of the truck.

Kay shoots me a knowing glance. She knows what I'm up to. I'm trying to give her time alone with Cassie so they'll have a chance to talk, bond, whatever.

Cassie offers Kay a hand when she notices her trying, unsuccessfully I might add, to climb up into the bed of the truck without flashing everyone. Her dress is kind of short, so let's just say it's kind of an amusing challenge.

When Kay and Cassie start giggling, I nudge Will and say, "Looks like our girls are getting along great."

"Yeah," Will says, sounding pleased. "It's cool they like each other. Cassie mentioned that Kay's easy to talk with. She thinks she's really nice." He play-punches my arm and adds, "So, how'd you land a classy chick like that, anyway?"

I call him a dick, and we pretend to spar as we start down to the squat cinder block building with the old-fashioned "concession stand" sign. We spend a minute or two just acting like typical guys, but when we knock it off, I tell him the story of how I met Kay.

After I give him an abbreviated version of events, I say, "It's kind of crazy, but we more or less found love in the parking lot."

"Sounds like the title to a bad country song, dude," Will jokes.

"Yeah, it does," I agree, laughing.

After a beat, Will says in a more serious tone, "So you, like, literally ran into her?"

"*She* ran into me," I clarify.

"Lucky you," he says.

"You got that right, bro," I reply.

Right before we reach the concession stand, Will slows to a stop. He lowers his gaze, and I turn to him. "What's up?"

Kicking at the gravel, he quietly says, "I was just wondering if you have to go back to work tomorrow?"

"Yeah, I do."

"That sucks," Will says. "Tomorrow's going to be boring out at the house without you around. I mean...Cassie will be there, yeah, but I've been having a good time hanging with you."

I'm flattered and touched by my brother's words. Shit, he actually wants to spend more time with me.

Suddenly, I have an idea. "Why don't you come to work with me? Father Maridale has been on my ass lately to get started on a mural over at the school. But I keep coming up with a major blank on what to paint."

Will's interest is piqued; I see it in his expression.

"Whatever I paint," I continue, "it has to be something kid-oriented. Anyway, you're good with cartoon characters. You know I think your comic book is amazing, right?"

Will nods once, his cheeks reddening. He has nothing to be embarrassed about, though. He's been working on creating a comic book line, and from what he's showed me thus far, it's incredible.

"So, come with me tomorrow," I say, "help me come up with something for the mural."

Will's green eyes brighten. "You mean, like, paint with you?"

"Yeah, why not?"

Little bro nods slowly, like he's really thinking this thing through. "Yeah," he says at last, "I'm down with that."

"Cool," I reply.

My brother has art in his blood like I do, even if his artwork is different. I have the ability to sketch anything, just as it is, whereas Will's best with distorting stuff, turning people and things into caricatures and cartoons, like the characters in his futuristic and war-torn Las Vegas comic book. The hero in his story is a badass character named Champion. Kay swears up and down that this Champion dude is a comic book version of me. I don't know about that, but I do know if Will actually based his hero on me, I am humbled. It's been a long fucking time since Will has viewed me as any sort of a good guy.

When we return to the truck, popcorn and sodas in hand, the movie is just starting. Kay whispers something to me quickly, before the four of us make ourselves comfortable on the blankets in the back of the truck.

The opening scene is an action-packed, testosterone-fueled car chase, complete with explosions. Needless to say, Will and I are pretty much engrossed within minutes. Kay and Cassie, on the other hand, are...not.

"Ugh, this is such a guy's movie," Cassie mumbles to Kay when yet another building blows up onscreen. At least ten have been flattened in the first forty minutes.

"They don't know what's good, do they, bro?" Will yells over to me.

Kay and Cassie, seated between us, simultaneously turn to Will and snap, "Shut up."

Everyone chuckles, and a short while later, I overhear Kay whispering to Cassie, "At least the guy playing the lead is hot."

I roll my eyes and grab another handful of popcorn.

Cassie replies, "Yeah, I guess he's okay, but he's a little too old for me."

My brother, who is obviously eavesdropping, same as me, leans in close to his girlfriend and kisses her cheek. "Good girl," he tells her in a completely patronizing tone.

That prompts me to launch a handful of popcorn over the girls' heads while calling him out. "Don't be such a Neanderthal, Will."

"You're one to talk," my brother retorts, brows raising.

Kay whispers in my ear, "Don't worry, Neanderthal is good. I like you untamed."

She squeezes my bicep, and I murmur back, "That's my girl."

Will grumbles to Cassie, "See what I mean?"

"Well," Cassie comments, "it's obvious you two are related."

I ignore their chatter and lean in to Kay. Our lips meet, and soon we're so lost in kissing the hell out of each other that I end up missing the big climactic finish on the screen. Not that I care. I'd rather taste Kay's sweet lips than watch the movie.

But I'm soon reminded we're not alone when Will mutters from a few feet away, "Dude, seriously, you two need to get a room."

Kay smiles against my lips. "Guess that's our cue to stop."

"Guess so," I quip.

Intermission arrives about three minutes after Kay and I quit making out, and as I regroup, which includes discreetly adjusting myself, I hear Cassie saying to Will, "I'm gonna go buy some candy. You want anything?"

In a very loud voice, Will announces he needs more popcorn, since, "Someone wasted a bunch, throwing it at my head."

His eyes slide to me, and I chuckle but refrain from commenting. Kay, meanwhile, offers to go with Cassie to the concession stand.

While Cassie is preparing to jump down from the bed of the truck, Kay turns back to me, pins me with a meaningful look. I catch on quickly—this is another opportunity for her to get through to Cassie. Kay plans to close the deal, so to speak, in convincing Will's girlfriend to talk with her mom before the week is up. Kay has already made good progress.

After Will and I returned with the popcorn, seconds before he and I became immersed in the movie, what Kay whispered to me was that Cassie told her she wants to go back to Vegas—she misses her friends and her mom—but she fears her twisted stepdad, Paul, will continue to harass her. As it stands, things have gone from bad to worse. He propositioned her in very vivid terms last week. That's what dragged Will away from the airport. That's why he didn't fly to Ohio to visit as was originally planned. And that fucker Paul's proposition is what led to Will and Cassie running away.

As far as I'm concerned, the sick fuck has to go—and

soon. I swear, if Kay can't convince Cassie to tell her mother what's been going on, I'm flying my ass out to Vegas and laying that motherfucker out myself. There was no tolerance for pedophiles in prison, and I uphold the same philosophy here on the outside.

Eventually, Kay and Cassie return, but there's no opportunity to get an update. Everyone is tired and ready to go home. We return to the house, and as soon as we're parked, Will jumps out of the truck.

"I'm exhausted," he announces as he heads straight to the house.

I linger in the driveway while Kay and Cassie fold the blankets, trying to assess if they need help.

"Hey, bro," Will calls over his shoulder when he reaches the porch. "Come on."

"Yeah, give me a minute," I yell back.

Cassie is fumbling with one of the blankets, so I take it from her and say, "Why don't you go spend a few minutes alone with your boyfriend before we all turn in?"

Cassie smiles thankfully and heads over to the porch. But before Kay gets started on telling me how sweet of a gesture that was, I drop the stupid blanket and grab her up in my arms.

Showering my love in hungry kisses, I say, "I've been dying to do this since we were interrupted earlier."

I am up—in more ways than one—for Kay sneaking over again, but I can tell she's beat. It's probably best if we don't push our luck. Two nights in a row of Kay calling out my name while I fuck her senseless is sure to wake up Will. Not that I care if my brother hears us. I'm just worried he'll take the opportunity of my being preoccupied to sneak over to the apartment and engage in the same sort of activities with his own girlfriend.

After a few more minutes of holding my girl and sharing with her how much I love her, we reluctantly part.

When I reach the porch, I yell in through the screen door for Cassie to come out. "Time to wrap things up," I say.

Will and Cassie are in the dining room, which is directly off to the left of the hall. That allows me to hear every word of them telling each other how much they love one another and can't wait to hook up. Kissing noises follow, and I roll my eyes.

Seconds later, Cassie scurries past me. She tosses a "Good night, Chase" over her shoulder before she catches up to Kay.

When I step inside the house, chuckling and shaking my head, Will is standing at the base of the stairs. "Hey," he says, yawning, "I'm going to take a shower before bed."

"Okay, cool."

"Good night." Will says, yawning again.

"'Night…and stop yawning." I stifle a yawn of my own. "That shit's contagious."

Will laughs and heads upstairs. Meanwhile, I make sure everything is locked up, since, unfortunately, there will be no visit from Kay tonight. When I'm done, I jog up the steps. But as I'm making my way to my bedroom, I just about trip over something that's lying on the floor. I turn on a light and discover it's Will's duffel bag that's in my path.

Standing at the bathroom door, it's clear that the shower is still running. I shake my head and start to toe the bag out of the way, but suddenly, this feeling comes over me, like maybe I should take this opportunity and check to make sure my brother's not toting around any drugs or alcohol. I hate to go through Will's stuff, but he did recently borrow money from me under false pretenses. Shortly after I (ill-advisedly) loaned him some cash, our mom found his stash—weed he had bought with my money.

With my foot, I push at the duffel bag. *What should I do… what should I do?*

I'm not so much worried about weed in particular. I already told our mom the kid's bound to try it. But I do worry bud will turn into a gateway drug for my brother. After all, he has the same genetics as Mom and me, and God knows, she and I have fought our addictions.

Mom spent years gambling. And me, well, I was into just about every drug you could name, except for heroin. That one exclusion didn't mean I wasn't in deep. Cocaine had me by the balls for a long time. And I sure as fuck don't care to stand by and watch my little brother follow in those same footsteps.

Despite feeling shitty for what I'm about to do—rummage through his things—I push all that shit aside and crouch down next to Will's duffel bag. With the shower water echoing in the background, I reach out, unzip the bag, and proceed to go through my little brother's belongings.

I'm relieved at once when I find no drugs—no alcohol, either. Will's bag is crammed with mostly clothes, in addition to some other things, like shaving cream, disposable razors, shit like that.

I chuckle when I come across a box of condoms. When I tuck them back under one of Will's T-shirts, I send up a prayer that my brother is actually using them.

With my search complete, I start shoving things back

into the bag. But in doing so, I discover a sketchbook at the very bottom. I pull it out, lean back against the wall, and start thumbing through a bunch of colorful comic panels Will has drawn.

A few of the scenes are familiar. I recognize them as the same pages Will e-mailed to me when we started talking again back in June.

Taking in the intricate detail of Will's futuristic, annihilated Las Vegas, I can't help but smile. Despite the bleak subject matter, Will's art is fucking impressive. It's good, really good—professional, even. My brother's comic book is definitely polished enough to be published. And *that* makes me feel so fucking proud of him.

I become so wrapped up in Will's creations that I barely notice when the water abruptly shuts off. But once I do, I hurriedly toss the sketchbook back into the bag.

When I start to pull the zipper closed, unfortunately for me, the teeth catch on a pair of Will's cargo shorts. "Fuck," I hiss.

I fumble a few seconds with the zipper, manage to get the shorts unhooked, and shove everything deeper into the bag. And that's when my thumb brushes over what feels like a folded piece of paper that's been jammed into an inside pocket. The paper feels like a page from a sketchpad. But it's too smooth, like in a worn-out way.

This can't be what I think it is.

But when I lift the piece of paper, carefully from the narrow inside pocket, I discover it is indeed a page from an old sketchbook, a page from one of *my* old sketchbooks. And it's exactly what I think it is.

With shaky fingers, I unfold the yellowed page. Still

feeling stunned, I stare down at the tree house sketch Will told me the other night he no longer had. This is the same sketch my brother once told me gave him hope. So that begs the question of why Will would lie to me. Why did he say the sketch I drew him all those years ago was long gone?

I blow out a breath. My brother has had his hope with him all along. But perhaps even more mind-blowing than discovering the tree house sketch still exists is the fact my brother took the time to pack it in his bag and carry it with him across the country.

Fuck, fuck, fuck.

My eyes tear up. I mean, shit, all this time I've been thinking my brother has been struggling to forgive me for letting my ass get locked up. But maybe he never really gave up on me in the first place.

Why else would he hold on to this sketch—one of the first things I ever drew for him?

I shake my head. I failed this kid, but he obviously never stopped believing in me. He held on to hope even when I'd forsaken it.

I run a fingertip over what I drew so long ago. The blue walls of the rooms are faded, and there's a double water ring on top of the green foliage on the tree, like someone used the sketch as a coaster once or twice. But despite the wear and tear, the truck parked at the base of the tree—Will freaking loved that thing—still looks good, all big, badass, and bright yellow.

More importantly, though, when I look past all the aesthetics, I finally see what Will has seen all along in this drawing, what he saw so many years ago. I realize why something created by my hand once gave him hope. Somewhere, in between faded blue rooms and water-marked leaves, every ounce of love I felt the day I sketched this for my baby brother is clear. My love for him resonates in every line, every curve of colored pencil. There's love even in the once-colorful shades. This sketch is something special. It's from a different time, a time when we all had different lives, lives filled with so much love it was fucking unbelievable.

But that was before everything changed.

The water stopped a while ago, but I make no move to stand. I don't really care anymore if Will finds me out here in the hall, seated next to his open bag on the floor. I just can't bring myself to put the sketch back where I found it. Not yet.

The bathroom door swings open and thick, hot steam wafts out. I don't look up, but my brother's bare feet step into my line of sight. He clears his throat, and that's when I tilt back my head.

Will's upper body is damp and bare, but his lower half is covered in basketball shorts that look familiar. "Those mine?" I ask with a quick jerk of my head indicating the shorts.

"Yeah, they were clean. Is that okay?"

I shrug.

Will glances down at the sketch in my hand, but his eyes dart away when he notices me watching him.

He sighs, loudly. I fully expect him to start yelling and calling me every name in the book. I deserve as much for so blatantly invading his privacy.

But Will does none of these things. Instead, he sits down next to me and leans his head back against the wall.

"So you were going through my shit, huh?" He motions lazily to his open bag.

He doesn't sound angry, just resigned.

I clear my throat. "Yeah, I was going through your stuff. Sorry, bro."

"I don't have any drugs, if that's what you were looking for."

"I know, Will. And yeah, drugs were exactly what I was looking for."

He doesn't say anything in return; he just accepts. My brother closes his eyes and rakes his hand through his wet hair. Yeah, I have the same quirk. I also notice Will's hair wet like this is the exact same shade as mine, the strands more of a light brown color instead of his usual dark-blond shade.

Will may resemble Mom the most, but like me, he's got a lot of Dad in him, too. It's becoming more obvious now that he's maturing.

With his eyes still closed, Will mutters, "I'm sorry, Chase."

"Sorry for what?"

"For lying to you about the money I borrowed."

Exhaling loudly, I say, "Yeah, that wasn't too cool, bro."

"I know." Will opens his eyes and shoots me a sidelong glance. "It won't happen again, I promise."

"You still smoking?" I ask.

He shakes his head. "Not since Mom found my stash."

I nudge his shoulder with mine. "Hey, you know why I worry about that shit, yeah?"

"I know, I know," Will replies. "You and drugs. Mom and gambling."

I sigh. He sighs. Sometimes there's nothing left to say.

But then Will gestures to the drawing still in my hand. "I see you found the sketch," he says softly.

After a beat, I ask, "Why'd you tell me it was gone?"

Will turns away and doesn't respond.

I can't see his face, but I see him swallowing hard. "Will?"

When he turns back to me, his eyes are brimming with tears. "Fuck, Chase, I don't know." He scrubs a hand down his face. "What's it matter, anyway? It's just a stupid sketch, right?"

It's not, but he sounds so distraught that I agree. "Yeah. Yeah, it is."

I start refolding the sketch, with every intention of putting it away, but Will smacks my hand. "Don't," he croaks. "Just…let it go."

Talk about a loaded statement.

Despite Will's protests, I finish folding the paper. He hits my hand again—hard. So hard that the sharp report slices though the silence in the hall.

I release the sketch and let it drop into the bag. "Happy?" I snap.

Will smacks my hand again, harder still. But I let him. He chokes back a sob. I know he's upset; this shit isn't about some old sketch.

"Hit me if it makes you feel better," I tell him.

I mean it. This one time, I'll let my little brother raise his hand to me. He can beat the fuck out of me if it makes him feel better. Just this once, I won't fight back.

But instead of hitting me again, Will grabs up my hand and clutches at it desperately. That shit just about guts me.

"Shit, bro," Will sobs, chokes on his words. "This is so fucking dumb. I'm such a fucking pussy." My brother's tears don't stop, despite him grinding his fist into his eyes. "Chase…"

"Fuck, Will."

I gather my brother in my arms. He resists at first, but I work to soothe him.

When he keeps trying to push me away, though, I say sternly, "Stop fighting me, goddammit. Just let go, okay? Let it out, Will. You're safe with me."

With a strangled sob, my brother gives in. He wraps his arms around me and lets his heart pour.

"I feel so alone all the time, Chase. I pretend like I'm okay, but I'm not. Most of the time, I'm just winging it. Really, I honestly don't know what I'm doing half the fucking time."

"Will." His words break my heart.

He chokes back another sob that reverberates in my own chest. "I mean, Mom… She tries." Will loosens his hold but still clings to me. "I know her intentions are there, but she's just… I don't know. She's just Mom, you know?"

"I know," I say, nodding.

God, I know all too well what he means. Mom's not been solid in the way we've needed since Dad died.

"I didn't know what to do when Cassie called," Will continues, "when I was at the airport. I didn't mean to blow off coming here that day. But what was I supposed to do? When I got to Cass's house, it was just so…bad. But I am sorry we ran away like we did. I didn't mean to show up here and put you on the spot. I'd never want for you to end up in trouble because of me. It's just that I...I can't keep doing this shit all on my own. I can't, Chase, I can't..."

Will trails off, and I lean down and kiss his head of wet hair.

"You don't have to keep doing everything on your own," I whisper soothingly. "I'm here. Even when you're in Nevada, Will, I'm always just a phone call away. And if things ever get really bad, I'll be there for you. I'll fly out to Vegas, bro, I swear, whatever you need."

"Thank you," he sobs.

I knew this fucking bullshit would catch up to my brother—this saving Cassie, this running away. Will can't save the world. He's only fifteen, for fuck's sake. With all this in mind, I hold on to my brother like I used to when he was a small child. I let him cry it out. He's practically curled up in my lap, so I bury my nose in his shoulder. He smells the same way he used to when he was a small child—clean. And it's not the kind of clean from just showering, though there is that, too. But my brother also smells innocent, unsullied by maturity.

We don't say a word for the longest time. There's simply no need to.

As if the sketch wasn't proof enough, the fact that my brother lets me hold him like I used to convinces me he still needs me—a lot. He may never call me "Chasey" again, like he did when he was little, but he'll always be my baby brother. To me, he'll always be that uncoordinated little kid who used to look up to me, who once longed to be like me, the little boy who needed me. And what's become glaringly obvious tonight is that Will *still* needs me.

I'm going to be here for him, just like I promised.

When Will calms and pulls away, he looks embarrassed. I punch him in the arm. Not hard, but not completely easy, either.

"Ow! What the fuck, dick." My brother rubs his bicep.

"That's for hitting me earlier, like multiple fucking times." I pause, catch his gaze. "And also...just because."

Really, I am giving my brother the chance to save face. Not to mention, it's my fucked-up guy way of letting him know I love him.

But he likes to press, so he says all cocky like, "'Cause why?"

I ignore his inquiry and stand up. He stands up, too. I try to stare him down, make myself look all stern, but hell, I gotta smile. The little shit is giving me attitude, all in good fun.

I reach out and fuck up his still-wet hair. "Don't worry about why," I tell him. "Just get the fuck to bed."

Will ducks under my arm, but not before grabbing up his duffel bag. I notice he makes damn sure the tree house sketch is secure before he takes off down the hall.

"Good night, Will," I call out over my shoulder.

When he doesn't answer, I turn around. He gives me the finger.

"Hey, Will," I say, more serious now.

He stops, but doesn't turn to face me.

"I fuck with you because I love you, all right? And I've missed being around you like this. I've missed being your brother."

Will's shoulders sag, and he starts into his room. But before he closes the door, I hear him say, "I've missed you, too, Chase. I love you, bro."

The next day, I take Will to work with me, and since Cassie has no desire to hang out all alone at the house, she asks Kay if she can tag along, too. Of course, Kay's cool with that.

All I can say is thank God Father Maridale is a laid-back kind of dude. He just shakes his head when he sees the four of us piling out of Kay's car in the morning.

Everyone waves jovially, and Father waves back. Kay and Cassie head over to the church office in the rectory, while Will and I walk over to the school.

"So...what do you want to paint?" my brother asks me a short while later.

We're standing side by side, staring at a completely blank wall in the school entrance area. The bright-white smooth expanse is like one giant, big-ass canvas, just waiting for our ideas to give it life.

I shrug one shoulder and glance over at my brother. He's wearing faded jeans and a plain white T-shirt, just like me.

"You got any ideas?" I ask him. "I'm thinking this is more your area of expertise."

"What do you mean?" he asks, chuckling. "You want me to draw comics on the wall?"

"No, smart-ass." I roll my eyes. "I was thinking of something more along the lines of a cartoon scene of some sort. Remember what I told you last night?"

"That kids go to school here," Will replies.

"*Little* kids," I stress. "This is a grade school."

We have drop cloths down, and there are paint cans all around us. There must be twenty different colors. Will picks up a brush, contemplates, and then dips the tip into a can of cinnamon-brown.

He holds the glistening paintbrush out in front of him. "Okay, I have an idea."

"Have at it," I say as I gesture to the blank wall.

Will steps forward and swashes a big curve of cinnamon brown onto the wall. Then, he starts to paint. I cock my head to the side, trying to figure out what he's up to. It looks to me like Will is painting the hindquarter and tail of a huge-ass squirrel.

"So, what are you thinking?" I have to ask, before he gets too far in on an idea that I may have to nix. Will's forte is action comics, and I suspect Father Maridale would frown on any ass-kicking wildlife animals gracing the school wall, cartoon or not.

"Don't worry." Will laughs.

He keeps painting, and it soon becomes clear his squirrel is nothing but cute and cuddly, kind of Disney-like.

He steps back after a minute and points his paintbrush at the far end of the wall. "Do you think you can paint, like, an old-fashioned school, place it at the end of a road? I think one of those red ones, with the bell at the top, would look good. We'll need some bright-green grass around it, too, and a few trees."

I pop the lid off of a can of schoolhouse red. "Sure, I can do all that."

My brother paints for a while longer, and then steps back to assess his work. He appears deep in thought as he brushes his hair back with his free hand. A drop of cinnamon brown drips from the paintbrush he's holding in his other hand. It lands on his jeans, a circular drop directly above his knee.

S.R. Grey

Will doesn't even notice. His eyes remain fixated on his giant canvas.

After a beat, he says, as if he's still working it out in his head, "I'm thinking maybe I'll paint a bunch of cute, cuddly animals. And, like, a cartoon kid who is walking to school." He pauses, ponders a few seconds more. "Yeah, and I'll make the kid look all happy and shit to be going off to learn. I'll paint the animals along the side of the road. They'll be cheering him on, wishing they could go to school, too." He finishes up with, "If you can paint all the background shit, I can paint the characters."

"No problem," I say. "And I like your idea, it's really great. The kids are going to love it."

We start painting together and end up working past noon. Kay and Cassie stop by, laugh at how involved we are in our masterpiece, and then offer to bring us sandwiches back from the diner so we don't have to stop painting.

Will and I are all about that.

"That'd be perfect," I say to Kay. "We're kind of on a roll here."

My brother and I accomplish a lot before Kay and Cassie return, and when they do, sandwiches in hand, they are impressed with how great the mural is shaping up to be.

Father Maridale stops by after Kay and Cassie leave. He gives his stamp of approval, as well.

"Keep up the good work," he says before he goes.

"This is fun," Will remarks a short while later, while he's wiping sweat away from his brow with the back of his hand.

He's beaming after hearing all the positive reinforcement, and truthfully, so am I.

We work so hard and get so caught up in our creation

that, by the end of the day, we're a little more than halfway done. And what we've created *is* amazing: blue skies, fluffy white clouds, swaying trees. There's a red schoolhouse on the far left side of the wall, and a happy cartoon kid traveling a path leading to the school, his cartoon-animal buddies encouraging him along the way.

Will's vision has come to life. My brother and I have created something upbeat that the kids at Holy Trinity are sure to love.

"Shit, I'm beat," Will says, wiping sweat from his brow for the umpteenth time.

It's a hot summer day and sweltering in the non-air-conditioned school. I chuckle when I notice how Will's dark-blond hair is sticking up off his forehead in a crazy way.

Doesn't matter, though, as I'm sure my hair is even more of a mess.

Even so, I tousle Will's hair, making it messier still, and say, "Hey, this shit looks fantastic, doesn't it?" I nod to the mural, my hand still on his head.

Will smacks my hand away, but he's laughing as he does so. "We did good, Chase," he says. "The little kids are going to love this shit. We make a good team, yeah?"

"We do, little brother, we do." I hold out my hand and make a fist. "Gartner brothers get it done."

Will bumps my fist with his and yells out, "Hell yeah!"

It feels right having my brother here at the school with me, working beside me on something so positive.

However, my natural high falters when I remember there are only two days left until Will has to go back to Vegas. *Fuck.*

Later that night, I'm standing in the upstairs hall, leaning against the doorframe, watching my brother while he sleeps. He's snoring lightly, sleeping soundly, worn out in the best kind of way, from an honest day's work.

For me, though, this is turning out to be tougher than I expected. Now that my brother is in Harmony Creek, I want him to stay awhile longer. Thirty-six more hours of having him here is not nearly long enough.

I hear a noise downstairs and cock my head. Someone just came in through the front door. But there's no cause for concern; I know exactly who's here.

Two minutes later, Kay is wrapping her arms around me from behind, and I'm smiling as I lean back into her comforting warmth.

"Hey," she whispers as she presses her cheek to my bare back.

"Hey," I whisper back. "Where's Cassie?"

"Sleeping," she mumbles.

I am freshly showered and have on nothing but boxer briefs. The clean scent of soap and shampoo fill my nose when I breathe in deeply, but it's not from me. This scent is feminine, flowery. "Babe," I murmur, breathing my girl in.

From the way Kay is pressed against me, I can feel she's wearing her sleep shorts and a thin tee. Her nipples, pronounced through the almost-sheer fabric, brush along my back when she shifts her body. She pulls back slightly, just enough so she can kiss the angel inked at the center of my back. Her soft lips linger at the angel, before traveling over to one of the spread wings.

I chuckle to myself. Kay sure loves my tattoos. Now, if I

could just talk her into having a small one inked right above where I love to—

"Hey," Kay says, breaking me from my wandering thoughts.

She slips under my arm, but in a way, that keeps us wrapped up with each other, only now we're face-to-face. "You seem distracted, Chase. What's up?"

I skim my hands down her back and sigh. "It just sucks that Will has to go back so soon."

She glances up, holds my gaze. "You missed him more than you realized, didn't you?"

"Way more," I admit.

She bites her lower lip and I lose her for a minute. "What are you thinking?" I ask.

"I was thinking maybe you should ask Will to stay awhile longer. Another week would be nice."

"Yeah, another week would be amazing," I agree. "And I'd ask Will to stay on in a heartbeat. But he'll never do it with Cassie heading back to Vegas with her mom. Not as long as the perverted stepdad is still in the picture. Will thinks his presence is the only thing keeping Cassie safe from that fucker."

"Actually"—Kay loosens her hold and takes a step back—"I wanted to talk to you about that whole situation."

There's hardly any light in the hall, but I can still detect a smile playing at her lips.

I can't help but smile right back at her. "What are you up to, Kay?"

Now she is absolutely grinning. "What if I told you I talked Cassie into calling her mom earlier tonight? And what if I told you she spilled everything?"

"Shit, I'd say you're fucking amazing."

She is amazing, beyond belief. But for so many more reasons than just this one.

However, this is certainly good news.

"So what happened?" I ask.

Kay's lips thin to a straight line as she recollects. "Well," she begins, "Cassie told her mom all the nasty things Paul has been saying. She detailed exactly what happened that prompted her to take off with Will." Kay takes a breath. "And Stephanie—that's Cassie's mom's first name, by the way—took action."

"What'd she do?"

"She kicked Paul out of the house, Chase. She told him to never come back."

"How'd she do that? I thought Cassie's mom was in New York this week."

"She is, but she called him from her hotel room. She used the landline phone so Cassie could remain on the cell and hear everything that was said. Bottom line, Chase, is that Paul has until tomorrow morning to get all his things out of the house, for good."

I'm still skeptical, so I inquire, "Yeah, but how will she know he really left?"

Kay replies, "Cassie's uncle lives near their house. He's stopping by tomorrow morning to check on things. He'll make sure Paul is gone. He's changing all the locks, too."

It sounds like everything is covered, so I breathe out a big sigh of relief. This is such great news—for Cassie and for Will, for all of us, really. I tug Kay closer to my body and shower her in featherlight kisses of appreciation.

"This is all because of you, baby," I say, my lips traveling along her jaw.

I move up to her ear, and I guess I hit a ticklish spot, because Kay starts to giggle.

Will, who sleeps through most everything, finally stirs. "I think we're getting too loud," I whisper. "Let's move this down to my bedroom."

It doesn't take anything more to convince Kay, as she practically drags me down the hall.

"Anxious?" I teasingly ask when we step into my bedroom.

Her response is to tug at the waistband of my boxer briefs. Chuckling, I reach behind me and close the door.

All playfulness soon subsides, as this raw need to connect with Kay becomes my driving force. I scoop her up into my arms, eliciting a surprised gasp from her.

She nuzzles my neck as I carry her over to the bed, and the whole way, I am telling her, "I love you so much, baby girl. You are my world."

"Mmm," she murmurs when I lay her down gently on the bed. "I love you too, Chase."

Want and need urge me to take her swiftly, but I corral those thoughts. Tonight, I want to love this woman who saves me again and again better than that, I want more than a rushed and hurried encounter. So I take my time undressing her. And as each piece of fabric is discarded, I worship her exposed skin...with my lips, with my tongue.

Kay makes the sweetest sounds as I do things to her that I know drive her crazy. I hear sweet anticipation in her every stuttered breath, sharpness in her every gasp, especially when I taste and explore where she's so fucking wet for me.

Her hands find their way into my hair, and she chants my name like a mantra. In response, I make her come and come and come.

When she finally stills, I trail a few sloppy kisses along the insides of her thighs, making them now wet from not just her, but from me too. Slowly, I begin to inch my way up her body. My boxer briefs were long ago discarded, so when my cock touches Kay, first dragging along her thigh and then pressing to her core, it is all me—bare...and hard as fuck.

Supporting myself with one arm, I handle myself by gliding the head of my cock back and forth along Kay's slit, spreading all of her wetness till she's writhing and begging, "Now, Chase, now."

"Not yet, baby, not yet."

I circle her clit with the tip of my dick, then press in slowly. When I still, only partway in, Kay circles her hips. My name falls from her lips, and I can tell she's close, but she's not there yet.

I lower my mouth to hers. "Say my name again."

As my name starts to form on her lips, I slide into her fully. My cock fills her pussy while my tongue invades her mouth. And the experience is so consuming, so fucking beautiful, that I swear I taste every muffled letter of my name. Kay is better than any drug I've ever done; she overloads my senses in the best kind of way. So I keep on tasting our love as I move my hips slowly, making love to my girl.

I discover loving like this has a taste all its own, the kind of taste that flavors your soul. Loving slow and easy is sweet, good, and pure. Going faster, picking up the pace, turns things tangy, like how spice adds dimension and depth. And climaxing is complex, multilayered, sweet and tangy, rolled into one huge fucking overwhelming experience.

Finally, when I collapse onto Kay and find her lips once more, I know what this flavor is. It's the best kind of taste— the taste of love, the taste of home.

CHAPTER FOUR

KAY

I fall asleep in Chase's embrace and don't wake until morning. My eyes blink open, and I promptly panic when I realize I'm in his bed, not on the sofa in my apartment.

"Shit, Cassie," I mumble as I jump up.

I stumble over a tangle of sheets and embark on a search for my sleep clothes. I didn't plan to stay the entire night in Chase's bedroom. Last night, I never even mentioned to Cassie that I was leaving the apartment. Poor girl. After she spoke with her mother, she went straight to bed. Last she knew, I was lying on the sofa, reading a book on my e-reader.

Chase wakes while I'm scurrying about. He yawns and stretches languorously, distracting me from my task. I take in the full view of his magnificent physique. Not only does he look amazing—hard, defined muscles and beautiful, sexy tats—but the things he can do to me with his body…

Besotted with lust, I snatch up one of the many T-shirts Chase has discarded on the floor. I ball up the tee and toss it at the object of my attraction.

Chase laughs and catches it easily. "What's this for?" he asks, holding up the T-shirt.

"You need to put a shirt on, like, fast. Before I come over there and jump you."

I catch sight of my own tee, grab it up quickly, and tug it over my head.

"And this is your incentive for me to get dressed?" Chase laughs, making no move to slip the shirt in his hands over his head. "'Cause I have to tell you, Kay, it's not very effective."

He lowers the little bit of sheet that's barely covering him and exposes his rather impressive morning wood. When he catches me staring and biting my lip, he raises an eyebrow in invitation.

I have no self-control when it comes to this man, so three seconds later, I am on him, riding him hard. It's nothing like last night, this is urgent and fast, but he still makes sure I come first.

"Always so considerate," I murmur in a post-orgasmic lazy tone.

He chuckles against my neck. "Let's take a shower together. I have one more 'considerate' thing in mind before we go to work."

"Oh, I'm intrigued," I shoot back.

"Oh, you'll be more than intrigued soon enough," he promises.

In the shower, Chase washes my body and shampoos my hair. He's so careful and gentle with me that I am soon turned on again. Surely this was his plan all along.

"Intrigued?" He cocks an eyebrow as he drops to his knees in front of me.

Before I can respond, his wet body leans toward me. On

his knees, with his head between my legs, Chase brings me to orgasm with his mouth.

Once I recover, I insist on returning the favor. "It's only fair," I say playfully, lowering myself until my mouth is inches from his hard cock.

Needless to say, Chase needs no convincing. He's pretty much down for head in the shower, and his cock is in my mouth within milliseconds.

When our morning sexcapades finally wrap up, Chase and I make our way downstairs. We slow up in the dining room, though, when we hear Cassie and Will in the kitchen, talking about Cassie's stepfather.

"Wait," Chase whispers, grabbing my arm.

I stop next to him, and we listen as, over the sound of a spoon scraping in a cereal bowl, Will asks Cassie, "Is that asshole really gone, though? Like, for good? Are you sure your mom's not bullshitting you?"

"Yeah, I'm sure," Cassie replies. "I heard her tell him he had to go. They're done, Will. Their marriage is finally over."

"Shit, that conversation must've been crazy," Will remarks, after emitting a low whistle. "How'd that go?"

"Not good," Cassie admits. "But all that matters now is that the pervert is definitely gone. In fact, I talked with Mom when I first woke up. She said my uncle went by the house late last night and Paul had already left. His shit was gone, every last bit of it."

"Fuck, that's good news, Cass." Will says, sounding relieved.

Chase and I choose that moment to make our presence known. When we step into the kitchen, Cassie and Will mumble simultaneous "good-morning" greetings, but otherwise fall silent.

Both kids are seated at the table, dressed and ready for the day. Cassie has on jean shorts and a bright-yellow tank top, while Will is wearing torn jeans and an old faded graphic T-shirt. As is often the case, Chase's brother is dressed the same as Chase is today, meaning both are ready to get back to work on the mural.

Chase grabs the orange juice out of the refrigerator. He pours a glass and hands it to me. I sit down at the table with Will and Cassie, while Chase hops up on the counter, juice carton and glass in hand.

"So, Will," Chase begins, filling his glass as he speaks, "now that everything's settled with Cassie's stepdad, what do you think about sticking around Harmony Creek for another week?"

Will must like the idea, his expression brightens immediately. He smiles at Chase, nods once, and then turns to Cassie and says, "Would you mind?"

She shakes her head. "No, not at all, I'm good with that. With everything going on, my mom decided to take off work next week. She already has a bunch of mother-daughter stuff planned. No doubt, I'll be running around with her once we're back in Vegas." She pauses for a beat, and then adds softly, "I think my mom feels guilty she didn't pick up on what was going on with Paul."

Cassie's mention of mother and daughter stuff reminds me that there's a message on my voicemail from my own mother, sent yesterday. I've yet to return her call. I now make a mental note to call her back sometime today. She sounded kind of urgent in her voicemail, but I don't know if that was nervousness showing in her voice, or something else entirely. It's hard to discern these things with stuff still weird between us. Sadly, though, I expect this is the way it will remain for some time. At least, until we have a break-though.

While I ruminate over my mother, everyone else is busy discussing the logistics of Will staying in town until next Friday. He still has the plane ticket he never used, so there's talk about when to call the airline to make the date-change adjustment.

"Clear it with Mom first," Chase says to Will. "Then we'll call the airline this afternoon."

"Yes, sir, big bro," Will retorts with a mock-salute. "Consider it done."

Some laughter and playful insulting ensues, but when Will falls into a murmured discussion with Cassie, I feel Chase's focus shift to me.

I am staring into my juice glass, only somewhat listening. Then again, I'm not really paying much attention at all. I'm too preoccupied, thinking about my mother. I guess, even after my talk with Father Maridale, I'm still all over the place when it comes to her.

I glance up at Chase, still on the counter, and his blues fill with concern.

"What's wrong?" he mouths.

I shake my head once to let him know now is not the time; I'll tell him about my mixed-up feelings later. But, first, I should speak with my mom so I know what she wants.

When I do have a chance to talk with her, later in the morning, while at work, she is nothing but kind to me. I speak to her on my cell outside the rectory office, and the sincerity in her voice alleviates my earlier concerns. I have to admit that I do feel better about my mom every time I speak with her.

So, there's no problem there, not like I initially feared. But the update she shares with me leaves me feeling more than a little queasy.

I step back into the rectory office, where Cassie is seated in the chair next to my desk, amusing herself on her phone.

Chase and his brother are putting the finishing touches on the mural, so Cassie has been hanging with me all morning.

"Is everything okay?" she asks when she looks up and sees my face drained of color.

I wave her off. "Yeah, yeah, everything is fine."

It's not, but it's Chase I long to speak with, not Cassie.

I sit back down at the desk, slowly. Cassie smiles at me, but there's concern in her eyes.

I decide to change the focus to lunch, but just as I'm about to ask Cassie what she feels like eating today, Will steps through the office doors.

He makes a bee-line to Cassie, leans down and kisses her cheek. "Guess what?" he says "Chase gave us money for lunch. Where do you want to go?"

Cassie twists in her seat to face me and asks, "Is it okay if I leave?"

"Of course," I reply.

"Kay, you can come with us, if you want," Will says, smiling. "Chase gave me more than enough cash for three lunches."

Will seems so much more relaxed now that Cassie is no longer in danger of being harassed, or possibly molested.

Plus, spending the past few days with Chase has clearly been good for him.

His smile, like Chase's, is very infectious, so I can't help but grin back.

But then I tell him, "I think I'm going to decline the lunch invitation. But thanks for asking. I'll just wait for Chase."

"Oh"—Will smacks his hand to his forehead—"I almost forgot. I'm supposed to tell you Chase is skipping lunch today. He has a few more details to add to the mural."

"Uh, okay," I say, "thanks for letting me know."

I place some papers into a file, straighten a few things on the desk, and then, just thinking out loud, add, "I should still probably stop over at the school and make sure Chase takes a break and eats something."

Will nods, "Yeah, good plan."

I can tell Will and Cassie want to get going, so I say, "You two go on ahead."

Before they leave, Cassie asks if it'd be okay if she and Will just do their own thing for the rest of the afternoon. She mentions the ice cream shop with the miniature golf course that's across from the church. "Do you mind if we hang out over there the rest of the day?"

Will chimes in, "Yeah, my part on the mural is pretty much done. Chase said he didn't care if Cass and I hung out in town this afternoon. He did say I should ask you, though. You know…to make sure you're cool with it."

"Yeah, sure." I shrug. "I don't mind. Just be back in time for us to leave."

"You got it," Will replies, "we'll be back by four or five."

After Cassie and Will leave the rectory office, I head over to the school. If Chase is still set on not going out for lunch,

I'll just buy him some food from the vending machines in the teachers' lounge.

After a walk across the sweltering parking lot—it's a scorcher today—I step into the entrance area of the school. Chase is hard at work, across from the main doors, intently painting some detail onto the red schoolhouse in the mural.

He spins around, paintbrush in hand, when he hears my approach. "Hey, babe."

His appearance is nothing short of stunning as he lowers the paintbrush to his side and wipes sweat from his brow with his other hand.

Sweaty Chase is übersexy Chase, and I take a minute to thoroughly enjoy the view. The man could truly star in one of those sweaty-gorgeous-guy-working-hard-on-a-hot-summer-day-and-needs-a-drink-of-water commercials.

That particular image prompts me to ask, "Are you thirsty?"

Chase chuckles, places the paintbrush sideways across a can of paint, and replies, "Maybe just a little."

I turn in the direction of the teacher's lounge. Pointing, I say in a rushed tone, "Let me go grab you a bottle of water. I'll buy some chips and pretzels for you, too."

With concern in his eyes—he knows something is amiss—he says, "You don't have to buy me anything, Kay. Will was supposed to give you a message that I plan to work through lunch."

"He did give me that message," I tell Chase. "But I still wanted to stop over and see you. Plus, you have to eat, you know?" I force a smile.

"Okay," he replies slowly, "but what about you? You sure you're okay with just pretzels and chips for lunch?"

Now, when I smile, it's for real. "Hey, that was good enough for the two of us before."

It's a clear reference to the lunch he and I shared following out first kiss, and he knows it.

Chase's eyes meet mine. "That was a great lunch," he agrees, "one of the best."

I say, "Yeah," and cast my eyes downward.

"Hey," Chase says softly, "what's wrong, sweetheart?"

I raise my eyes to his. "Ugh." I frown. "I talked to my mother today."

Chase comes to me without hesitation. "What happened?" he asks, placing his hands on either side of my face.

Just his touch comforts me, so I close my eyes for a few seconds to savor the feeling of being so well cared for. I know Chase thinks my mother has upset me. And she has, but not in the way he's probably thinking.

Chase worries my mother will disappoint me, like she's done before. As a result, he doesn't fully trust her. Not that I do either, not completely, but I have to say that today my mother gave me hope that she and I can move forward. She's *trying* to make amends for choosing my ex-boyfriend, Doug Wilson, over me for so many years. In fact, she's trying so hard that jerky Doug was the purpose of her call. Seems she wanted to give me a heads-up on what the asshole is planning.

His plan is what has me so upset. It's also the news I now share with Chase.

"My mom was great," I begin, "but it's what she told me that has me feeling like I might puke."

"What'd she tell you?" Chase asks with concern in his tone.

79

"Doug is coming to town tomorrow," I blurt out in a rush of words. "He'll be here for a week, maybe two."

Chase tries to hide it, but I see his fists clenching when he lowers his hands down to his sides.

"Why's that fucker spending time in Harmony Creek?" he grinds out.

Chase hates my ex-boyfriend almost as much as I do. Doug was at my house, uninvited and unwilling to leave, the night my sister died. I've always placed partial blame at his feet—Sarah never would have been left alone if he hadn't showed up that night. And she wouldn't have been left unattended long enough for her to wander out to the backyard pool, where she drowned. But Doug had me trapped upstairs, keeping me from her and thus allowing my sister to end up in that damn pool.

As if all that wasn't horrible enough, I recently found out—through my mother—that Doug played a much bigger role in the awful tragedy. He was the one who left the back patio door unlatched. If he hadn't forgotten to re-latch the door when he went out to dispose of a beer can, Sarah never would have snuck outside. She wouldn't have ended up in the water.

There's no doubt in my mind that my baby sister would be alive today if it hadn't been for Doug Wilson and his acts of stupidity.

"Kay?" Chase cups my cheek when I sway a little. "Are you all right?"

"Yeah, I guess." I look up at the man I love, the man who keeps me together, the man who steadies me at times like these. "To answer your question," I continue, "my mom said Doug's coming into town to help his mom. I guess he has vacation time or whatever."

Doug's mother was in a serious car accident recently. Doug was in Harmony Creek directly following the accident, but he had to return to where he lives now—Columbus, Ohio, same as my parents—because of work.

I was glad he left town so quickly, as it meant no chance of running into him. But if Doug remains in town longer than a day or two, the possibility of my running into him increases exponentially, especially if he's striving to make that happen. Personally, I don't care to come face-to-face with Doug Wilson ever again, not for the rest of my life. It might be unavoidable, though, considering the other thing my mother told me.

"There's more," I say to Chase.

"What?" He eyes me warily.

I breathe in deeply, then exhale slowly. "My mother said I should be on the lookout."

"What the fuck does that mean?" Chase narrows his blues, and I'm reminded why I once christened the color of his eyes gunmetal blue.

In times like these, when he's upset or angry, the gray flecks in his eyes become more apparent, making his gaze cold and hard. But his reaction is not directed at me. Chase's ire is solely focused on my ex-boyfriend.

I continue, though I know, in doing so, Chase's irritation will increase tenfold.

"I guess Doug has it in his head that he needs to seek me out, so he can, like, apologize in person." I roll my eyes. "He's about four years too late, right? Besides, I have no desire to hear his lame apology anyway."

I finish speaking and sigh, relieved to have everything off my chest. Chase remains quiet, his lips pressed together. The look on his face makes me think he may have plans for Doug Wilson. I should discourage my boyfriend from violence. But, like with the junkie situation, a part of me yearns for Chase to kick the shit out of my ex. Sure, I want to be a good person, and for the most part, I am, but I can't deny there's a level of darkness in me, just like there is in Chase. Our good *and* bad bind us. Chase almost killed a man in my defense, the junkie who attacked me not so long ago. But instead of being appalled by the level of violence Chase meted out on the guy—and it was substantial—I was pleased, not to mention turned on. So now, instead of making Chase promise to leave Doug alone, I request nothing. I keep my mouth shut and think, *Let the chips fall where they may.*

Chase's eyes meet mine. I don't know what he's looking for, but he must find it. He nods and then heads back over to the mural.

When he starts closing up paint cans, I ask, "What are you doing? I thought you wanted to work through lunch."

He shakes his head and continues to clean up. "No, this can wait." He stands and turns to me, holds out his hand. "Let's get out of here for a while."

I place my hand in his. "You sure?" I ask.

He nods and that's that. We go to lunch down at the diner. We eat and talk. My worries leave me and we have fun, just like we always do.

My make-everything-better guy brings out my best.

Consequently, when I return to the church grounds, I'm in a far lighter mood than before we left. Chase deposits a light kiss on my cheek, and we go our separate ways.

Unfortunately, when I reach the church office, the bright mood I'm hanging on to by a thread snaps. Or more succinctly put, it's snipped away when I see who's waiting for me in the chair next to my desk.

"Missy Metzger," I mutter to myself. "Oh, yay."

Missy can't hear me through the glass doors, but she glances up nonetheless and gives me a little wave.

I wave back, taking in her attire. Her clothes snag my attention, since they're so vastly different from what she's usually wearing.

"What a change," I whisper.

Missy is dressed in conservative clothing, a long navy skirt, a light-blue blouse buttoned up snugly over her substantial cleavage, and plain flats. Her dishwater blond hair is pinned up tightly and her makeup is minimal.

I sense something has changed in Missy's life. I sense that's why she's here—to give me an update.

"Might as well get this over with," I mumble, before I push open the double doors and step into the church office.

My approach to my desk is hesitant. This is the closest I've been to Missy since I found out she shared an intimate encounter with my boyfriend one night back in early June. She and Chase hooked up (not all the way, but enough) behind the Anchor Inn.

I've successfully avoided Missy since the night I overheard her and Chase arguing about their encounter at the church carnival. Their intimacy happened before I met Chase—like a day before—but it still feels awkward every time I see Missy. Anyway, the week after the church carnival I got lucky and only saw Missy at Mass. I've never been so happy that Missy sits in the front of the church as I was that

Sunday. I used to sit there, too—right between skinny Missy and her far-from-skinny mom—but, nowadays, I sit with Chase where he feels most comfortable, in the back pews.

So the first week of Operation Avoid-Missy was a breeze.

The following two weeks, right up until today, running into Missy wasn't even a concern. She was down in Virginia visiting with her dad. He moved away years ago, following his breakup with Missy's mom.

But clearly, my successful run of avoiding Missy has come to an end. She's obviously back from her trip out of town. And it's not like I can turn around and run away, even though I long to do exactly that. And I don't do anything of the kind.

Instead, I offer up a cheery "Hey, Missy" as I slip around the opposite side of the desk from where she is seated.

I put my purse in a drawer, sit down, and with a fake smile in place, inquire, "So, how was Virginia?"

Missy fidgets nervously with the scalloped-edge of her blouse sleeve. "It was good," she drawls, eyes down. "Dad's doing okay. Still loves to bitch about Mom, of course." She glances up and gives me a little roll of her eyes. "You'd think after all the years that have gone by, he'd move on. But…guess not."

I really don't know how to respond, so I just nod once.

Silence descends and the awkwardness between us increases tenfold. "Uh"—I move some random papers around on my desk—"I really have a lot to do this afternoon, Missy. I'm glad you're back and all, but I should probably—"

"Look, Kay," she interrupts, "I know you hate me now that you know about the…stuff that happened between me and Chase."

I flinch, thinking, *Stuff?* This woman blew my boyfriend, and he fingered her to orgasm, twice. Ugh.

"But we still have to work together," Missy continues, oblivious to my thoughts. "The rummage sale is coming up in August. And Father Maridale has already said he expects us to work on it together."

"I know." I sigh, resigned.

What Missy is saying is true; we do have to work together. Maybe it's time I get over my jealousy, especially with something that occurred before I even knew Chase. I can hold on to this forever, or I can move on. I feel like I've been making progress on the forgiveness front, so I let it go.

"For the record, Missy," I say, "I don't hate you."

Missy plucks at a wrinkle in her skirt. "I wouldn't blame you if you did," she mumbles. "I should have told you when you first started dating Chase. I guess I just didn't know how to bring something like that up. If it helps, the things he and I did that night meant nothing, I swear."

I cringe. I may be up for forgiving her, but that doesn't mean I care to rehash the details of what she and my boyfriend did to each other, even if it was before I met him.

"Just let it go." I wave my hand around, swishing the air. "I'm over it, okay?"

Missy looks doubtful, but I really am trying.

I tell her that, and she replies softly, "Well, since we're putting it all out on the table, I also need to apologize for the night you and I were at the Anchor Inn. I swear, Kay, I never would have hit on Nick Mercurio if I'd known you two used to date. All I knew that night was that he was your boss last summer when you worked at Pizza House. I honestly didn't know you two ever had a thing."

"He was my boss, yeah, but we never really had…a thing," I reply, floundering with discomfort.

How do I explain I never had sex with Nick?

I go with, "He and I were never *involved*-involved."

Truth be told, I only went out with Nick a few times. And it was *mostly* platonic, apart from a few chaste kisses. Oh, and one night, we messed around in the back of his car. But we didn't go too far, just some groping. I've always known Nick would've liked much more, though. He'd been crushing on me since we started worked together.

Right now, though, I just want to end this line of conversation with Missy. I clearly recall the night she and I were at the Anchor Inn. It was a girls' night out, and we ran into Nick and his cousin Tony.

To say Missy, Nick, and Tony hit it off would be a major understatement. The three of them hooked up, and I ended up overhearing their threesome in a back stairwell at the bar.

Despite my repeated attempts to squelch the conversation, Missy insists on explaining the Nick-Tony thing. "Kay, you need to know I never had sex with Nick." Missy is emphatic. "I mean, sure, we messed around some, but I was only with-with Tony."

"Whatever, Missy," I snap.

And that's when she starts crying, like bawling.

Shit, now I feel bad. I'm not upset with Missy, not really. I think I'm just overly emotional this afternoon, what with worrying about Doug, my mom—just everything.

I touch the edge of Missy's sleeve, the one she was toying with earlier. "I'm sorry," I say. "I didn't mean to upset you."

She shakes her head, while big tears roll down her cheeks. "It's not you, Kay," she sniffles.

Truth be told, I am a little worried about Missy. This outburst isn't like her. She takes things in stride; she has a thick skin. Something is dreadfully wrong for her to be this upset.

"What's really wrong?" I ask. "Did something happen in Virginia?"

She takes a tissue out of her purse and dabs at the corners of her eyes. "No, Virginia was fine, just like I said."

"Then what's going on?"

Missy hesitates, twists the tissue in her hand. After a beat, she blurts out, "I'm pregnant, Kay."

"Oh...God."

A million things run through my mind: *Does Missy know who the dad is? How far along is she? She's not still doing drugs, is she?* But ahead of all those thoughts, I'm just thankful Chase never stuck his dick in Missy. I'd die if there was a chance he was the father of her baby.

"Don't look at me like that, Kay," Missy snaps when she catches me staring her way. "I haven't been with as many guys as you're thinking. I know who the father is."

"Tony?" I venture, since she just told me she and Nick never had sex.

Missy nods. "We used protection, but I guess it's true when they say condoms aren't one hundred percent effective." A tear trails down her cheek, and she swipes it away impatiently.

"Have you talked to Tony yet? Does he know?"

Missy scoffs. "No. I've only told my mom—and now you."

"How'd it go with your mom?" I inquire, genuinely interested in the answer.

I guess my feelings for Missy are softening already. She was my friend at one time. Not a close friend, but still, enough of a friend that my heart now goes out to her. In the situation she's in, she faces a rough road ahead.

"My mom was pissed as hell," Missy says. "That's why I'm in no hurry to tell the father the"—she coughs sarcastically—"happy news."

I lean forward and put my hand on her arm. "But, Missy, you have to tell Tony. He has a right to know."

She doesn't answer, and I whisper, "Unless you're thinking of—"

"No," Missy barks out, and even more vociferously, she adds, "I'm keeping this baby, Kay. And I will tell Tony. I just have to get the nerve up, okay?"

Any leftover anger I was harboring towards Missy evaporates. I can't fathom what she's going through, so I say as comfortingly as I can, "Yeah, Missy, I get it. Just talk to him when you're ready."

Missy seems so, I don't know...deflated, maybe. She's clearly a little broken. Maybe she thought her wild behavior would never bear any consequences. Speaking of which, I carefully inquire, "Um, you quit all the drugs, right?"

Missy narrows her eyes at me. "What drugs?"

"Missy..." I impart a "come on" kind of gaze in her direction.

"Chase," she spits. "I should've figured he'd tell you I was using the night we—"

"Yes," I interrupt in a rush, "he told me you had cocaine in your purse that night."

Missy sighs and averts her eyes. "I did have cocaine with me," she whispers, "and, yes, I snorted a bunch that night. He told you the truth."

Before I can respond, hers eyes meet mine, and she says, "I'm not doing that shit anymore, though. I quit everything, Kay. I plan to be a good mother. I want to be the kind of mom my kid can look up to." Her eyes fill with tears. "I just want him or her to love me, you know?"

There's so much yearning and hope, even desperation, in Missy's voice. And it's then that I realize all she's ever wanted was to feel loved and accepted. I am no different—no one is. I can't condemn Missy for desiring the same things we all ultimately crave.

"Hey." I place my hand on Missy's hand. "I'll be here for you—that is, if you want me to."

She nods, prompting me to go on.

"You'll get through this, Missy. And you'll come out stronger. You're going to be a great mom, I know it."

She looks surprised. "Do you really believe that?"

I think about it, and I realize I really do. I think Missy has had goodness in her all along. She's never done anything to hurt anyone, only herself. But she seems to have conquered those demons.

So I say, "Yeah, I do believe it."

She inquires softly, "Does that mean you've fully forgiven me for not telling you about what happened between me and Chase?"

I'm truthful and sincere when I say, "All that stuff is in the past, Missy. It doesn't matter, anyway. I didn't even know Chase back then."

Missy suddenly leans over and gives me a hug. It feels like one from the heart.

"Thank you, Kay, thank you. I have a feeling I'm going to need a friend to get through this."

I close my eyes and realize I want to be there for Missy. I want to be her friend.

CHAPTER FIVE

CHASE

On Friday morning, the day Cassie's mom is due to come into town to pick her up, Kay is in a great mood. I ask her what's up when I find her in the kitchen, cooking up a big country breakfast.

She smiles and keeping her eyes on a skillet filled with scrambled eggs as she stirs, says, "I don't know, nothing in particular. I just feel happy today." She turns away from the stove and stands on her tiptoes to kiss my cheek. "Now, sit down. I sent Cassie upstairs to get Will. The eggs are almost ready."

"Who can argue with that?" I remark as I follow my girl's instructions.

When Will wanders into the kitchen a minute later, I pay close attention to his demeanor. He seems to be in pretty good spirits despite the fact his girlfriend, who is trailing behind him, is leaving in a few hours.

After we're seated and have started to eat, Will glances my way. I've been watching him from across the table, but he's only just now noticed.

He raises a questioning eyebrow, but I just shake my head and smile. I give him a "Life is good, yeah?" kind of look, and his lips curve up into a smile of his own.

Cassie scoots her chair a little closer to Will. She places one hand on his knee and picks up her juice glass with her other hand. "Everything is really delicious," she says to Kay. "Thank you for doing this."

Cassie proceeds to nod to the assortment of breakfast foods on the table, and Will and I chime in with our own gracious sentiments.

Following the compliments to Kay's cooking, Cassie says to her, "I wish you could have taken off work today, like Chase. I was hoping you could meet my mom when she gets here."

"I know." Kay sighs. "I wish I could have, too. I planned to take today off, but Father Maridale has an out-of-town meeting that will last all day, and someone has to man the office."

"Well," Cassie replies, toying with a crispy piece of bacon, "if you and Chase ever make it out to Vegas, you'll have to stop by our house and visit. You can meet Mom, then."

Kay promises that when—not if—we fly out to Vegas, we will most assuredly visit with Cassie and her mom.

"And on that note"—Kay glances over at the digital clock on the stove—"I better get going."

"Hey," I mumble to Kay through a mouthful of pancake, "hold on a sec and I'll walk you out."

I finish off the last bit of syrup-covered goodness from my plate and push back my chair. "You two get started on cleaning up in here," I say to Will and Cassie as I stand.

Will groans and insists he's too full to move, but Cassie elbows him and quickly interjects, "Of course we'll clean up, Chase."

Out in the driveway, when we reach Kay's car, I lean

forward to open the door for her. But when she places her hand over mine, stopping me, I ask, "What's up?"

She sighs. "I didn't want to say anything last night, or this morning in front of Cassie and Will, but Missy stopped by the church office yesterday afternoon."

I roll my eyes. "What the fuck did she want?"

Yeah, I'm still a little aggravated with the way things went down at the church carnival, the night Kay learned of my hookup with Missy. And I'm less than thrilled when I think of how Missy blew off Kay at the Anchor Inn to go fuck around with Nick Mercurio and his cousin. But, hey, when it comes right down to it, who am I to judge?

Kay stares down at the keys in the hand not still on mine and mumbles, "Uh, Missy wanted to talk about next month's rummage sale."

Kay's acting a little strange, like there was more to Missy's visit, so I ask, "She didn't upset you, did she?"

"No, not at all. But she did have some…news."

"Oh yeah? What kind of news?" With Missy, I can only imagine.

But even I'm shocked when Kay blurts out, "The baby kind of news, Chase. Missy is pregnant."

"Holy fuck."

There are these few drawn-out seconds where Kay and I just stare at each other. I squeeze her hand, all the while, thinking one thing: *Thank God I never fucked Missy Metzger*.

Kay glances away, probably thinking the same thing. She says, "For the record, Missy knows who the father is— Nick's cousin, Tony."

"How does she know it's not Nick's?" I chuckle, recalling how Kay told me Missy had been with both Tony and Nick.

Kay explains that she's since come to learn Missy was only with Tony.

"Nice," I say, smirking, "so Nick just watched the show."

Kay frowns. "Chase, please, be nice."

Moving my hand from hers, I cup her chin and urge her to look up at me. When she does, I want to know, "So you're friends with Missy now?"

"Actually, I do want to be her friend. I think she needs people to support her."

I have a sinking feeling this includes me. "I guess that means she's my friend now, too?" I raise an eyebrow.

Kay smacks me in the chest. And I suppose to show me she's not holding my indiscretion with Missy against me—or Missy—she teasingly says, "Not too good of a friend, buddy."

I laugh, but then, just to make things clear, I lower my lips until they're touching hers.

"Hey, it's you I love," I murmur against her mouth. "I have no desire to ever be with anyone other than you. You know that, right?"

"Mmhmm," she replies, before placing her hands on my sides, standing on her tiptoes, and kissing me with everything she's got.

Shit, Kay's enthusiasm has me muttering between heated kisses, "Fuck, I wish we could go back inside right now."

Kay lets out a little moan that does nothing to make me want to stop. But before I end up lifting her pretty summer-green dress, pulling down her panties, and fucking her against the side of the car, I pull away.

Giving her a light swat on the ass, I say with a sigh, "You better go."

After Kay's on her way, I head back into the house. In the kitchen, I happen upon Cassie and Will, who are apparently having an R-rated moment of their own. Cassie is sitting in Will's lap, her mouth on his. They don't even notice me. I chuckle to myself on my way to the sink. But when things threaten to turn X-rated, my brother shifting Cassie's hand from his thigh up to his crotch, I clear my throat—loudly.

Cassie jumps off Will so fast it takes all my self-control to keep from laughing out loud.

"Sorry to interrupt," I say with a smirk directed at my brother.

He's smirking right back, cocky bastard, while Cassie, who's blushing profusely, busies herself with gathering the plates from the table.

Something is clearly wrong with this picture, though, as I distinctly recall telling Cassie *and* Will to clean up after breakfast.

Turning to Will, I say, "You're supposed to be cleaning, too. Help your girlfriend."

"Dude, she's got it," he whines.

I then insist Will help his girl.

"You could use the distraction," I say, nodding to where he's adjusting an obvious hard-on.

I decide it's probably prudent to stay in the kitchen, so I start cleaning up, as well. My presence, however, doesn't deter Will from feeling up Cassie every time he thinks I'm not paying attention.

Damn, it's a good thing she's leaving today. I don't know how much longer I could keep those two apart.

But I need not worry. Mrs. Sutter arrives shortly before noon, right on schedule, to pick up her daughter. Will, Cassie, and I meet her out in the driveway. Will carries Cassie's suitcase over to her car as the taxi Cassie's mom arrives in drops her off and backs out of the long driveway.

Mrs. Sutter then rushes over to her daughter.

"Mom," Cassie cries out as the two meet in a reunion embrace.

On his way back from Cassie car, Will glances over at the mother-daughter love-fest. When he reaches me, he says, "Mrs. Sutter is kind of hot, dude. Am I right or am I right? She's like an older, curvier Cassie."

I roll my eyes, refrain from commenting. Will's teenage-boy hormones are in overdrive this morning. But it is true that Mrs. Sutter is attractive. And like Will commented, she's definitely an older version of her daughter, with long blond hair and a thin body, but, also like Will pointed out, she's far curvier. Another striking difference between mother and daughter is their attire. Cassie has on cutoff, white denim shorts and a graphic tee, while her mother is dressed for success. She's wearing a smart business suit and expensive-looking pumps.

Following what feels like a five-minute hug, along with a few tears and apologies, Cassie and her mom finally break apart. They step over to where Will and I are standing.

Will introduces me to Cassie's mom, and she kicks off the conversation by thanking me for letting Cassie stay at my house, to which I reply, "It was the least I could do, Mrs. Sutter."

Cassie's mom juts out her hip, then places her hand on my forearm and squeezes lightly.

"Still," she says softly, "it was very kind of you, Chase. And I really appreciate that. Oh, and please just call me Stephanie."

Cassie's mom is clearly hitting on me. She continues to thank me and thank me for keeping an eye on her daughter all week. I mostly just nod and brush it off, prompting her to move closer to me, all smiling and giggly.

Lord help me. It isn't the first time I've been hit on by an older woman. And in another life, I would have been all over that MILF shit. But I am not that guy anymore. I'm with Kay—body, heart, and soul. My girl is it for me.

So, while Cassie and Will talk amongst themselves, I casually ignore every last one of Stephanie's come-ons.

Eventually, though, I've had enough. To get her off my dick, I pointedly ask, "You sure you have everything straightened out at home? That deviant who was harassing your daughter is definitely gone, yeah?"

Apart from tiring of the misplaced affections, I figure I have a right to make sure my brother won't have any reason to run away with this woman's daughter a second time.

The serious turn in which I've steered the conversation is effective. Stephanie drops the flirty act and says somberly, "Yeah, Paul is gone for good. He didn't even leave a forwarding address, which is just as well. He isn't coming back."

"Well, let's try to keep it that way," I strongly suggest, hoping she's not the kind of woman who will eventually forgive him and let the dick move back in.

Perhaps detecting my skepticism, she says, "I'll never let that man back in my house."

Cassie and Will have quit talking, and she says quietly, "Come on, Mom, we better get going."

Before they depart, Will gives Cassie a good-bye kiss that makes Stephanie clear her throat. And then mother and daughter are off.

When Cassie's car, with her mom at the wheel, disappears from sight, Will's eyes remain downcast. Wearing the same scuffed, black Chucks he arrived in, he grinds his toe into the gravel.

"You okay?" I ask.

He nods once. "Yeah."

"Would you want to do something this afternoon," I throw out.

He nods, and I ask, "Like what?"

"I don't know, Chase," Will says impatiently. "But, shit, let's do something."

He glances over at me. He's squinting from the sun, and his eyes are watery. But, fuck, that wetness isn't from the bright summer day.

"Hey." I pretend to punch his shoulder to lighten shit up. "Let's go fishing down at the creek. There's a great spot right over the hill." I point to beyond the tree line. "I took Kay there a while back. We didn't catch much that day, but she still had a blast."

"Yeah, sure, fishing, okay," Will mutters dejectedly.

I drape an arm around his shoulders and nudge him toward the house. "Come on, let's go grab the gear. Hey, you never know, you may actually catch something."

I'm trying to get Will to laugh, but he just gives me a sad smile. "Yeah, maybe I will."

Little bro remains mopey as we trudge down to the

creek. He perks up considerably, though, once we're set up and he does indeed start catching fish.

The hours pass. We don't talk a lot. We're content to just kick back and savor the tranquility of sitting side by side on the creek bank, casting lines and enjoying the day. As the sun shifts in the sky, and late afternoon nears, we begin to pack up our gear, along with the several fish we caught.

Out of the blue, Will asks, "Hey, Chase, can you do me a favor?"

I close the latch on the tackle box. "Sure, what do you need?"

"I was wondering if you'd take a look at some stuff I've been working on for my comic book. I need an opinion from someone I trust."

I am touched as hell that Will trusts my opinion, that he cares what I think of his work.

But when I respond, I just leave it at, "Of course I'll check out what you've drawn."

"Cool," Will says, nodding, like this is a burden off his mind.

We walk back from the creek to the house, and as we approach the back porch, Will wants to know, "What's for dinner?"

I hold up our catch. "Fish?"

"Nah…" Will shakes his head. "Kay shouldn't have to cook again. She just made us that great breakfast."

"Good point. We can always just fry them up ourselves," I offer.

But when my brother shrugs, I sense he's not in the mood to eat what we've caught.

"You got something else in mind?" I ask him.

"Yeah, what about takeout?" We reach the back porch and set our fishing gear down. "I could go for some pizza."

I instantly think of Pizza House, since it's the only game in town if you want really good pizza. Kay and I tend to avoid the place, though. For one reason only—Nick Mercurio. Kay used to date him—kind of—so she isn't entirely comfortable dining there. She thinks our presence at the restaurant might make Nick feel uneasy. I really don't give a shit how the dude feels. Fact is, Kay is with me now, and Nick will never again have a chance with her. Not that the guy ever really had a shot in the first place. *Jackass.*

I guess when I really think about it, I, like Kay, am not too into the idea of hanging out at the place where Nick Mercurio works. But if Will is set on pizza, then Pizza House it is.

Of course, as luck would have it, Nick is standing behind the front counter, ringing up an order, just as Will and I walk in the place.

Great.

I try not to picture the fucker's hands on my girl, but it's tough. Kay told me they never had sex—thank fucking God—but there was one night when he did get half her clothes off in the backseat of his car. I bristle at the thought, but remind myself that, like my hookup with Missy, it's all in the past.

Still, so I don't fly off and sucker punch Nick just for the hell of it, I divert my attention away from him, focusing instead on the clean-cut guy who's at the counter paying for the takeout order.

Even with only a view of the back of Clean-Cut guy's head, there's something vaguely familiar about him. His neatly trimmed dark-blond hair, athletic-build… I feel like

I've seen him before. He's not someone I know well, I'm sure of that, but I sense he's from this town. Hell, if he's here at Pizza House, he has to be from Harmony Creek. Only, his nice attire doesn't fit in. A suit and tie on a hot day like today just screams out-of-towner.

But the mystery remains when guy-I-can't-place never turns around. He slips out a side door with his pizza.

"Someone you know?" Will jerks his thumb toward the guy's departing form.

I shake my head. "No, I don't think so."

At the counter, Nick's dark eyes widen slightly when he sees me. Unlike with me and the dude at the counter, Nick obviously knows who the fuck I am. And he surely knows Kay and I are a couple. That juicy tidbit has made its way around this small town too many times to count.

Despite the awkwardness, Nick takes our order with efficiency. He jots down everything on an order pad, then excuses himself to "personally" take the order back to the kitchen.

"I want to make sure they get everything right," he explains.

"Great, that's cool," I snort.

I know Nick just doesn't want to get stuck making small talk with my brother and me while we wait for the two large pizzas we ordered to bake.

A waitress who looks like she's worked at Pizza House for the past twenty years comes around the corner, just as Nick is heading toward the back.

He stops her midstep and tells her what we ordered, then adds, "Can you ring them up, Vi?"

"No problem, sweetie," Vi replies warmly as she reaches

for an order pad in the pocket of her apron. She removes a pen from the big bun on her head—dark hair streaked with gray—and recites the items we ordered while she writes them down.

When she steps over to the register, her eyes following her fingers as she taps in our order on a touch screen, she asks me, "So, young man, you being good to our girl?"

Clearly, Vi recognizes me as the local bad boy dating the beloved former Pizza House employee.

I smile charmingly when she looks up and I hand her the money. "Yes, ma'am, I am."

She smiles as she peruses my face and my body. *These older women are killing me today.*

She takes the cash from my hand and says, "I swear, that Kay is one lucky girl. It's been like a gathering of her good-looking men—past and present—in here this afternoon." She proceeds to count off the list with her fingers. "Let's see, there's you, Nick, that last customer—"

Whoa...wait. "The last customer? What are you talking about?"

She hands me my change and gives me a look like maybe I've missed something important. "That man who was leaving just as you arrived...he used to date Kay."

Oh shit.

I sure did miss something important. Now I know why the dude looked so familiar. Doug-motherfucking-Wilson was no more than eight feet from me less than ten minutes ago. If only he'd turned around, then I would've recognized his face.

Fuck, this is bad. Kay's mother wasn't bullshitting; Doug is in Harmony Creek, right on schedule. And that means he'll be looking for Kay so he can spew forth his four-years-too-late apology.

Yeah, right. Not if I have anything to say about it. That fucker is not going to unload his guilty conscience onto my girl. She's finally at a place of peace, coming to terms with Sarah's untimely death. And Doug-fucking-Wilson isn't going to be bringing that shit back to the forefront of sweet girl's mind.

Kay doesn't want to see him anyway, she's told me as much. And she sure as fuck doesn't need Doug's phony apologies.

I had considered taking preventative action when Kay first told me about her ex's plan, but now I am certain—I'm going to make sure that dickhead stays far away from Kay. Too bad he left the restaurant, or I'd nip that shit in the bud today.

Vi misreads the displeased look on my face. She says in a low but consolingly voice, "Aww, don't you worry, gorgeous. You're definitely the most handsome."

I roll my eyes, and Will laughs out loud.

Nick returns a minute later and shoos away Vi. "Sorry about that," he says apologetically. "She's quite the talker."

Will shakes his head. "Bro, this is one small fucking town."

He doesn't even know the half of it.

Nick chuckles like he's agreeing with Will, but he shuts the fuck up when he sees my expression. I don't have a problem with him, not at the present. Nope. But I do have an idea. And I'm about to enlist Nick's help in taking care of the problem I presently face.

"So"—I lean forward on the counter—"the guy who

was leaving with the takeout when we first got here, that was Doug Wilson, wasn't it?"

"Yes," Nick replies slowly, eyes wary. "Why?"

I shrug. "I hear he's in town for the next week or so. Does he come in here much when he's around?"

Nick's concern with my question is obvious, his expression is grim. But he answers nonetheless, "Yeah, Doug picks up a lot of takeout whenever he's around. I'm sure he'll be back."

I grab an order pad off the counter and scribble down my cell phone number. "Do me a favor"—I tear the slip of paper from the pad and hold it out to a reluctant Nick—"give me a call next time he places an order. Hold him up a little, if you can. Give me some time to get here."

Nick takes the slip of paper and stares down at the number I've written. "Is there some reason why you want to see him in person?" His voice is a mere whisper.

"Yeah, I got something I need to talk to him about."

Knowing my background and my temper better than anyone, Will whistles under his breath. The kid knows what's up.

I ignore Will, and raise a questioning brow Nick's way. "Are you cool with helping me out with this?"

He folds the piece of paper and slips it into a pocket of his pants. "Yeah, sure. I'll let you know when Doug orders again." His eyes dart from me to Will, and then he points to the back of the restaurant. "Uh, your pizzas are probably ready. I should go check."

After Nick is out of sight, Will says, "You look pissed. What was that all about?"

I mess with the order pads on the counter, stacking them up. "Nothing."

"You got some ass to kick, I can help," Will offers.

"Hey"—I turn abruptly and point a finger at my too-eager-to-fight brother—"you are doing nothing of the kind. This next week is all about you staying *out* of trouble, not getting into it. Got it?"

Will shrugs. "Sure, bro, whatever you say."

I don't mean to be so harsh with Will, especially after he's already had a rough morning with Cassie leaving. But I sure as fuck don't want him involved in my mess. Or what will probably end up turning into a fucking mess.

Because one thing is certain: Doug Wilson is not going to be searching out and upsetting Kay. I'll do whatever it takes to make sure that motherfucker stays far, far away.

CHAPTER SIX

KAY

I come home from work on Friday, swap out my summer-green sundress for denim shorts and a peach-tone baby-doll tee, and then head across the driveway to the house.

"You look cute," Chase says when I walk into the living room, where I find him and Will eating pizza and watching TV.

I plop down on the sofa next to Chase, lean over and grab a slice of pizza from his plate. "I see you started without me," I say, before biting into a big glob of cheese and pepperoni.

"Sorry, babe," Chase says.

Will looks up from where he's stretched out on the floor in front of the TV. "Don't be mad at Chase. It's my fault we started without you. I was starving." He takes a large bite of pizza, as if to illustrate the point, and once he's finished chewing, he adds, "I couldn't wait."

"I'm not mad," I say, smiling at Will. "I'm just teasing you two."

After a few more bites of pizza, I recognize the distinctive flavor. I turn to Chase and ask, "Did you pick this up from Pizza House?"

I'm surprised Chase chose that particular restaurant. On account of Nick, we tend to avoid the place.

But, sure enough, Chase replies, "Yep."

His short response, though, leaves me with the impression he doesn't care to discuss his Pizza House run. I have to wonder why.

Chase suddenly reaches over to the end table and grabs an unopened can of soda. "Thirsty?" he asks, his lips curving into a mischievous smile.

When I see he's offering me a lemon-lime soda—of course, it's Chase's favorite—I decide to have some fun.

Accepting the can from Chase, I make a show of reading the label. "Oh, big surprise, lemon-lime." I huff and roll my eyes mock-dramatically. "I swear I can never get anything else in this house."

Will, poor kid, misreads me once again. He sits up and offers to get me something else.

"There're other things in the fridge," he says, his expression serious. "Juice, water, beer—do you want any of those?"

Chase chuckles. "Kay is just giving me a hard time, Will. She loves the lemon-lime shit." His eyes slide to me, and he winks. "Don't let her tell you anything else."

Will then takes the opportunity to endorse his brother's love of lemon-lime soda. He sings the praises of how that particular flavor is "truly the very best."

"God," I interject, "you two are so much alike it's scary."

"I guess," Will mutters, glancing away. "Whatever."

Will acts like he doesn't care, but it's evident in the smile he's trying to hide that he's pleased by my comment. Chase picks up on Will's satisfaction and smiles over at me. For some reason, though, Chase's smile doesn't quite reach his eyes. I know something has to be weighing on his mind. But, for the life of me, I can't imagine what could be bothering him. He spent the day with Will, and they seem to have gotten along well. Heck, from what I've observed thus far, they're getting along great.

That leads me to wonder if something happened at Pizza House. I hope there was no trouble with Nick Mercurio—or anyone else, for that matter.

Chase interrupts my reverie when he asks if I want to watch a movie. "Sure," I reply.

Chase, Will, and I pick out a comedy and spend the evening in front of the TV.

Later, when Chase and I are going up to bed—no need to tromp over to my apartment and sleep there since Cassie is gone—I ask, "Everything went okay today, right?"

He replies, "Yeah, fine...today was great. Cassie left with her mom, Will and I went fishing down at the creek, and then we picked up the pizzas."

I slow to a stop at the top of the stairs. "No problems at Pizza House, then?"

Chase drapes his arm around me. "Of course not, Kay."

"Did you see Nick?"

"Yeah," Chase says slowly, "he was there."

I glance up at him, but instead of meeting my eyes, he urges me to start down the hall. "Let's go to bed, Kay."

"All right," I acquiesce.

We stop by the bathroom to brush our teeth. But Chase finishes up before me and says, "See you in bed." He then heads to the bedroom.

Hmm, something is definitely off.

A few minutes later, when I enter the bedroom, the first thing I notice is how the small lamp by the bed illuminates Chase's tattoos, as well as all the hard muscles in his back. He looks so good, even when turned away.

I decide I'm done worrying about possibly nothing. If Chase claims things are fine, then I should take him at his word.

I crawl into bed and lean over him to switch off the light. As the room goes dark, Chase rolls onto his back. He grasps my waist and pulls me down on top of him.

I giggle as he nuzzles my neck.

"Something funny, sweet girl?" he asks, shifting so I can feel that he's naked and, not surprisingly, hard and ready for me.

"Not at all," I say.

Chase lifts the hem of my tee and says huskily, "How about we lose this shirt?"

"Sounds good to me."

I sit up and swiftly pull my shirt over my head, and when I lean back down, I press my bare breasts to his warm chest. Chase groans and lifts his hips so he can push his hard cock into me. My panties, however, prevent us from joining.

Not for long, though, as Chase makes short work of my underwear, tossing it off to the side. He then, with no warning, sheaths himself in me. I gasp and he winds his fingers in my hair, tugging roughly, and then urging me down to his mouth.

Chase is rougher than usual tonight, but I have no complaints. I revel in his hungry kisses, relish his frenzied touches. His urgency leaves me breathless, particularly when his fingers find my clit, where he plays and plies me in all the right ways.

I hold on to wide shoulders, riding Chase's hand and his cock. When I come, I cry out and bury my face into his neck. His pulse throbs against my lips, while a far different part of him pulses inside me.

"That was so good," I rasp once I've recovered.

It's always good like this, whether it be a session of lingering lovemaking or, like tonight, a quick fuck. Chase is just amazing when it comes to all things sex. But a little part of me is left wondering if this quickie was his way of distracting me.

Whatever the case, it worked.

When I start to move off of Chase, I am held in place. "We're not done yet,." he informs me.

"Oh really?" I trail a hand down his taut abs, straight to where he's once again hardening fast. Wrapping my hand around his length, I begin to stroke. "It's amazing how you can get so hard again so fast," I comment.

"It's all because of you, baby," he rasps. "You turn me on so much."

Chase closes his eyes and pushes his head back into the pillow. His breaths quicken and his mouth opens slightly. I move down his body, take him into my mouth. But after a few thrusts between my lips, he stops me.

Rolling me onto my back, he says, "I need to feel *you*, Kay. Not just your mouth." He then pushes into me, telling me, "I love how you stretch and open for me when I first slide into you."

When Chase is in as far as he can go, he stills, letting me

feel his fullness, how he swells and hardens even more, just from being inside of me.

"God," I groan.

"I could stay here all night"...he whispers..."never move."

I want to respond that I could too, but, truth is, I *have* to move. I need to feel him; I have to create friction with what is filling me to capacity.

Chase, of course, is only too happy to give me free rein. He sits back on his heels while I raise my hips and slowly work his shaft in and out of my sex.

Chase watches, smirking and amused.

"Letting me do all the work?" I gasp as I slide up and down his length...over and over again.

"I like watching you fuck my cock" is his simple response.

"Ah, say it again," I demand, glancing down to where we are so intimately joined.

I like when Chase talks dirty. And he's very good at it. He knows what turns me on. He tells me now, in the raunchiest terms, the things he likes to do to me...and then he does each one.

His words, not to mention what he's doing to my body, get me close to release. But I hold back. I want to keep fucking his cock, keep feeling his hands roam all over me, keep feeling his lips and his tongue. Everything he is doing feels so good, so right. There's raw honesty in Chase's actions.

How could I have doubted him earlier tonight?

"I wish we could keep doing this all night," I say as I slow my pace.

"There's nothing stopping us," Chase replies.

He lowers his body down over mine, his hands lifting my ass so he can take over and drive into me. There's no more talk, but I get what I want. We fuck—soft, hard, fast, slow—well into the wee hours.

Needless to say, we sleep in late the next day. Lucky for us, it's the weekend.

Despite the late start—or maybe because of all the phenomenal sex that resulted in our sleeping in—Saturday begins as an exceptionally good day. Everyone is in a fine mood. Not just Chase and me, but Will, too. Plus, it's a perfect summer day to match our moods, all blue skies and soft breezes.

Throughout what's left of the morning, Chase and his brother spend time together out on the back porch, looking over Will's latest pages for his comic book. I plop down in the kitchen, e-reader in hand, all set to read. But I find myself smiling more than reading as I listen to Chase and Will, laughing and talking. I hear Chase suggest some changes to the plot direction of Will's comic, and then his brother thanks him for taking the time to look over his work.

When they come back into the house, I set down my e-reader.

Will follows my movement and says, "It's too nice to sit inside and read, Kay. We should all do something fun."

I shrug and say, "Hey, I'm up for anything."

Will arches an eyebrow at his brother. "What about a day trip?"

Chase glances at me, and I nod. He then says, "Day trip it is."

Chase doesn't give us any details right away, but Will

digs out our destination when we drive out of Ohio and into Pennsylvania.

"Where are we going?" Will asks as we travel on the turnpike.

"Pittsburgh," Chase replies.

When we reach the city limits, we head into the downtown area. Chase informs us that there's a festival of some sort going on. We park in a garage nestled among the tall buildings, then walk to where this event is taking place. Turns out, it's some artsy event, complete with vendors selling their artsy wares and prominently displayed professional art of all genres everywhere.

Art is on display across a wide expanse that starts at the edge of where the buildings end and extending out along a piece of land—a park—that narrows to where three rivers converge.

"This is right up your alley," I say to Chase as we walk past several stands all in a row.

Each one in this area appears to be selling sketches and paintings.

Will catches sight of a teenage girl with an easel in a clearing nearby. She's drawing caricatures for passersby. He turns to us and says, "Hey, I'm going to check that out, okay?"

"Sure," Chase replies, but not before Will is halfway to where the girl is set up.

Chase and I smile at each other. "Kids," he says.

"I know, right?"

We stick close to where Will is speaking with the girl about her craft. Chase and I peruse the stands in the area.

Most of the artwork is amazing, but I can't help but think Chase's art is better.

"You should do something like this," I say when we step into one artist's tented area.

Numerous sketches, mostly city scenes, line the walls, and some sit propped up in tiny easels on a table. Chase picks up a sketch that's for sale. It's of the Eiffel Tower in Paris. It's similar to the one he drew for me, the one that hangs above his bed, the one we make love under all the time.

As he peers down at the sketch, I lean into his shoulder and truthfully say, "Yours is so much better."

"Thank you," Chase replies softly, and then he places the sketch back on the table from where he picked it up.

Chase asks the artist how one goes about securing a spot for an event like this. The man, an older gentleman with wild gray hair, is very helpful. He gives Chase a card and some other information printed out on a sheet of paper.

Will returns just as Chase is pocketing the information. He sees the card and printed form and says, "Thinking of selling some artwork, bro?"

"Yeah..." Chase blows out a breath. "...maybe."

"You should," Will says excitedly. "You're good enough that I bet you'd pull down some fat stacks."

"Fat stacks, eh?" Chase chuckles at his brother's slang, not to mention his enthusiasm.

I agree with Will, though. Chase *is* extremely talented. The sketchbooks from his time in prison are a testament to his skill. Some of the artwork contained in those books is disturbing, but every last one is nothing short of amazing. Encouraging Chase to sell his sketches, however, might take some doing. He's shy about his talent. And he's not exactly pressed for money. He doesn't make a whole lot working for the church, but his grandmother left him some cash in the bank, as well as all that property and the house.

"Chase," I say to him, "it is something to consider."

While we start over to the next artist's stand, he quietly replies, "Maybe."

I don't press any further. Chase is stubborn, and if and when he decides to sell his artwork, it will be on his own terms. In any case, the rest of our afternoon in Pittsburgh goes well. We spend the whole day at the arts festival, where we have an incredible time, and then it's back to Ohio that evening.

The next day, after church and a visit to Sarah's grave, we embark on another outing.

Chase, Will, and I drive a little north of Harmony Creek, to the closest multiplex in the area. The plan is to catch a matinee movie. We do exactly that, and after the show, on the ride back home, we stop at a family restaurant along the highway to grab dinner.

It's there in a booth, as we're laughing, talking, and eating, that I realize I honestly feel like I am part of their family. I feel like I belong, like I'm a part of something. I may only be Chase's girlfriend at the moment, but I feel like his wife in so many ways. And Will feels like my young brother-in-law. It makes me curious as to what life will be like when Chase and I start a family of our own. The thought of Chase as the father of my children fills me with the warmest, most contented brand of joy, making me wish we could have children sooner rather than later.

I know it's probably too soon to be thinking these sorts

of things, though. So I push my yearnings aside...for the time being.

Once the weekend is behind us, Monday arrives in full glory. And it feels, at first, as if the happy times are set to continue.

First, Will comes down to breakfast in an exceptionally good mood. He grabs a slice of toast as it pops up in the toaster and slides into the chair next to Chase.

"Good morning," he says jovially to Chase, and then to me.

"You're up early," Chase comments as he leans back in his chair.

"Yeah, Cassie woke me up. She and her mom are back in Vegas."

"Already?" I inquire.

At the same time, Chase interjects, "Wow, they must have hardly stopped."

I place a plate of over-easy eggs in front of Will, smiling since I know they're his favorite.

He thanks me, holding my gaze long enough to express his gratitude, and then he continues his conversation with Chase. "Yeah, they didn't stop much. Plus, you should see, dude, Mrs. Sutter drives like a maniac."

"Clearly," Chase remarks.

Will then asks his brother if it'd be okay if he stayed home today, as opposed to spending the day with us at Holy Trinity.

"Tired of working for free?" Chase teases, referencing the unpaid work Will did on the mural.

"No, that's not it at all," Will replies. "It's just that Cassie and I met this kid who lives in town. He was at that miniature golf place across from the church the day we hung out over there."

Will leaves it at that, saying no more, which prompts Chase to ask, "Okay, and…?"

Will continues, "Well, he called me last night. Seems like an okay dude, so I was wondering if maybe it'd be all right if he comes out to the house today."

This is uncharted territory for Chase, and it shows in his uncertain expression. "Uh, I don't know. What's this kid's name? How old is he? Where's he live?"

Will laughs. "Jesus, Chase, you're worse than Mom."

But when Chase shoots him an I-am-not-messing-around glare, Will hastily provides some background on his new friend.

"Jared is the kid's name, okay? Jared Knox. He's sixteen and lives somewhere not far from the church. I think he called the area South of Market, wherever that is."

Chase glances over to where I'm standing by the stove. South of Market is the nicest part of town. Jared is probably from a wealthy family, though the name Knox doesn't ring any immediate bells.

Chase turns back to his brother. "Yeah, I guess it'd be okay. How's he planning on getting out here? Are his parents okay with driving him out?"

"Not necessary." Will picks at his eggs with his fork. "He actually has his own car."

Further evidence the kid's family has money. Chase's blues find my eyes again, and I know he's thinking the same exact thing.

"Fine," he says to Will. "You can stay here today. And it's fine with me if you have your friend over."

"Cool," Will mumbles through a forkful of eggs he shovels into his mouth.

When Chase and I leave for work, he asks me when we're in the driveway if I think he made the right decision.

"Sure," I say. "Jared is probably a nice kid."

"Probably," Chase echoes, and then he says, "But I'm thinking maybe I should drive separately to work. If I wrap up early today, then I can head back here and hopefully meet this Jared guy. I better make sure he's not trouble."

"Yeah," I agree, "that's probably a good idea."

Chase and I then leave for the church in our respective vehicles.

Later, at lunchtime, Chase and I are down at the diner as usual. He reminds me again of his plan to leave work early. "Just so you don't wonder where I am," he says, a second before taking a bite of his burger.

"Great, I'll see you back at the house, then," I reply.

The rest of my workday is uneventful, but late in the afternoon, all hell breaks loose.

It all starts when I receive a frantic call from Cassie.

"Oh my God, Kay," Will's girlfriend sobs when I answer. "I'm so sorry to bother you when you're probably still at work, but I didn't know who else to call."

She sniffles, and I assure her, "It's fine, sweetie. What's wrong?"

Cassie chokes up when she tries to speak. In the background, I can hear traffic whizzing by.

"Where are you?" I ask, worry creeping up my spine.

"I just pulled off the road," she says, her voice hitching

as she suppresses a sob. "Mom and I were supposed to go out to lunch today, but she forgot she had some conference call for work that she absolutely couldn't miss. Anyway, I told her I'd pick something up for us. So I went to this restaurant we like, and when I was coming out, I noticed Paul's car parked a few spots away. I hurried and got the hell out of there, but he followed me." She lowers her voice, adding, "Kay, he was right on my bumper. I was terrified."

"Oh, Cassie."

"I turned into a residential area," she continues, "and I just kept turning and turning until he finally gave up and sped off."

Cassie breaks down as she finishes her story, and I, as kindly as I can, say, "Cassie, listen to me, okay?"

"Okay," she says in a stuttered breath, still choked up.

"You have to call your mom right away. Tell her everything you just told me."

"I did call her," Cassie chokes out. "I called her first, but she was still on that stupid call and couldn't talk. I'll tell her everything when I get home, I promise, but what should I do *now*?"

"Can you go to a police station?"

After a long pause, Cassie says in a whisper, "I don't think I want to do that."

I'm floored. "Why not?"

She takes a deep breath. Cassie's not crying anymore, but she still sounds upset.

"What if I go to the cops and it makes things worse?" she begins. "Paul is obviously mad I ruined his marriage to my mom. Besides, I've seen those crime shows. He didn't do anything illegal. It's just my word against his. If I tell the police what happened, maybe they'll question him, yeah, but they can't do anything, not really. There's no proof he did anything wrong. And what if my telling the police makes that psycho even angrier? Then what? I'm scared, Kay, for myself and for my mom."

Cassie has a point. It's her word against Paul's. Surely, he'll deny he was anywhere near her. Needless to say, I'm officially lost here.

While I'm trying to think of an effective solution where there appears to be none, Cassie throws out that she needs to call Will and tell him all that has happened.

Calling Will is a very bad idea.

"Please don't do that, Cassie," I plead. "Will can't do anything from here. Please, just talk to your mom. She can file a restraining order based on how Paul has been harassing you. And ask her to talk to your uncle. He can keep an eye on you and your mom, right?"

"I guess," Cassie mutters.

"So you'll hold off, for now," I qualify, "on telling Will?"

Cassie promises she won't call her boyfriend, but I have a bad feeling she's just saying what she knows I want to hear.

"I gotta go," Cassie says softly, and then she ends the call.

I immediately text Chase: *Are you still over at the school? I think we may have a problem.*

I gather my things and lock up the office. But by the time I reach the parking lot, I still haven't heard back from Chase. My Neon is the only car in the lot, so I assume that he's left work early as planned and that he's either on his way home or already at the house.

But then again, maybe Chase is somewhere else entirely. I mean, why else would he not reply to my text? Maybe something turned up, something unexpected. It'd have to be important, though, for him to skip going home to check on Will and his new friend, Jared.

"Shit," I mutter to myself.

Cassie could be calling Will at this very moment, getting him all worked up. And here I am, with no idea where Chase might be.

I try to call him before I leave the lot, but his phone goes straight to voicemail.

Still, I leave a message detailing Cassie's call. "Maybe I'm panicking over nothing. I mean, maybe you're home, after all," I say hopefully. "I'm heading there now."

When I reach the house, I pray Chase's truck is in the driveway. But it's not.

Chase definitely left work early, so where in the hell did he go?

As I park in my usual spot near the garage, I notice there's a shiny black sports car parked around the side of the house. It's a really nice car—a Jaguar. Will's friend Jared's car, I assume. It's not funny, but I have to laugh. Chase thinks Cassie has what he terms a "too-nice-for-a-kid car." Wait till he sees this flashy thing.

Unbelievable.

Shaking my head at the blatant display of wealth, I walk past Jared's Jag and let myself in the house through the back door. When I step into the kitchen, I am greeted by a tall, gangly kid with a mop of messy dark hair.

"Hey," he says from where he's seated at the table, his long legs kicked out in front of him.

He's alone in the kitchen; there's no sign of Will.

"Hi," I reply, making my way to the table, "you must be Jared."

"Yeah," he slowly replies, glancing up at me. "Who are you?"

"I'm Kay." I smile. "I live in the apartment next door."

His face lights up with realization. "Oh, yeah, you must be Will's brother's girlfriend."

"That would be me," I confirm as I glance around. "By the way, is Will around?"

Jared frowns and I know before he speaks that Cassie has called. Sure enough, he says, "Uh, Will's girlfriend called, like, ten minutes ago. I could hear her crying. She was upset about something, so Will went upstairs to talk to her."

"Damn," I curse.

"Is something wrong?" he asks.

He seems like a nice enough kid, so I tell him the truth. "I don't know. Maybe."

As it turns out, things are indeed wrong—very, very wrong.

Will returns to the kitchen just as I finish speaking. His stressed-out expression, not to mention the way his lips are pressed together in a straight line, tell me all I need to know. Cassie has definitely told him about Paul. And just as I feared, Cassie sharing the unpleasant stalker-stepdad update with her overprotective boyfriend has set off a chain of events, the likes of which I soon discover I have absolutely no control over.

Where the hell is Chase? I think when Will starts freaking out.

He paces the kitchen floor like a caged animal, muttering things like, "I need to get the fuck out of here. I should be in Vegas. Cassie needs me. She can't handle this shit on her own. That motherfucker is one sick dude. He needs to be fucking put down."

The whole time Will is ranting, Jared sits quietly at the table, staring down at his hands, his face obscured by his mop of hair.

Suddenly, surprising both Jared and me, Will skids to a halt. He scrapes back a chair from the table and plops down in it. Then, he whips out his phone and starts to make a call.

"I'm calling the fucking airline and changing my ticket," he announces.

But when he finds out how much it costs to make a last-minute adjustment to an existing ticket, he disconnects and slams his phone down on the table.

Jared glances from the phone to Will. He mumbles, "Dude, be cool."

Will ignores Jared and states to no one in particular, "I gotta call my mom."

He leaves the phone on the table, hits speaker, and dials. When his mom answers, things spiral from bad to worse.

Abby informs her son that not only is she not giving him any money to change his ticket, but his flight home has actually already been changed!

"What the fuck are you talking about?" Will spits.

"Don't you swear at me, young man," Abby states calmly.

And then she proceeds to inform her youngest son that she has *extended* his stay in Harmony Creek. Now Will is not due to fly back to Vegas until mid-August, which is two and a half weeks away.

"Greg and I are booked on a cruise to Mexico that leaves Los Angeles in two days," she says, dreamily, as if there's not a care in the world. "We figured, with you gone, this would be the perfect time to travel."

"Well, it's not perfect, Mom," Will says, his voice cracking.

His anger has turned to an emotion I can only describe as despair.

"My life does not revolve around you," Abby replies dryly. "Anyway, we're flying to LA tomorrow, so it's too late to change our plans. Everything is set."

"You can't fly to Los Angeles tomorrow," Will whispers into the phone. "I need to come home, like, *today*. Why would you do this?"

"I'm sorry, Will, but I have a life to live, too." His mother sighs. "I thought you were having a good time in Ohio. I figured I was doing something nice in extending your ticket. I thought since you and your brother are getting along so nicely, you'd enjoy the extra time with him."

"You don't care about me or Chase," Will croaks out, defeated. "You always put yourself first, Mom, always." My heart breaks a little at the depth of sadness in Chase's brother's tone. You can just hear how this is breaking him.

But sadness turns to anger when, suddenly, Will snatches the phone up from the table and whips it across the room. The cell whizzes past me and hits the pantry in the corner. It skitters across the linoleum as Will's fist comes down on the table.

My heart hurts for Will, yes, but I need to take control of the situation before things get too out of hand.

I clear my throat and say in what I hope is an authoritative voice, "Settle down, Will."

He turns slowly to glare at me. "Really?" His eyes fill with defiance. "*Really?* And who the fuck are you, Kay? Do you seriously think you have some right to tell me what to do?"

Holding my ground, I reply, "I'm your brother's girlfriend. And since he's not here, I'm the closest thing to family."

Will laughs derisively. "Sorry, Kay, but just because my brother sticks his dick in you doesn't make you family."

I am momentarily speechless, not to mention completely saddened. So much for feeling like a part of the Gartner family, the way I felt yesterday at the restaurant. My silly feelings were obviously way off base.

"Will"—Jared glances over at me, his expression apologetic—"that wasn't cool, dude."

Will scrapes his chair back and stands up. "Come on," he says to his friend. "This is bullshit. Let's get out of here."

Jared reluctantly stands.

Finding my voice, I say, "Wait, where are you going?"

He shrugs. "I don't know. Obviously not Vegas, if that's what you're worried about."

With Jared on his heels, Will starts toward the door. I follow.

"You can't leave yet," I say pleadingly. "You should at least wait until your brother comes home."

Will opens the back door, and Jared steps out.

"Please don't do this," I beg Will in a last-ditch effort to stop him.

For a few brief seconds, I think I've reached him. He looks as if he might reconsider.

His whole demeanor softens, and he says, "Look, I'm sorry I said that shit to you. It was rude, and I didn't mean it, okay? You are kind of like a big sister, and, well, big sisters sometimes get shit too, you know?"

I place my hand on his arm. "Will, listen. It's okay, I understand, I'm fine. But please don't go. Please just stay until Chase comes home. You can talk to him about everything."

Will shakes his head and gently pries my hand from his arm. He holds my hand in his grasp, so carefully, so gently, so at odds with his earlier outburst of anger.

My gaze meets his. So many emotions pass in his green eyes—eyes that have seen far too much sadness, betrayal, and loss for such a young age.

Will squeezes my hand lightly before releasing it. "Hey, don't worry too much. I'll be back. I'm not running away or anything."

"What are you going to do?" I whisper. "What should I say to Chase when he returns?"

Will scrubs his hand down his face. "I don't know. Just tell him I needed to forget for a while, all right?" He sighs, deflated. "Chase is going to be pissed, no doubt, but trust me, Kay, I don't plan on doing anything my brother hasn't done a thousand times."

"That's what worries me," I whisper as Will steps out the door.

CHAPTER SEVEN
CHASE

Just as I am hurrying to finish up with an electrical issue over at the school, all the while hoping I can get home in time to meet Will's new pal Jared, my cell buzzes. I answer immediately when I see the caller is none other than Nick Mercurio.

"Hey, what's up?" are the first words out of my mouth.

Getting right down to business, Nick replies, "I'm at Pizza House and thought you might want to know Doug Wilson just placed an order."

Nick, who has given me the impression he isn't exactly on board with my plan to corner Doug, alone, to talk with him, suddenly sounds like a fucking coconspirator. Good, I need someone who has my back.

I take a deep breath, exhale slowly. "Great," I reply. "Can you hold up his order?"

"I can try," Nick tells me.

"I'm close by, over at the school. But I'm gonna need about ten minutes or so to reach the restaurant."

"Ten minutes is not a problem. I can do that." Nick pauses for a beat, like he's covering all the bases. I guess, in a way, he is, as he adds, "Doug usually parks in the back. There are a few takeout spots. He's got a silver sedan. A late-model Lincoln. Looks like a company car or something to me."

"Got it," I say.

"Okay, then I'll keep him here long enough for you to get here."

Our conversation up to this point has been rather stilted, but I relax and say sincerely, "Hey, Nick, thanks. I really appreciate you doing this."

"You're just going to talk to him, right?" he asks, wariness creeping into his tone. "I don't mind helping you, but I don't want trouble blowing back on me or the restaurant."

"I have no plans to fuck Doug Wilson up, if that's what you mean."

Nick's silence tells me that's exactly what he means, so I say reassuringly, "I just need a few minutes alone with him to make a point."

"Uh," Nick lowers his voice, "does this, by chance, have something to do with Kay?"

Nick is still hot for my girl, but she's mine, so I see no point in being dishonest.

"Yeah," I retort, "it has something to do with Kay."

"Okay, man." Nick sounds like he's back on board. "I'm going to trust you on this."

He's about to disconnect, but I have one more thing to say.

"Hey, Nick, hold up a sec."

"Yeah, what is it?"

"If you happen to run into Kay, I'd appreciate it if you didn't mention anything about me wanting to talk to Doug alone—and definitely nothing about today specifically."

Nick is quiet for a beat, but then says, "Yeah, sure. She won't hear anything from me."

Everything is set, time to go. There is one more thing, though. I don't want Kay to catch me leaving the church grounds. She's expecting me to head home early to meet Jared, but with Nick's call coming in, that plan is out the window.

I check the time on my phone. It's after four, and there's a good chance of running into Kay in the parking lot. Lucky for me, though, when I walk out of the school, the coast is clear. Kay's car is in its usual parking spot, but my girl is nowhere to be seen.

I hop into my truck without delay, but before I drive away, I decide to turn off my phone. I don't need Kay calling me while I'm setting her ex-boyfriend straight, especially since I plan to keep this little excursion to myself.

I am pretty calm driving to Pizza House, but I begin to slip into a shitty mood when I'm a couple of blocks away. This fucking day hasn't gone as I'd anticipated. Maybe if I'm quick with Doug, I can get back on track. Maybe I can make it back to the house before Will's new friend leaves.

I don't know why I'm so worked up about a teenager, but I just have this strong feeling that I should make sure this Jared guy isn't trouble. His being from a family with money means shit. Back in my drug days, some of the biggest hell-raisers and hardest users I knew came from wealthy families. I sure don't want Will hanging out with someone shady like that.

When I reach the old yellow-and-green frame building with the pizza house sign out front, I signal and slowly turn into the lot. In the back, just as Nick has said, Doug's silver car is parked in a takeout spot.

I make sure I park right the fuck next to it.

A few quiet minutes pass, and then dickhead Doug comes sauntering around the side of the building, not a care in the world, just a pizza box in hand. Little does he know, I'm about to change that carefree bullshit attitude.

Just as Doug reaches his driver's side door, I step down from my truck. He looks my way and recognizes me immediately.

"Hey, look," he stammers as he slowly backs away, "I know who you are"—*No shit*—"and I don't want any trouble."

He looks like he might just piss his fancy khaki pants, so I hold up my hands in a placating kind of way. "I don't want any trouble, either. I just want to talk to you, man," I try to assure him.

Guess Doug doesn't believe me. The pizza box drops to the ground, and he attempts to flee. But he only makes it a few feet before I have him pinned up against his car door.

His shifty eyes dart from side to side, and, in response, I say in a low voice, "There's no one around to help you, if that's what you're hoping for."

Standing this close to the guy whose actions led to Kay's little sister's death, I feel like exploding. It takes everything I have not to lay him the fuck out. But I promised Nick. And more important, I promised myself. I am not the same man I once was. I'm trying to change. And aside from the episode with the junkie who jumped Kay, I've cleaned up my act. No more fucking people up, no more taking a chance on getting caught and going back to prison, especially for something stupid like assault.

Considering all this, I loosen my hold on Kay's ex.

"What's this all about?" Doug squeaks out. "I got no problems with you."

I chuckle. "That's not exactly true."

"I don't know what you're talking about," he protests, sweat beading on his brow.

"Well, let me enlighten you. I heard about your little plan to contact Kay."

Doug blanches. "Oh…um…uh…"

I laugh. "Yeah, that's right. I know what you intend to do…and it's not happening. Kay doesn't need you searching her out, dredging up shit that happened four years ago, and throwing around a bunch of empty apologies."

This man who used to get off on upsetting the woman I love starts to shake. "Okay, I won't do it," he says. "I promise I'll keep my mouth shut. I'll stay away from her."

With my hand fisted in his pressed polo shirt, I yank him to me and then shove him back, hard, against the car. I want so badly to break his fucking face, but I settle for just holding him in place.

"You better fucking stay away," I growl. "Or next time, we'll be doing more than just talking. Got it?"

I let go and step back. Doug nods and nods, like some preppy bobblehead doll. "Yeah, I got it," he states in a quivering tone. "I won't go near her—ever."

"I think I might just believe you, you preppy mother-fucker."

Doug ignores my insult. He's too busy straightening the clothes I've wrinkled.

I take him in. And then I glance down at myself, my paint-stained jeans, my faded black T-shirt, the ink exposed where the short sleeves end.

When I shake my head and make a scoffing sound, Doug says, "What? I said I'd stay away."

"Just get the fuck out of my face," I mumble. I'm already tired of dealing with this douche.

Doug fumbles with his keys, but I notice he never makes a move to pick up the pizza box from the ground. He just gets in his car and takes off.

Rich, littering motherfucker.

I walk over to the dropped pizza box, pick it up, and toss it in a Dumpster.

Then I get in my truck.

But I don't leave right away.

I know, despite all my faults, I am a better person than Doug Wilson. I'd never hurt Kay the way he did. But seeing him dressed like some upper-middle-class dude that has made something of his life leaves me feeling unworthy of my girl. Kay deserves so much more than what I'll ever be able to give her. And based on the things I'm still compelled to do, like intimidate the fuck out of her ex-boyfriend, I am apt to say Kay is too good for me. She is kind and pure-hearted. Me? I'm a different story. I remain what I've always been—fucked up. I'll forever be damaged—a former druggie and an ex-con. For as much as I try to fool myself that I've become someone different, and I have in some ways, there's a part of me that will always be the kind of man who settles things with his fists, the kind of man who's not above using his strength and power to intimidate.

I sit in the truck for a while, riding out all these unsettling feelings until I feel closer to right than wrong. When I finally turn the key in the ignition, ready to go home, I power my cell back on.

And that's when I discover I have six frantic messages from Kay.

Fucking hell.

Kay's increasingly panicked messages get me up to speed on all I've missed, which is a hell of a lot, including Cassie's urgent call to Kay about her stepdad tailing her, then her call to Will relating the same information, and finally, Will's (not surprising) subsequent meltdown.

I call Kay on the ride home, and understandably, she's a wreck.

"Will's gone," she sobs. "Chase, I have no idea where he went. I tried to talk him out of leaving, but he took off with Jared." She pauses, sniffles, and tentatively asks, "Where were you, anyway? I thought you were coming home early."

"Uh, something came up."

"Like what?"

"Just something," I hedge.

Slowly, Kay asks, "Is everything all right, Chase?"

"Yeah, everything's fine—now." I sigh. "I'll be home soon, babe. I'm on my way. Maybe my brother will change his mind and come back. Then we can get this clusterfuck straightened out sooner rather than later."

I hope I'm right, but of course, I'm not. When I arrive at the house, Will's not yet returned. There's no straightening out to do, not just yet. Kay fills me in again on everything I've missed, just in case she's forgotten something in all the messages she left.

We're both too wound up to eat, so we skip dinner and settle in on the couch in the living room.

And then the wait begins for Will to return, a wait and a watch of the clock.

As time passes, Kay and I slowly lean into each other, her shoulder to mine. We eye the grandfather clock in the corner, watching minutes, then hours, tick away. It's like we're these substitute parents of my mixed-up brother, trying to navigate these uncertain waters, these thrust-upon-us roles.

Kay holds the cell Will threw across the kitchen in her lap. He never bothered to pick it up and take it with him. The phone is banged up, but it still works. We found Jared's number in the contacts awhile ago, and we've tried to reach him too many times to count. He has yet to answer.

"Should I try him again?" Kay asks, holding up the phone.

I pinch the bridge of my nose. "Sure, why not?"

Kay hits *Call* for the umpteenth time, and like every time before, no one picks up.

"Should we call the police?" Kay says as she slides the phone onto the coffee table.

"Fuck no."

That is the last thing I care to do. Involving law enforcement in my life—or Will's—is a last resort. With my background, there's no love lost between the police and me.

"But, Chase, what if he doesn't come back tonight?"

"He will," I assure her. But, really, I don't know any more than she does.

Fucking hell. I start bouncing my leg up and down, feeling edgy as shit.

"How can you be sure?" Kay presses. She turns and faces me fully. "Didn't you say your mom told you Will has stayed out all night before?"

Kay's questions are not helping my shitty mood. I feel helpless in this situation with my brother, and fucking guilty that I was at Pizza House, busy confronting Doug and missing the things that were happening here at my home. Maybe my presence in the house would have made a difference. Shit, of course it would have. My brother wouldn't have made it three steps out the door before my ass would've been dragging him back in. And then there's the unfortunate fact that I'm keeping my "meeting" with Doug a secret. That just makes everything worse.

Without her even realizing it, when Kay says my name, prompting me to respond to her earlier question, I feel more boxed in than ever.

Before I can censor myself, I snap, "Jesus Christ, enough already!"

Kay's mouth snaps shut, and I wince. Yeah, I'm the world's biggest asshole right now.

I stand and say with what I hope is an apologetic tone, "Look, I'm going out to the back porch to get some fresh air. I'll be back in a few minutes."

Kay nods curtly and looks away.

Out on the back porch, I slump down on the old swing hanging from the ceiling. I sigh audibly and scrub my hands down my face. Leaning back, I whisper to myself, "Get it together, man."

In an attempt to relax, I listen to frogs down at the creek, singing their songs. Meanwhile, the crickets chirp in the surrounding fields, adding to the fray. It may be dark out back, but the land is alive, teeming with activity. It's like a fucking symphony out here, in fact, reminding me that life goes on even when your own world is spinning out of control.

Eventually, I'm calm enough to go back in the house.

When I step into the living room, Kay lowers her head. She starts absently tugging at a loose thread in the hem of the pretty floral dress she's wearing today. Everything about her reminds me that she is vulnerable, especially when it comes to me.

I sit down next to her and notice her eyes are wet.

"Shit, Kay." I place a hand on her knee and squeeze lightly. "I'm sorry. I'm such an asshole. I should have never snapped at you like that."

She wipes at her eyes and twists on the couch till she's facing me. "Chase"—she covers my hand on her knee with her own hand—"thank you for apologizing, but you're not why I'm crying, not really. I just, I don't know, I guess I feel like this all could have been avoided if I could have kept Will from running off."

"Aw, babe, that was impossible," I reply. And it's absolutely true. "Will is just like how I used to be." I nudge her knee with mine. "Maybe how I sometimes still am, yeah?"

With our knees touching and our hands now interlocked, my sweet girl smiles this tiny but absolutely adorable smile. "Yeah, maybe," she agrees, her voice as soft as she.

We sit quietly a moment, then Kay asks, "What should we do now? I mean, with Will, after he comes home."

"I honestly don't know."

"Cassie's stepdad is going to continue to be a problem," she states.

I blow out a frustrated breath. Kay is right. A guy like

Paul isn't going to stop until he gets what he wants, which, in this case, is Will's girlfriend.

Fuck. I lean forward and rest my elbows on my knees.

"That guy needs to be locked up. That would solve the problem."

"Unfortunately," Kay says, "that's not going to happen unless he does something more than follow Cassie around."

"Her mom could always file a restraining order," I suggest. "That would be a good first step."

Kay sighs. "Yeah, I agree. I actually said the same thing to Cassie when she told me what happened."

But Kay knows the same as I: a restraining order is only a temporary fix to what appears to be a permanent problem.

I scrub my hand down my face. "And then there's Will. He's not going to let up on going home."

"But he can't go back to Vegas," Kay says. "No one is at the house. He can't stay alone. God knows what he'd do. Your mom won't be back from that cruise for almost three more weeks."

"Ah, yes," I say, "the other surprise of the day, courtesy of dear Mom."

Kay sighs, and I mutter, "Fucking Abby. I knew she'd pull something like this. She was gunning for Will to spend the rest of the summer in Ohio way back in June. Guess she saw her chance and grabbed it."

"Guess so," Kay says while shaking her head.

We lose ourselves in our own thoughts for several minutes, but then Kay yawns. She looks over at me, and I lean back into the corner of the sofa and make a spot so she can curl up with me.

As she crawls into my arms, I say, "Just get some rest. It's after midnight. Will has to come home eventually."

Kay dozes off, and some time later, as I predicted, Will stumbles through the front door. I don't see him, since I'm in the living room, but I sure as hell hear him. Spare change falls on the hardwood floor, while Will curses up a storm. Next, I hear him kicking off his shoes.

When he bumps into something, he shouts, "Fucking hell."

I don't have to witness all that shit to surmise my little brother is totally fucked up.

I ease my arm out from under Kay, smooth back her hair, and kiss her on the forehead while she sleeps. Then I go out to the hall to see just how annihilated my brother is.

As it turns out, Will is pretty far gone. He's stumbling up the stairs, barely navigating each step.

I go to my brother before he loses his balance and tumbles backward. All I need is for him to break his fucking neck.

I offer him a steadying arm, say, "Come on, Will, let's get you to bed."

He leans into me, and I smell alcohol and weed. "You don't wanna talk?" he slurs.

"Not when you're high and drunk," I reply. "We'll talk tomorrow."

"Yeah, sorry about that," Will says, not sounding apologetic at all. When we get to the top of the stairs, he adds, "Hey, I gotta take a piss."

I maneuver Will to the bathroom, close the door to give him some privacy, and wait for him in the hall. I hear him pissing, but when the stream stops and he doesn't come out, I panic.

Frantically knocking on the door, I yell, "Hey, everything okay in there?"

For these couple of crazy seconds, I imagine Will in the bathroom, cutting up a big rock of coke—just like I used to do. That's enough to prompt me to bang on the door with more fervor.

"Will, open the fuck up."

When my brother finally swings the door open, I push past him and rush into the bathroom. To my relief, there's no coke. At least, there's none in sight.

I turn to Will. He's stripped down to his boxers and wavering on unsteady legs.

"I don't feel so good," he slurs. His bleary, green eyes try to focus on me.

Shit, I know that look. I get him to the toilet just in time.

Will pukes and pukes. And midway through all the retching, there's a knock on the door.

"Don't let her see me like this," Will mumbles, and then I open the door a crack.

"Do you need anything?" Kay asks.

"No, he's just sick. He'll be fine in the morning."

"Okay. I'm going to bed, then."

I lean forward, open the door another inch more, and then place a soft kiss on her lips. "Go get some sleep, Kay. I've got this covered." I jerk my head toward the sounds of retching. "Looks like it'll be awhile."

Kay tells me I'm a good brother, taking care of Will like this. Then she heads down the hall. Meanwhile, Will is croaking out my name. So I turn my attention back to my sick brother.

After he's puked out most of what he's ingested, I help him clean up.

Despite all the vomiting, Will is still fucked up. He needs help to his room and assistance getting into bed. Once he's settled, I turn on a lamp in case he has to get up. I also cover him with a light blanket.

When I start to leave, though, Will pleads for me to stay. "Please," he whispers, "just for a little while."

"Sure." I step back over to the bed and sit down on the edge.

"Mom's a bitch," Will suddenly blurts out, his eyes fixed on the ceiling, but still somewhat unfocused. "She set this up. That's why she said I could stay the extra week."

Will is probably right, but I say nothing one way or the other.

"You think Cassie will be all right?" he asks, his voice tight. "I mean, since I'm obviously going to be stuck here in Ohio for a while."

Raking my fingers through my hair, I say, "I don't know, Will. But I think her mom and her uncle are capable of handling things out there."

"Yeah, I guess you're right."

Since I have my brother talking, I ask, "Where'd you go tonight? Who gave you the booze and weed?"

Will glances at me, then returns to staring at the ceiling. "We went to a party," he says offhandedly. "Just some dude Jared kind of knows."

"Will…" I blow out a breath. "Look, I know you're not a

child. But I can't have you staying here and going out party-ing. No one even knew where you ran off t—"

"Bro," Will cuts me off, "it's not like I was at some stranger's house. The guy who was having the party said he knew you."

Will eyes me now, his stare penetrating, asking the question of whether I've been the one lying here. Even though I'm pretty fucking sure I know whose house my little brother was partying in tonight, I still feel compelled to ask, "Who was this guy? Where was his house?"

"It was in some shitty part of town," Will replies, mak-ing my chest tighten. "Jared said the house belongs to some guy named Kyle."

I close my eyes and count to ten. I need to count to some-thing more like three hundred if calming down is the goal.

"Christ, Will, stay the fuck away from Kyle Tanner."

His bleary eyes narrow. "Ha, so you do know him."

"Yeah, I know him, all right."

Will shoots me a curious glance.

"From a long fucking time ago, okay?" I add.

"Not what he said, bro."

"Oh yeah?" Now I'm getting pissed. "And just what did that prick have to say?"

"He said you were at his house just a couple of Fridays ago, said you smoked with him. Some girl told me you went upstairs with Kyle that night. She said Kyle only goes up to the bathroom when he's cutting coke." Will eyes me up and down. "You lecture me all the time about drugs," he snorts. "And, all the while, you're still using."

Fucking Kyle and his big-mouth party friends. What am I supposed to tell Will? The night my brother is referring to is the night he blew me off, the night he was supposed to come to Ohio. I did smoke that night, I can't deny it. But I didn't touch the cocaine. I came close, true, but I stopped before it ever went up my nose.

I take a breath and tell Will the truth.

"So you really didn't touch the coke?" he asks disbelievingly, like he knows how much of a hold that shit used to have over me.

Wow, that shit saddens me. Though I made every attempt in the past to keep my heavy drug use from my brother, he obviously knew all along just how deeply involved I was. And he knew enough to ascertain cocaine was my biggest demon. He's mentioned it before, but tonight I get that he actually always knew how bad off I was.

My eyes meet my brother's. "Yeah, Will, this time, I really didn't touch the coke."

My brother then breaks my heart a little when he sighs and says, "I've done it, you know."

"Coke?" I croak out.

He nods. "Yeah, once... No, actually, I tried it twice."

"Fuck, Will." I shake my head.

"I didn't do any tonight, if that's what you're thinking. I could have. It was there. But the two times I tried it was back in Vegas. Once, I did it with Cass, and the other time, I snorted some at a party."

My brother is fifteen years old and snorting cocaine with his girlfriend, and at parties. I have to try to talk some sense into him. Maybe I'll get through to him, maybe I won't, but I have to try.

"Will," I begin, "no matter what you do, you absolutely have to stay away from coke. That shit will fuck you up, you and Cassie both. Whatever you think is bad now, it will be a million times worse when you start adding cocaine to the equation."

"Well, Cassie didn't like it," Will says. "So she's done with it. And I wasn't all that impressed with it, either. But even if I try it again, I'd never let myself get under it."

Will is such an innocent in so many ways. He has no fucking clue.

"It doesn't work like that. I know you're young and want to try things. But you're going to end up with less than what you started with if you start messing with hard drugs. I've been there, kid, you know I have. I know what I'm talking about."

Will solemnly nods. "I know, Chase, I know."

"So?" I prompt.

"So, okay, I'll stay away from the hard shit."

"Promise?"

Will promises, but his eyes skitter away so quickly that I have to wonder if he'll be keeping his promise for long.

All I can do is hope and pray that my brother doesn't succumb to the same demons that robbed me of four years of my life.

CHAPTER EIGHT

KAY

The morning following Chase's brother's evening of revelry, I feel like I am the one who was out partying the night before. But for tired as I feel, it doesn't come close to how exhausted Chase appears to be as I drive us in to work.

Poor guy, he was up half the night with his brother. Chase didn't come to bed until an hour before we had to get up. He couldn't really sleep, so we talked. He told me seeing Will messed up like that hit a little too close to home. Since he was so tired, I decided not to question him about where he was yesterday when I couldn't get a hold of him. And, once again, I choose not to ask him now. He's had a rough enough past twelve hours.

So instead of an interrogation, I gently ask, "Are you working on that electrical problem in the school again today?"

I turn into the church parking lot, and Chase continues to do what he's done the whole ride to work. He stares out the side window, seemingly lost in thought.

I repeat the question, a tad louder this time, and he replies, "Oh, sorry, I didn't hear you. Uh, I finished that project. But I think Father Maridale has something for me to do in the rectory today."

"Figures." I laugh. "The one time I won't be in the rectory office, and you'll be right down the hall from where I'd normally be sitting."

"That's right," Chase says, stifling a yawn. "I forgot you'll be in the school gym all day. Organizing stuff for the rummage sale, yeah?"

"Yep." I place my dilapidated Neon in park and turn off the ignition. "Me and Missy, sorting and pricing all the things people have been bringing in." I twirl my finger, and add sarcastically, "Woo-hoo."

I don't mind working with Missy, but sorting through a multitude of boxes and bags filled with donated items promises to be tedious.

"You and Missy, eh?" Chase chuckles. "Try not to kill each other."

"Hey." I smack his arm. "I think she and I are past that, smart-ass."

"Yeah, I guess so," he murmurs distractedly. Chase's attention is starting to waver again. "That's good, babe."

I know Chase is worried about Will, especially since we have to leave him all alone out at the farmhouse today.

"Hey, your brother will be all right." I place my hand on his forearm. "He'll probably just sleep all day. He has to still be hurting. Nursing a colossal hangover, I imagine."

"Yeah, I'm sure you're right," Chase replies. "But I'd just feel better if we could wrap up early and get back to the house."

"Yeah, sure." I nod. "Of course."

Chase and I eventually go our separate ways, with him

heading to the rectory and me meeting up with Missy in the school gym.

In the gym, Missy and I accomplish a lot in getting things ready for the rummage sale. Together, we sort through dozens of bags and boxes, each one overflowing with an assortment of items. Clothes, appliances, knickknacks—you name it, we come across it. We find a kind of rhythm of sort and price, sort and price, and then, at one point, as we're kneeling on the gymnasium floor we come across a big box filled with baby clothes.

"Aw, Kay, check this out." Missy shakes out and holds up a tiny blue onesie with tumbling and romping puppies adorning the soft-looking fabric.

I reach out and touch the material. It's soft as can be. When I rub my thumb across a rolling-over puppy, I coo, "This is so precious, Missy."

Missy folds the adorable onesie and places it on the floor. She continues to dig through the box. "There are so many cute things in here," she gushes. "Damn, I wish I could have some of this stuff for when the baby arrives."

I pause and sit back on my heels. "You know, I'm sure Father Maridale won't mind if you set a few things aside. You know how generous he is. I bet if you ask him he'll say, 'sure, take whatever you want.'"

Missy shrugs and starts to put baby clothes back in the box. "Yeah, maybe," she mumbles.

I assume her reticence means she hasn't yet told Father Maridale about her pregnancy.

"Missy, you have to tell Father Maridale eventually. He's bound to find out." I gesture to her still-flat tummy, covered by a dress far more conservative than the strappy sundress I have on today. "Your stomach won't stay flat like that for long, and he'll know for sure then."

"He already knows, Kay," Missy replies softly.

"Oh?" I raise an eyebrow.

"Confession," she states. "I went last week. So, yeah, he knows."

I reach over and touch her hand. "Speaking of confession, Missy, have you talked to Tony yet? Does he know he's the father of your baby?"

She shakes her head and focuses back on the baby clothes.

"Missy?" I prompt, squeezing her hand before releasing. "Are you ever going to tell him? I think it might be better to get it over with as soon as possible."

"Yeah," she says on a sigh, "you're right. And I'll talk to him soon. I guess I'm still just not quite ready."

Something is off with Missy. But since I have no clue what all she's going through, I let it drop.

The rest of the afternoon flies by. Father Maridale stops in to check on our progress. He, of course, gives Missy the green light to keep the baby clothes she's picked out. And since we're pretty much done sorting and pricing, he tells us we can go home for the day.

I text Chase to let him know I'm done early.

Great, I'm outta here too. Meet you by your car in five.

Missy and I walk out to the parking lot together. I offer to help her carry the baby clothes she's stuffed into a big plastic bag, but she insists she's got it.

As we near my Neon, I notice Missy's car is only a few spots away. I then notice Chase has arrived. He's leaning against the driver's side door of my car, looking delicious.

Damn, Chase is exceptionally hot in his faded jeans and snug black T-shirt. And working over in the rectory all day must have involved some heavy lifting, because the muscles in his arms bulge, all hard and ripped, as he fidgets with his phone.

Chase pays no heed to our approach—or my perusal of his body. He's too preoccupied with texting or something.

"Hey," I call out, garnering his attention.

He lifts his head and slips his phone into his back pocket. He then starts to smile but falters when he notices Missy is with me.

"Hey," he says flatly when Missy and I reach him.

Missy places her bag of baby clothes on the ground and quietly mumbles, "Hi, Chase."

She crosses her arms, while Chase squints and looks up at the sky.

"Oh, Lord," I lament.

This is the first interaction the two of them have had since the night at the carnival, the night I overheard them arguing and, consequently, found out they'd hooked up. But if I can get past what happened between them—which I have—then they surely can, too.

I go on to state those exact words, eliciting two surprised expressions. But I get my point across. The tension begins to lift, and soon enough, the three of us are chatting about the rummage sale.

When the conversation falters, though, Missy says softly, "Well, I guess I better get going."

I catch Chase's eye and nod to the plastic bag on the ground.

He catches on quickly and says to Missy, "Hey, you want me to carry that over to your car? It looks kind of heavy."

"Oh, okay." She appears genuinely surprised, but also pleased. "Thanks."

Chase hoists the bag up with ease and heads toward Missy's car. Missy hangs back, and when I glance her way, she suddenly throws her arms around me.

"Whoa, what was that for?" I ask, taking a step back when she finally lets go.

"Sorry." She giggles. "I get a little carried away with the pregnancy hormones and all, but I just wanted to say thank you."

"For what?"

"For everything, Kay," Missy says, sighing contentedly. "For being so nice to me, for forgiving me"—she lowers her voice—"for getting Chase to forgive me."

Before I can respond that there's no need to thank me, Chase turns around and yells over for Missy to pop open the trunk. Two minutes later, Chase is back. Missy says good-bye and walks over to her car, and Chase and I take off.

When we arrive back at the house, to both my surprise and Chase's, Will is up and about. He doesn't appear to be sleepy or hungover—at all. In fact, he's downright lively for a kid that, by all rights, should be recovering from his night of hard partying.

But, no, Will is seated at the kitchen table, earbuds in his ears, husking fresh cobs of corn while his foot taps to the beat. He adds an ear he's just shucked to a huge pile of husked corn that covers the entire surface of the table. He then promptly picks up another.

Chase and I skid to a stop in the entryway to the kitchen,

and when Will catches sight of us, he takes out his earbuds and says loudly, "Hey, you're home."

Before either Chase or I can respond, Will continues to talk, his speech rapid.

"Yeah, so you're probably wondering what I'm doing, huh? See, there was this farmer selling corn at a stand on the side of the road, so I bought a bunch." He holds an ear aloft. "Can't get shit like this back in the fucking desert."

"Wow, that's a lot of corn," I say as I realize that, apart from the corn on the table, there are two more bagfuls under the table.

Chase doesn't comment on the corn, though I know he notices all of it. Instead, though, he leans against the doorjamb, crosses his arms, and says to Will, "You went out?"

Will nods as he absently plucks silk off a cob he's just shucked.

"You were supposed to stay in today," Chase continues tightly, "stick around the house."

Will returns to the shucking, his fingers working faster than ever. "Yeah, I know," he says. "But Jared stopped by, and we decided to go out for a while."

Chase's eyes meet mine. There's worry in his blues. And why wouldn't there be? Will went out with Jared today, just like last night, and also like last night, Will's behavior is indicative of being high on something.

"So, where'd you go?" Chase asks his brother.

Will's fingers falter, but his eyes remain on his task. "Uh, just out."

When Will resumes shucking, his legs start to bounce.

Chase whispers to me that he wants to check Will's

room for drugs, see if he can find anything that might help him figure out what Will is on.

I nod once, and he then comments loudly enough for Will to hear that he's going up to the bathroom and that he'll be right back.

When Chase is out of sight, I head into the kitchen, hoping to keep Will occupied.

I open the refrigerator door, and say, "Well, since we have plenty of corn, how 'bout we pick out something to go with it?" I grab a package of hot dogs and hold them up above the door so Will can see. "Hot dogs work for you? We can grill them."

"Sounds good to me," he replies. "In fact, I can get the grill started, if you want."

"Sure, give me a sec."

I cut open the package of hot dogs and put some water on for the corn to boil. After I place the wieners on a plate, I hold them out to Will. When his hand touches the plate, his eyes meet mine. His usually clear green eyes are dark, dilated, and bloodshot.

Quickly, he averts his gaze.

I draw back the plate. "Wait."

"What?" Will's eyes dart around the kitchen, all skittish-like.

I touch his shoulder. He has on a thin tee, and I immediately feel how hot his skin is beneath the cotton. "What'd you take?" I ask. "Were you and Jared snorting cocaine?"

Will shakes his head. "No."

"Please don't lie," I whisper. "You know this is killing your brother."

"It wasn't coke, okay?" he huffs. "We took some speed."

"Like, amphetamines?"

"Yeah."

"From Kyle Tanner?"

Will nods. He reaches for the plate of hot dogs again, and this time, I let him have it. He doesn't say anything else, just heads out to the back porch. After a minute, I hear him messing with the grill.

I sink down into a chair near the table and pick up an ear of corn.

Damn. I know in my heart that, when Chase finds out Will was buying drugs from Kyle Tanner *again*, he *will* go talk to his former dealer. And I hate that I won't be able to stop him. Because if there's one thing I've learned, it's that Kyle is bad news—for both Gartner brothers.

Chase walks back into the kitchen just as I'm absently toying with a pile of corn silk on the table.

"I didn't find anything," he says. "But I know Will's on something."

I watch as Chase walks over to the refrigerator.

When he opens the door, I tell him what Will shared with me. "You're right, Chase," I say, sighing. "Will is on something. But it's not cocaine."

Chase's hand on the top of the refrigerator door tightens, but he doesn't look up. I stand immediately and go to him. I touch his back, rub his shoulders. I'm trying to do anything to make all this awfulness just a little less horrible.

And it works, a little. Chase relaxes slightly. He turns around, and the refrigerator door closes softly.

"What'd he take?" he asks flatly.

"Amphetamines."

Chase rubs his hand down his face. "Christ."

"It's okay," I say. "We'll get through this."

I don't know what the hell I'm talking about, but I know Chase needs some kind of reassurance right now.

And, as I expected, Chase declares, "I have to talk to fucking Kyle Tanner. Will's in town for two and a half more weeks. I need to nip this shit in the bud before things get out of hand."

"I know." I touch Chase's chest, the outline of his pecs so defined beneath the cotton. His body is so hard, but his heart is so soft. "Just be careful, okay?"

Chase catches my hand and holds it tightly. "Don't worry, Kay, there's not going to be any violence. But I will be making sure I get through to that motherfucker."

Despite his trying to soothe my fears, I have a bad feeling. All I know is that Chase calling on Kyle—violence or not—never results in anything good. Last time he spent time with his former drug dealer, Chase ended up drinking, smoking weed, and coming dangerously close to snorting cocaine.

But he has to do this. I know that.

Resigned, I ask. "When are you planning on talking to Kyle?"

"As soon as possible," Chase says. "In fact, I think I'll head over to his house tonight."

CHAPTER NINE

CHASE

I have no desire to pay a visit to Kyle Tanner, but if I don't talk with him as soon as possible, who knows where shit may land. Will is spiraling fast.

Fuck.

Damn my mother and her selfishness; damn Cassie's perverted stepfather who can't control his sick urges; damn Cassie for running to Will every time shit in her own life falls apart. I'm not surprised Will has chosen to turn to the same things I once sought—drinking, drugs. It's all about seeking fucking oblivion, dude. You don't have to deal with shit when you're fucked the hell up.

But if Will thinks I'm just going to stand around and watch him fall, he's sadly mistaken.

In my truck, I tug a flannel shirt on over my T-shirt and then drive away from my house. I travel back to the bad side of town, head down the worn dirt road that leads to Kyle's house of deeds best forgotten.

It's early, dusk, so the party has not yet begun. When I get out of my truck, I notice there's no one around outside the old dilapidated frame structure Kyle calls home. The screen door is propped open, though, so when I reach the small porch on the house, I push open the front door and let myself in.

"Gartner," I hear Kyle breathe out, along with a very loud exhale of smoke, and then a cough.

I turn toward the living room and find my former dealer reclining on the couch, meth pipe in hand. He lights a flame under the glass bulb, takes a hit, and while trying to hold in his smoke, chokes out, "You want some, man?"

I shake my head and laugh. "No fucking way."

Kyle exhales the rest of the smoke from his lungs. His dark, suspicious eyes meet mine. "Whatcha doing here, then, Gartner?"

"We gotta talk."

Kyle sits up and sets the pipe he's been smoking from on a coffee table cluttered with other drug paraphernalia. "Okay," he snaps, "then talk."

My former dealer is looking worse than ever these days, skinny and haggard. He's on his way to becoming used up.

After my ex-perusal, I get down to business. "I don't want you selling any more drugs to my kid brother."

Kyle laughs. "Little Gartner? Aw, dude, he's one cool kid. No need to get all bent out of shape. I only sold him some weed, man."

"You sold him more than that," I grind out, my anger rising. "He got pills from someone, and unless the local pharmacy is selling speed over the counter these days, I'm guessing it was from you."

"Oh, that," Kyle mutters. "I forgot."

Yeah right.

Kyle is such a cocky piece of shit that what I'd really like to do is smack the smug look off his fucking face. But I don't want to make things worse. Kyle knows he has the upper hand in this situation. I have no real way of stopping him from selling whatever he wants to my brother.

So I take a breath and rein in my rage. "Yes, *that*," I sarcastically mock.

Kyle smirks and I continue to plead my case.

"Look, Will's only staying with me the next couple of weeks…and then he'll be back in Vegas. Don't sell him anything else, man, or there's going to be trouble." I level Mr. Ex-Dealer with an I-am-not-fucking-around look. "After all, Tanner, it's not like you're establishing a steady customer here."

I may as well appeal to Kyle's business side. Better than losing it and pummeling the fuck out of his face, right?

He seems to ponder what I've said. Then again, maybe he's just fading in and out because of the meth he just smoked.

When he finally replies, he says, "I got an idea that might just make us both happy."

The cocky look on his face tells me before he even has a chance to say another word that it's something I won't like.

"What's your idea?" I ask warily.

Kyle starts to say, "It's a business thing—"

—And I cut him off with, "I am not muling drugs for you."

A tense moment of silence ensues. Kyle knows it was his X that sent me away for four years.

"Don't worry," he says lightly, trying to diffuse the tension, "it's nothing like that."

"So, what is it?"

"Well, the way I see it"—Kyle lights up a cigarette and sits back—"I have a need here. And so do you."

I roll my eyes.

"You don't want me supplying little Gartner, right?"

"That's right."

It's fucking killing me to hear this prick call my brother "little Gartner," all familiar like, over and over again, but I keep my mouth shut. Best tread lightly.

"Here's what I propose," Kyle says on an exhale as he leans forward and stubs out his barely smoked cigarette. "Next time little Gartner comes a-calling, looking for a little bud or something stronger, I'll turn him away. But I need you to take care of something for me. Quid pro fucking quo, man, that's what shit's all about."

"What is this *something* you need?" I ask warily.

Kyle chuckles. "See, there's this guy who owes me a shit-ton of cash. He's not gonna pay up anytime soon without some, shall we say, encouragement."

"Whoa, whoa, whoa." I throw up my hands. "Fuck that. I am not your fucking muscle."

Kyle leans back and puts his feet up on the coffee table. "Fine, it's your call, Gartner. But, remember, no favor from you, no favor from me."

I take a menacing step toward him, and he puts his legs down in a hurry. He cowers back when I growl, "I should fuck you up for even saying something like that."

"Be cool, man," Kyle says, his eyes widening with fear. "Why don't you use all that righteous anger and just take care of my problem? That way, we both win. I promise, Gartner, you do this for me, and I won't sell your brother a fucking aspirin even."

I scrub my hand down my face. Fuck, I'm at an impasse. This guy who owes Kyle money, I don't have to hurt him. I could just scare him a little. Like what I did with Doug Wilson. I got my point across without laying him out, right?

I don't see where I really have a choice, since I'll basically do anything to keep my brother from following a path that will lead him to problems far worse than the ones he's currently facing.

Reluctantly, I agree to "talk" to this customer of Kyle's who owes him money. "Okay, I'll do it," I say quietly.

Kyle gives me the guy's address, and it comes as no surprise that he lives in the apartment building Kay used to live in.

"You could probably find him there later," Kyle offers, all helpful-like. "He hangs out in the alley next to that building every night."

"I know where you mean," I reply. And sadly, I do. In fact, I know the place all too well.

"Here's a picture I got of him." Kyle picks up his cell phone. "He didn't know I was taking it when I snapped it last week."

He holds out the phone. I put my hand on it but don't take it right away.

He glances up. "What?"

"How long have you been planning on having someone fuck up this guy?" I want to know.

"Hey, he's owed me money for a while now," Kyle says defensively. "I've been exceptionally patient, trust me."

"Whatever."

I grab the phone and take a look at the photo. The guy looks pretty strung out. He's pale and gaunt, with long, stringy blond hair covering part of his face. Even so, it's clear he's hitting a pipe in the picture.

"He looks like a real winner," I say to Kyle as I nod to *his* pipe that's still on the table.

"Fuck you, Gartner," he spits. "Just get this shit done."

Kyle starts to get up, like we're done here. But he's not calling all the shots.

"Not so fast." I shove him back down to the couch. "I'll do this for you, but we're doing it on my terms, my timetable."

"What does that mean?"

"It means I'm waiting till at least Friday night to talk to him."

"That's three fucking days away," Kyle protests.

"Too fucking bad. I need to make sure you're holding up your end of the bargain. I already checked Will's room, and I know he doesn't have any drugs at the moment. So, if I see him staying clean the next few days, I'll assume you're keeping your word and not selling to him."

"Okay," Kyle agrees, albeit reluctantly. "I guess that'll work for me. But what am I supposed to do if your brother stops by with that Jared kid? That's who he's always with. And before you ask me not to sell to Jared, just know that rich boy buys all the time. He's a consistent customer, and you'd be stepping on lucrative business if you have a problem with me selling to him, too."

"I don't care about Jared," I honestly state. "But anything my brother asks for, you tell him you're out of it."

Kyle agrees to my terms, and I get the fuck out of his house. There's something about Tanner's place that triggers the part of me that craves drugs. Spending time at his place makes me want to get spun right the fuck out of my head. And that's not good. So I take a breath and squash that shit down before I head back to the house.

On the way home, I decide it's probably best to keep my brother away from Jared for now. I hate to fuck up his new friendship, but I feel a little pressed. I, at least, want Will away from Jared until Friday.

But a short while later, when I announce to Will that he's not allowed to see Jared until I say so, he's beyond livid.

"That is so fucked up," he yells, before he storms up the steps. "You think I don't make my own decisions?" he yells down from the top.

"Jared's a bad influence," I yell back from the bottom of the steps.

Will calms slightly, and offers in a placating tone, "What if I promised not to touch any drugs, no matter who I hang with. Could I hang out with Jared then?"

"I don't know," I respond. "Maybe."

Will stomps off, and I turn to Kay, who has witnessed the whole exchange. Her eyes meet mine, sympathetic.

"I don't know what I'm doing here," I admit. "It's not like there's some rulebook."

"You're doing the best you can," she says.

My sweet girl is so accepting of my decisions, so unwaveringly supportive. She knows I talked to Kyle, but she has no idea I made a deal with that devil so he won't sell my brother drugs anymore.

And though here's my chance to tell Kay, to come clean now, I don't say a thing.

Three days pass, and since my brother remains drug-free, I consider loosening up on the no-hanging-with-Jared rule. Will pleads his case a few more times, too. He insists his decision to stay away from drugs is solid, no matter what happens or whom he hangs around with.

I inform Will I'm still thinking it over.

Meanwhile, the time comes for me to hold up my end of the bargain I made with Kyle Tanner.

Around nine thirty on Friday night, I am striding toward the front door, as stealthily as I can. No one knows I'm heading out. Kay is in the kitchen, cleaning up after a late dinner.

Unfortunately, she hears me in the front hall and catches me by the door.

"I thought I heard something," she says, the dish towel she was using to dry the dishes still in her hand.

She glances to where my hand is on the doorknob.

"Where are you going?" she asks, frowning. "It's almost ten o'clock."

"Uh…" I drop my hand to my side. "I have something I gotta do, babe." I lean her way and deposit a light peck on her cheek. "I promise I won't be gone long, though."

I start to turn away from her, but she grabs my arm. "What are you doing, Chase? You didn't say a word all evening about having to go out tonight."

I glance toward the stairs. Will is up in his room, listening to music. The low bass beat fills the heavy silence around us.

Kay glances to where my eyes are focused on the stairs, and says, "This…your leaving…it has something to do with Will, doesn't it?"

"Yes," I admit. "I have to take care of something I promised Kyle Tanner."

She blanches and asks, "Nothing to do with drugs, right?"

Kay knows why I went to prison, and she doesn't want the same thing happening again.

"No, it's nothing like that." I try to smile to reassure her.

Kay crosses her arms. She's waiting for more information, but I can't bring myself to tell her the details, that I'm going out to fuck someone up.

"Kay, trust me," I say, ignoring the irony of those words, "you're better off not knowing."

When I turn away, I add softly, "I'm so sorry."

Then I am out the door before she can stop me. I don't look back, either. I know if I turn around and see Kay's sure-to-be-disappointed expression, I won't be able to do what needs to be done. I hop into my truck and leave quickly, focused solely on the task at hand.

At the apartment building, after I park somewhere my truck won't be recognized, I start my search for the gaunt meth addict with the stringy blond hair. Several pairs of blank eyes follow me, distrusting, as I slowly make my way down the alley. There's not a lot of light, but the flickering flames from lighters as the junkies hit their pipes provide an eerie orange glow that illuminates the darkness, enough so I can see.

I have no luck, though, in locating the junkie I'm searching for—that is, until I reach the end of the alley. And there he is, right in my fucking path. He's sitting down, leaning back against the wall, legs outstretched, head lolling.

I say, "Hey," and his only reaction is to open his eyes slightly.

When he doesn't answer, just stares up at me blankly, I yank him to his feet. Amid his protests, I drag him around to the back of the building.

"What's this about, man?" he shouts, finally coming to life. "Get the fuck off me."

I throw him up against the brick side of the building. "You owe Kyle Tanner money, right?" I ask, getting right up in his business. "I'm afraid the time has come to pay up."

"I ain't got no money," he cries.

"We'll see about that."

I search the pockets of his dirty pants and discover he's not lying. He has drugs, of course, but no money.

"See?" he whines after I pat him down some more. "No money, just like I tried to tell you."

And that's when I throw a right hook, falling oh so easily back into my old patterns. My fist connects with the poor slob's face, creating a sickening sound. Fuck, I've just become who I used to be, a man resorting to violence to solve problems and exert his will. And just like that, it feels like everything good I've been striving to be has just gotten thrown out with the fucking trash.

The guy drops to the ground.

He covers the side of his rapidly bruising face and cries out, "Why'd you go and do something like that?"

I pull him up to his feet. I can't lie, I long to hit him again. Truth be told, it feels good to break a man.

But I refuse to lose myself completely tonight.

So instead of swinging, I take a step back and ask the guy, "You got a place where you can get some money?" I nod at the building he's slumped up against. "You live here, right?"

"Doesn't matter, man," he mutters. "I ain't got nothing to give you." The man then starts to sob. "You may as well just finish the job."

He stands there, waiting for me to strike him again, waiting for me to pummel his ass. His easy acceptance that he has no chance against me makes me feel really fucking bad. I think of Kay and how disappointed she'd be in me. I think of how far I've come from the bloodlust I used to carry around in me. And though I've faltered and succumbed to doling out some violence tonight, I am nowhere near where I used to be. And I don't want to back fall into that state of mind. But if I lay this dude out, I *will* fall. Right along with him, though in a different way.

I let him go.

"Just get out of here," I say, moving farther away so he can get away from me.

He doesn't hesitate. He runs off.

Meanwhile, I lean my forehead up against the side of the building. "Fuck," I hiss.

Kyle will be fucking fuming when he finds out I let the junkie go without getting any money from him *and* without a thorough beating. That love tap I gave the guy, he'll probably forget by morning. He's high, and I'm sure he'll remain fucked up throughout the night. Once he finally notices his bruised face, if he even does, he'll think he fell or something.

Whatever.

My problem now is that the deal with my ex-dealer is off. Kyle will have no reason not to sell to my brother once he finds out. And I can't be around every second of every day to make sure Will doesn't go to Kyle's house or contact him some other way.

"Fuck!" I clench and unclench my fists.

My frustration and anger build and build. This feels like just another way I'm failing Will.

I need to lash out. If I don't, I will likely do something worse. Like turn to drugs or go find the junkie who I've just let go and finish the job.

Absolutely not.

Neither is an option. But slamming my fucking fist against the brick wall in front of me is.

So that is what I do. I hit and hit, even though it hurts like hell. My knuckles crack open and bleed. I feel my skin bruising. But I continue.

Because relief comes when, as the entire time I am hitting the unforgiving bricks, I imagine Kyle Tanner's smug fucking face on the receiving end.

CHAPTER TEN

KAY

When Chase returns to the house, his right hand is a bloody mess.

"Oh my God," I gasp when he steps through the front door. "What happened to your hand?"

"It's nothing," he mutters as he tries to move past me.

I step in front of him, blocking the base of the stairs. "Chase," I implore, "please don't do this. Don't shut me out. Where were you tonight? How'd your hand get messed up?"

"Kay…" He sighs, leans back against the wall.

"Are you going to tell me what happened?" I whisper.

He shakes his head. When he sees my surprise—we don't keep secrets—his eyes fill with guilt. Leaning forward, he lowers his head to rest against his injured hand that he's placed on the banister.

I see him wincing, and say softly, "Will you at least let me take care of your hand?"

He clears his throat and states dismissively, "It's not broken."

I step closer to him. "Still, Chase, we need to clean up those cuts and get some ice on it." I gesture to the kitchen. "There's still an icepack in the freezer, right?"

The icepack I'm referring to is the same one Chase held to my cheek the night I was attacked at my old apartment.

He nods once quickly, his eyes distant, like he might be recollecting the same thing. And that's when he agrees to let me help him.

Just like when I was hurt, but with the roles reversed, he says, "We should go up to the bathroom to take care of this."

"Okay, I'll grab the ice. I'll be up in a minute."

Chase jerks his chin toward the top of the stairs before he starts up. "Where's Will? Sleeping?"

"Yeah," I reply, "he stayed up there most of the night, listening to music in his room. It's been quiet for a while now, though, so I guess he fell asleep."

"Good. He doesn't need to see this shit." Chase holds up his bloody hand, and this time, I'm the one wincing.

"That looks terrible." I shake my head. "Go on up. I'll be there in a sec."

Chase heads up the stairs, and I grab the icepack from the freezer.

A few minutes later, when I step into the bathroom, Chase is seated on the edge of the tub, head in his hands. With one good hand and one bad hand, he reminds me that there are two sides to this man I love. The side he is most of the time—good. And the side he fights—bad.

Sighing, I decide not to press for details on what happened tonight. He'll tell me when he's ready—I hope.

I set the icepack next to him, grab a bottle of rubbing alcohol from the medicine chest, and run a washcloth under warm water. When I kneel down in front of the tub, I say, "Chase," to get his attention.

He raises his head, and I take his right hand in mine.

"Thank you," he murmurs as I begin to clean out the worst of his cuts with the washcloth.

When the time comes to apply the antiseptic to his wounds, I pause to warn him, "This may hurt." I hold up the bottle of rubbing alcohol and raise an eyebrow.

Chase sort of nods, like he's ready, but he turns his head away quickly. His tawny hair is messy as hell, and I long to run my fingers through the strands, to comfort him—and me—in our way. But, instead, I just start dabbing an alcohol-soaked cotton ball to his marred skin.

Chase suddenly becomes impatient with my slow process of dabbing. "Kay..."

He shifts, and I stop what I'm doing to look at him. "What?"

"Here"—Chase grabs the bottle of rubbing alcohol from the edge of the tub—"I'll take care of this."

He proceeds to dump half the bottle right on his hand. And then promptly grinds out from between clenched teeth, "Jesus-fucking-shit-fuck, that shit stings like a motherfucker."

I hand him the icepack. "That's why I was trying to be careful," I say under my breath.

He sits the ice next to him, and when I look up, his blues are on me.

"What?" I ask.

He looks away. "Nothing."

Chase rakes his fingers through his hair, picks up the ice, and then says, "No, there is something. Truth is, I'm worried about Will, babe."

I already sense that whatever happened tonight, it had

something to do with Will. But since I know Chase is not going to give me any specifics right now, I focus instead on a bit of positive news we found out before dinner today—there's now a restraining order out on Paul.

"Chase, I think your brother will be fine now that Cassie's mother took out that restraining order."

Thankfully, Cassie took my advice and told her mom about Paul following her from the restaurant. When Mrs. Sutter heard that story, she took action immediately, hence the restraining order. And, so far, Paul has abided by it.

"I think he'll leave Cassie alone," I continue. "He doesn't want to violate that order and end up in huge trouble."

"And what happens if he violates the order and the police can't find him to pick him up?" Chase throws out, cocking an eyebrow my way. "That happens in a lot of these cases, Kay."

I blow out a breath. "Let's just hope it doesn't happen in *this* case. But if it does, I guess we better pray Cassie doesn't tell Will."

Our eyes meet, and it doesn't need to be spoken that we're both worried about what Chase's brother might do if Cassie finds herself in any real trouble with Paul. Something extreme, no doubt.

Chase puts his face in his hands. "This is so fucked up."

"I know." I wrap my arms around his wide shoulders. "But we're doing the best we can."

I place my hands on his and lower them from his face. I kiss his forehead, his cheeks, his beautiful aquiline nose.

"Baby…" He sighs.

He pulls me close to him, and things heat up immediately. We express our love through sex, but sex sometimes becomes our escape from reality as well. With the urgent, needy way Chase is kissing me, there's little doubt in my mind that tonight will be about escape.

His hands skim and ply my bare legs, then move to my ass, and finally settle on my breasts.

After a few minutes of Chase groping me roughly, I pant, "God, Chase, don't stop."

I stand and lift my dress, tug down my panties. My plan is to straddle Chase right on the side of the tub, let him sheath himself in me.

But he halts my progress by grasping one of my hands. "Not here," he says, squeezing lightly.

"Why not?"

Chase chuckles and releases my hand. His hand moves to the back of my thigh. He skims his fingers along the sensitive skin. My panties are still partway down, and he nudges them down a little farther. He trails his fingers back up my thigh and then cups my ass...firmly. I slump against him, and he pinches one cheek lightly. When he pinches a little harder, I yelp.

"That's why I don't want to fuck you here," he rasps, his fingers moving dangerously close to my core. "I want you to get loud if you want. In fact, I want to *make* you get loud, Kay. And I don't want to worry about my brother hearing us. Not tonight."

He slips two fingers into me, not gently, and I gasp.

"Are you going to get rough with me?" He twists his fingers inside of me, and I add, "Rougher than that?"

He raises an eyebrow. "Do you want me to?"

I nod slowly.

No one knows how to give it rough like Chase Gartner.

It's never too much, but it's more than enough, enough to definitely remind me of who's in charge in the bedroom.

Oh, do I love that, I think as my mouth finds his, our lips bruising as we kiss heatedly. .

"Let's go over to your apartment," Chase whispers when we finally slow down enough to take a breath.

It doesn't take us long to get next door. And in my bedroom, things pick right back up where we left off in Chase's bathroom. Our kisses remain raw and hungry, and my hands roam and grasp as much as his. But after a few minutes of frenzied and rushed foreplay, Chase slows things down.

"Gentle first, baby girl," he whispers in my ear, a sexy promise. "Gentle, then rough."

His breath, warm and silky, seduces, as do his words.

Chase moves his lips to my mouth and kisses me slowly and deeply. Without breaking his sensual kisses, he sits down on the bottom end of my bed and pulls me onto his lap.

After a minute, he leans back slightly, and tells me, "I'm going to make you very wet for me tonight, Kay. Wetter than you've ever been before."

"I think I'm almost there," I whisper.

"Let me see, then," he rasps in return.

Chase positions me on his lap until my back is pressed to his chest. We're both facing forward, in front of us is a full-length mirror that hangs on the back of the closet door.

"Watch me, baby, "Chase says. "Watch everything I do to you."

His uninjured hand disappears up under the hem of my dress.

My breath catches. I slump against his chest. Seeing what's he's doing to me in the reflection of the mirror, while I feel every sensation, makes me squirm in his lap, seeking friction, seeking release.

But Chase stills my body when I move too much. His eyes meet mine in the mirror, burning hot. "Slow," he commands..

Watching my reaction intently, he starts to peel my panties down my legs. When the tiny swath of fabric falls to the floor, my eyes flutter, threatening to close.

"No, no, sweet girl," Chase says firmly.

He lifts my dress higher and higher, until my sex is fully exposed.

"No closing your eyes," he chastises when I throw back my head.

I like this game, so my eyes return to the mirror. And I watch as Chase's fingers dip into my glistening folds. When a moan escapes me, lazy and low, he bounces his knee once to make sure I'm not closing my eyes.

"Tell me you're not missing any of this," he says.

"I'm not missing any of this," I assure him, my breaths ragged.

And, hell, I am not missing a thing. This might be one of the hottest things Chase has ever done to me.

"Spread your legs for me—wide—so I can see all of you."

I slide down a few more inches and arch my hips. I spread my legs as far as I can.

"There you go," Chase says huskily, his breaths as ragged as mine. "Like that."

All of me is on display, and with anyone else, I'd feel embarrassed. But Chase makes me feel beautiful, sexy.

He groans, emboldening me to lift my hips another inch so he can see even more.

Chase likes what he sees, I assume, since he groans huskily. I know for sure that he likes what he sees when he shifts me in his lap. I feel how incredibly rock-hard he is. The rigid outline of his cock presses into my ass, and I silently curse that he's still wearing his jeans.

"You like this, don't you?" Chase asks.

My eyes meet his in the mirror. "I do."

I make a move to touch myself, but Chase grabs my wrist. Kissing down my neck, he whispers against my skin, "No, not yet."

With my sex fully on display—and aching to be touched—Chase slowly pops open all the little buttons trailing down the front of my dress. He rests his chin on my shoulder as he works, and I lean my head back against him and watch.

When my dress gapes open, exposing my simple white bra, I quickly say, "Oh, sorry, I should have worn something sexier."

His fingers brush over the swell of my breasts. "You don't need shit like that." He unclasps the front closure of my bra. "I prefer you with nothing on, anyway."

He tugs at the bra until it falls away and my breasts are exposed. He cups one breast and begins to massage the sensitive flesh, all while his other hand moves down to where I am desperate to be touched.

But he does more than touch. He ravages my pussy with his fingers.

Watching while he slams his fingers in and out of me, hard, I plead, "Oh, God, make me come."

His pace increases and my body responds almost immediately. I come apart for Chase, again and again.

Unable to speak, I collapse against him. He wraps his arms around me, shifts his body to the side, and lays me down on the bed. Slowly, he slides the material of the dress, which now barely covers me, off completely. Chase then stands and undresses. When he settles his body on top of mine, his cock teasing at my entrance, I expect him to take me. But he doesn't, not yet.

"Remember why I wanted to come over here?" he asks.

I glance up from beneath him, his body dwarfing mine. His face is dark, his blues intense.

"So I can get loud?" I venture.

"And," he prompts, "what else?"

"So you can be rough with me"

"You want more of that, baby girl? More than what I gave you just before?"

I nod, and without warning, Chase slams into me, so hard and rough that I cry out. His cock is so much more than his fingers, and it hurts for a second. But then, like always, it feels amazing.

Chase's fingers thread through my hair, and he tightens his grasp. He tugs hard, harder, while pounding into me fast, faster.

"Is this too much?" he asks when I become breathless.

Is he kidding? I shake my head.

"Good"—he chuckles—"'cause I don't plan on stopping anytime soon."

And he doesn't stop, not that I want him to. The things

he does to me don't allow me time to think. And I like not thinking, because, when I think, I'm forced to remember that there are now *two* secrets Chase is keeping from me: where he was the other day when I couldn't get a hold of him and how he ended up with a bloody hand tonight.

CHAPTER ELEVEN
CHASE

The day after I fail to get Kyle his money, I fully expect to hear from him. But he doesn't contact me. Thank God for small favors.

At breakfast, Will eyes my hand suspiciously. "Dude, what the hell happened? You fuck someone up?"

Kay is at the stove, her back turned to me. Her shoulders tense. She's still waiting for an answer, too.

I try to blow Will's question off by saying, "I hurt my hand at work."

Kay knows that's not true, and I see her shoulders slump when she realizes I'm not going to divulge a thing.

"How?" Will asks, skeptical.

"I did something really stupid. And I really don't want to talk about it."

Hey, both things are true.

Will's no dummy, though. He shakes his head and says, "Yeah, sure, dude."

Despite my hot night with Kay—and, shit, it was fucking scorching—things are subdued throughout the rest of the day. A weird tension permeates the air. Kay still sleeps in my bed Saturday night, but there's no sex. By Sunday, I just want things to return to fucking normal.

When Kay wakes, I smile over at her. She smiles back, snuggles into my grasp. *That's better.*

We just lie quietly in bed for a while, until I ask her if she wants to do anything today. "It's Sunday, you know, and we're both off."

She glances up at me from in my arms. "What did you have in mind?"

"There's a fair over in the next county," I say. "Want to check it out?"

"Yeah, sure," she replies, and then adds, "Why don't you ask Will if he wants to come with us?"

"Good idea, babe."

Five minutes later, I am walking into my brother's bedroom, unannounced.

Will is just waking up, stretching and yawning. But when he catches sight of me, he sits up quickly.

"Dude, what the hell?" he yells. "Haven't you ever heard of knocking? Or do you just make it a habit to walk into rooms like you own the goddamn place?"

I arch an eyebrow.

"Oh, right," he says. "Guess you do kind of own the place."

"No 'kind of' about it," I snort.

Despite our five seconds of banter, Will's behavior is a tad sketchy. It's not like him to get all worked up about me coming into his room.

So I ask, "Why are you so concerned with me knocking first? You got something you're trying to hide?"

I don't *think* he's been using these past several days, but you never know.

"I'm not hiding any drugs, if that's what you're asking," he replies.

I nod once and decide to take him at his word—for now. "Okay," I quietly say.

A moment of tense silence descends, enveloping the two of us, until Will laughs and says, "All I was trying to say, bro, was what if I'd been jacking off or something?"

I roll my eyes. "Good point. Next time, I'll knock."

"So, what's up?" Will asks, swinging his legs over the side of the bed. He starts to tug a pair of low-hanging jeans he finds crumpled at the base of his bed up over his boxers.

"There's a big fair over in the next county. Kay and I are going to check it out." I toss what appears to be a clean T-shirt in Will's direction when I see him scanning the floor for clothes. "What do you say, little bro? You up for spending the day riding some amusement park rides and eating a shitload of greasy fair food?"

Will tries to play it cool, as usual, but the smile he tries to hide lets me know he likes the idea.

"Yeah, sure," he says. He pulls the T-shirt I threw him over his head. "And maybe I can learn how to milk a cow, something I'm sure might someday be useful." He rolls his eyes.

"Hey, smart-ass, you never know when shit like that could come in handy," I deadpan.

Will laughs, and then he pretends to be milking a cow. Like the hormonal kid that he is, he quickly turns it into something sexual.

"Hey, Cass might appreciate a skill like this," he says as he tilts his head and pretends to be sucking on a make-believe udder.

"You, my friend,"—I point at him, try to keep from laughing—"are one sick pup,"

Wills cracks up, but then his expression grows serious.

He rubs a hand down his face. "If I go with you and Kay, would it be okay if Jared tagged along?"

Will knows I am currently not the biggest Jared fan around. But since Will has kept his promise—he hasn't done any drugs for days—I decide to cut him some slack. After all, I did promise him I'd think about letting up on the *no-Jared* rule.

Shrugging, I say, "Sure, give him a call."

Will's brows shoot up. "Really?"

"Yeah, really. He can come with us." I turn and start toward the door. "But we're leaving in an hour," I call back over my shoulder, "so make sure Jared's here by then. Tell him we'll leave without him."

"You will not," Will says.

I swing open the door. "Maybe we'll leave without you, too," I retort, completely in jest. And before Will can respond, I continue teasing. "That'd be a shame, too, since then you'd never learn that milking technique. Poor Cassie."

Will throws some article of clothing my way and yells, "And *I'm* the sick one, bro?"

I duck out the door, laughing, before his cotton projectile makes contact.

A couple of hours later, the four of us are making our way down the crowded midway at an expansive fairground in the next county. Kay and I are in the lead, walking slowly, with Will and Jared lagging a few feet behind.

"Guess they're too cool to be seen with us," Kay whispers, leaning into me.

I drape an arm around her shoulder. "Yeah, probably," I reply.

But then I reconsider. Kay is wearing really short denim shorts and a red shirt that she informed me earlier is something called a "baby-doll tee." The whole outfit is hot as fuck, and I have a feeling that's why my brother and his friend are hanging back.

So, I amend, "Hate to break it to you, but I think the boys might be checking out your ass."

"Chase!" Kay elbows me.

I chuckle. But just in case I'm right and those two hormonal teenage motherfuckers are indeed ogling my woman, I turn my head and shoot a warning glare over my shoulder.

They don't even notice me. Will is too busy saying to Jared, "Dude, quit staring. That shit's just wrong. You do realize Kay is probably going to be my sister-in-law someday, right?"

I smile. Will's got it right, except for one thing. There is no "probably" about it. I will be definitely be making the beautiful woman at my side my wife. Of that, I have no doubt.

I glance over at Kay. She's blushing, surely because she heard Will's statement.

I lean down and place my lips near her ear. "He's right, you know?" I pause. "That is, if you'll have me."

Kay, keeping things light since we're in the middle of a crowded fairground, replies in an exaggerated Scarlett O'Hara voice. "Why, I do declare, Chase Gartner. Is that a proposal I hear?"

Chuckling, I assure her, "You will definitely know when I'm proposing. And it sure as hell won't be somewhere between"—I glance around—"the shooting gallery and the Tilt-A-Whirl." In a very bad Rhett Butler impression, I add, "Because, frankly, my dear, I *do* give a damn."

Kay laughs and shakes her head. "Oh my God, Chase. That was so terrible. Are you sure you've seen *Gone with the Wind*?"

"Sadly, Kay, thanks to 'movie nights' at Gram's, the answer is yes, I've seen that movie more times than I care to admit."

It's true, too. On the rare occasions Gram decided to watch a movie with me and my dad—or my mom, dad, and me—we let her choose. And she always chose the same movie: *Gone with the Wind*. Rare or not, Gram's participation in "movie night" resulted in multiple viewings of that film.

The rest of the night at the fair is great. We play games, ride a few rides, and eat greasy fair food. We even come across a demonstration on how to milk a cow. Will and I just look at each other and bust out laughing. Kay and Jared want to know what's up, but my brother and I reply in unison, "Nothing."

Things are good—really fucking good—that Sunday. And they remain so right into the work week.But somewhere around midweek, things start to go awry.

Trouble begins Wednesday morning. Kay leaves extra early for work, since the big rummage sale is starting. That's how I find myself in the kitchen, attempting to make breakfast for Will.

I am trying to get the food right. I mean, shit, I want Will to eat a decent breakfast before I shove off for work. Problem is, I suck at cooking.

"What the fuck?" I grind out as I scrape away stuck-on egg from the sides of a frying pan. "So much for scrambled eggs. I thought this was supposed to be, like, a nonstick skillet or some shit?"

No one is around to hear me or respond; I'm just griping to myself.

Eventually. I conclude the skillet is most definitely *not* nonstick. Resigned that it is what it is, I dump half the eggs onto a plate. The other half remains stuck in the pan.

I needn't worry, though, about the salvageable amount, or the quality, of my eggs.

Will rambles in, sits down without saying a word, and mindlessly begins to shovel my sad excuse for scrambled eggs into his mouth.

"Good morning to you, too," I grumble as I cross my arms and watch my brother stuff his face.

He barely glances up, so I adopt a more serious tone. "Hey, is everything all right?"

Will finally makes eye contact. "Not really," he says listlessly.

Something is going on. It's not drugs—his eyes are clear. But I know my brother, and this is how he acts when he's upset.

I sit down at the table. "What's going on, Will?"

He sets down his fork. "Cassie called a little while ago."

"She's up early," I remark. It's eight o'clock in Harmony Creek, which means it's only five a.m. in Vegas.

"She never went to sleep last night," Will offers as explanation.

I know immediately that something has happened. Worse yet, I have a strong suspicion that whatever has gone down, it has to do with that perverted stepdad of hers.

Sure enough, Will says, "Paul followed Cassie to her friend's house last night."

"I thought he was leaving her alone, abiding by the restraining order?"

"Nope." Will takes a deep breath. "He must have just been laying low or something. Dickhead re-emerged last night, like the fucking vermin he is. And this time he ran Cassie off the road out in the fucking desert. No one was around, dude." Will shakes his head.

"Shit."

"Yeah, shit is right. The prick yanked her right out of the fucking car. He grabbed her ass, Chase, grinded up against her." Will sucks in a breath. "And then he made her kiss him."

"Fuck...Will."

Will pushes away his eggs, puts his head in his hands. "He let her go," he says quietly. "But only after he groped her some more. Fucking dick. And he would have gone further, he had his hand halfway down Cassie's shorts, but, thank fuck, someone drove by."

I don't even know what to say to make Will feel better. I conclude there are no words, so I just listen as he continues.

"Chase, that prick had the balls to tell Cassie that, next time, he's finishing what he started."

Will pushes his plate farther away and eggs spill over the side. "Cassie's beyond upset," he says, his voice catching on emotion. "This prick is serious. Paul's not going to give up. I swear I'm going to kill that motherfucker before he makes another move."

"Will—"

He puts his hand up. "I don't want to hear it, bro. I *have* to go back to Vegas. I can't hang around here for another week and a half. Cassie has no one watching her back. Her mom's back to work and gone all the time. Cassie needs me to take care of this shit."

I don't even want to know what "take care of this shit" entails according to Will.

Dragging my hand down my face, I say, "Listen, Will, you have to remember there's a restraining order out on that dick. The police can pick him up now that he's violated the order. They can take him in now."

"Yeah, that'd be nice," Will replies, "if the police could find him."

"What are you saying?" I ask as a sick feeling builds in my gut.

"Paul's gone. No one can find the asshole, least of all the cops."

As I'm shaking my head, at a loss for words, Will reiterates, "I have to go home. Like, today. I know people in Vegas who can help me find Paul."

People in Vegas? I don't like the sound of this.

"What kind of people, Will?"

"Just…people."

From the guilty look on my brother's face, I already know the kind of people who'd be willing to help a fifteen-year-old kid search for an adult man, a potentially danger-ous man. Unsavory people, people involved in illegal activities, like drug dealers and users, that's who would be willing to "help" Will—for a price, of course.

Shit. It pains me to think Will even has those kinds of contacts. But he's bought drugs from someone in the past, right? Not to mention, who knows who Cassie is involved with. After all, it was with her that Will first tried cocaine.

"You're not going back," I say with finality. "You're going to let the police handle this shit."

Will makes a scoffing noise and says, "*Now* you're suddenly a fan of the police?"

"Doesn't matter what my personal thoughts are. This is about what's best for you—and Cassie—in this situation."

"Whatever, dude," Will replies dismissively. "I'm changing my ticket today. Can you or Kay take me to the airport tonight?"

"Will, no!" I slam my palms down on the table and stand up. "You can't go back. Mom and Greg won't be home until next Friday. Not to mention, Mom doesn't even know what's going on. Just hold tight till next week. You can go home then."

Will shoves his chair back, the legs scraping the linoleum. "Really, Chase?" he snorts. "You want me to wait until next Friday to go home? That's nine fucking days away. You know all the shit that could happen to my girlfriend in *nine* days?"

"The cops will find Paul," I say as reassuringly as I can. "Cassie will be fine."

Will doesn't seem to know what to do. He runs his hand through his hair, turns left and right, and finally plops back down in the chair.

I glance at the clock on the stove. "Shit. I have to leave. I'm going to be late for work."

Will shrugs.

"Look, I hate to do this, but I *have* to go. We'll talk later, okay?"

Will glances up, his greens shaded by a swath of dark-blond hair that's fallen to his face. "Just promise me you'll think about letting me go back early," he whispers, his voice pleading. "I'll be fine alone at the house in Vegas." He gestures around. "I'm here alone all the time. What am I going to do there that I can't do here?"

I sigh and say nothing. There are way too many answers to that loaded question. The first of which is that my hot-headed brother will probably make a deal with some unsavory person the second his flight touches down, in an attempt to find Cassie's stepdad. Then, he will go after him.

I reiterate that we'll discuss it further when I get home from work. "I'll think about it," I say. "Maybe we can call Mom later and work something out."

That seems to appease Will. However, do I really plan to contact our mother so my brother can go home early? Hell no. But if allowing him to believe I'm considering it means he'll cool down and not do anything rash, my false words are justified.

The thought of how easily Will finds trouble reminds me to add, "No going out with Jared today."

"Can he come over, at least?" Will responds.

"Not today. Find something to do around the house by yourself. Play video games on the computer...or work on your comic book."

Will mutters, "Yeah, okay, whatever." When he sees me

glancing again at the clock, he adds sarcastically, "Better get going."

I ignore his attitude and hit the road. But the whole way to work, I have this incredibly sick feeling, the kind that clutches at your throat and makes you feel like you can barely catch your breath.

I almost call Father Maridale to take the day off, but I'm needed at the school today since the rummage sale is starting. I can't expect Kay and pregnant Missy to lug a bunch of heavy shit out to people's cars.

When I get to the church grounds, I search out Kay. She's in the gymnasium, standing behind a long table, setting up calculators and blank sales receipts. I take her aside and fill her in on what's going on with Will.

"Do you want me to call Cassie?" she asks. "I could probably talk her into making sure Will doesn't do anything stupid, like run off to Vegas or something."

I rake my fingers through my hair. "I don't know, Kay. I just don't know what to do anymore."

She touches my arm. "Hey, I'll call Cassie. If anyone can make Will stay put, it's her."

"Will staying put isn't the only thing I'm worried about." My eyes meet hers, and she knows my immediate concern is that my brother will seek out drugs today. This latest development is the exact kind of trigger to send him off in search of a high.

Kay presses her lips together determinedly. "Well, if that's what you're worried about, I think I have an idea to make sure Will doesn't leave the house."

"I'm open to anything," I tell her. And, damn, I am.

Kay then tells me her idea. And, as it turns out, the plan

isn't bad. But it requires rapid action. Kay's plan to keep Will from taking off is for the two of us to basically take turns babysitting him.

"That way," Kay says, "he won't have an opportunity to go out."

I hope she's right.

"If you can help Missy this morning," Kay continues, "I'll head home now and stay with Will until lunchtime. Then we'll switch."

It's not optimum—and I am less than thrilled to be stuck with Missy Metzger all morning—but Kay's plan is better than leaving Will to his own devices all day.

After we review the plan particulars, Kay says, "Okay, great. I'll tell Father Maridale what's going on. I'm sure he'll understand."

I grab her arm. "No, wait. I should be the one to tell him." I nod to Missy, who's clearly trying to eavesdrop. "You go fill her in on what's going on. She looks like she's dying to know."

"I'm on it," she says.

Kay heads over to the table Missy is sitting behind, and I leave to go find Father Maridale. I locate him in the church; bring him up to speed while we're standing next to the confessionals. Of course, Father is fine with our plan—he's always so easy-going. I then return to the gymnasium to let Kay know she can leave. But to my surprise, she has already left.

The rummage sale appears to be going full-speed ahead. There's already a line a mile long of people waiting to buy stuff.

Missy glances over at me, tilts her head, and mouths one word: "Help."

Chuckling, I nod and approach the table.

As the morning progresses, Missy and I don't have an opportunity to talk much, but we work well together. She sells the stuff, and I carry anything exceptionally heavy out to the buyers' cars.

Shortly before lunch, as I'm returning from carrying an outdated, heavy-as-fuck TV out to the parking lot for some little old lady, I take note that the line has finally ended. Everyone is gone.

Slumping down into the seat next to Missy, I exhale loudly and say, "A break, at last."

Missy smiles and says, "I know, right? I thought that line would never end."

"Seriously," I concur as I lean back in my chair.

Missy glances over at me. "Um," she says softly, "Kay told me about what's going on with your brother, and I know you have to leave soon, but I just wanted to say I hope everything turns out okay."

Missy is trying to be nice, and I feel kind of bad for her that she's knocked up with the kid of some guy she barely knows, so I decide I may as well be cool with her.

I run my fingers through my hair. "Yeah, I hope so, too."

Missy falls silent. She starts straightening some things on the table. I can tell she's nervous, especially when she knocks over a small, flimsy box filled with golf balls. The lid pops open, and golf balls roll out all over the table.

Missy stands quickly and grabs at the balls, but they're rolling every which way and she has no luck collecting them.

"I-I'm sorry, I'm sorry," she stammers. "God, I'm such an idiot."

I gather the golf balls with one swoop of my hand and place them back in the box. "Missy"—my eyes meet hers—"it's fine."

She glances away, and I look down. She's standing right in my line of sight, though, and I can't help but notice that the dress she's wearing is far more conservative than the sleazy shit she used to wear. In fact, the light-brown, sheath-like thing she has on is far more conservative than the dresses Kay reserves for Mass. Even though the dress is loose fitting, the fabric is stretched tight in the waist area. Missy is not really showing—according to Kay, she's only eight or nine weeks—but her stomach is no longer completely flat.

When she catches me staring at her midsection, Missy covers her abdomen with her hand and sits back down quickly.

"I guess you think I'm, like, the town whore, huh?" she asks. "Especially since we"—she waves her hand between us—"have a history of our own."

"Missy, I don't think you're a whore."

"Yeah, you say that, but I know Kay told you what happened the night she and I went to the Anchor Inn."

"She did," I confirm.

Missy sighs. "I was out of control that night, Chase. But that was the drugs, not me."

I don't reply, and Missy continues.

"Anyway, I swear I was only with one of those guys—just Tony. Not Nick. Tony is the father of my baby. I already told Kay that. She believes me, doesn't she?"

I shrug since I have no idea why what Kay believes is so important to Missy.

But she's waiting for a reply, so I say, "I'm sure she believes you, Missy."

"Good," she says, nodding.

Missy seems pretty fucking emphatic here, the way she's insisting Tony—not Nick—is the dad. But I can't imagine why it matters so much.

To end the weird conversation, I say, "This is really none of my business."

"I know, but I have one more thing to say about my behavior." Missy glances down. "I just don't want you and Kay thinking I am someone I'm not. I mean, I know you and I hooked up, but like my night with Nick and Tony, that wasn't really me. I had snorted a ton of coke the night you and I—"

"I know," I interject. How could I forget the packet of white powder in her bag?

"I was doing a lot of things back then." She sighs. "Things I now wish I hadn't."

"Listen, Missy," I reply gently, "you don't have to keep explaining yourself to me. Trust me, I'm no saint."

She smiles sadly. "Thanks, Chase."

"For what?"

She shrugs. "I don't know. For not judging me, I guess."

"I have in the past," I admit.

"That's okay. I probably deserved it at the time. But I don't want that rep following me around forever, especially after this baby is born." She touches her abdomen again. "I already told Kay that I don't want my kid thinking bad things about me. I want to be the kind of person he or she can respect. Like, I want to be a good mom, you know?"

"I'm sure you'll be a great mom, Missy."

When I say it, at first I think I'm just being nice. But then I realize I mean it. I think maybe Missy getting pregnant happened at just the right time, before she sank too low to recover. Now she's away from drugs and getting her life in order.

And, like all of us, she definitely deserves this second chance.

CHAPTER TWELVE
KAY

When I return to the farmhouse and walk into the hall-way, the first thing I notice is the silence.

You can almost hear a pin drop.

I immediately assume Will has already left, taken off to God-knows-where, and that my plan is a bust before it has even begun.

But then I hear noise from the living room, like some-one tapping at a keyboard. Sure enough, when I go in to see who's here, I find Will seated at the computer.

I breathe out a sigh of relief. "Hey, Will."

Will spins in his seat. "Kay, what are you doing home?" He's clearly startled, but his tone quickly turns sarcastic. "I thought today was the big, important junk sale."

"It's a rummage sale," I snap, bristling at his smart-ass attitude.

He laughs, turning back to the computer screen. "Yeah, like I said, a junk sale."

I choose to ignore Will's snide remark. He's still pissed at Chase, and the world. He's just taking it out on me since I'm the one here.

I take a step closer to where he's working on the computer, and when he notices, he quickly closes the window he's viewing.

"What were you doing?" I question.

"Nothing," he mutters, before snatching up a piece of paper lying in the printer tray.

Quickly, he jams the paper into what appears to be a boarding pass–type folder, leaving me to conclude Will has made some sort of change to his ticket to fly to Vegas.

"Will," I begin, sighing. "You know you can't go back to Vegas until your mom returns from her cruise."

"Yeah, I know," he remarks nonchalantly. "Don't worry, Kay, everything's cool."

I start to reply, but he talks right over me.

"Why, again, are you home before ten o'clock in the morning?"

I ignore his question. "I'll only be here till lunchtime," I say. "Then I'm heading back."

Despite my attempt to be vague as to why I'm at the house, Will figures it out.

"Oh, let me guess," he snipes, "my brother is taking the afternoon babysit-Will shift."

"Hey, it's not like that."

"Oh, but it is." He holds up his hand and stands. "Save it, Kay. I'm going up to my room."

He brushes past me, and not two minutes later, loud music is blaring from his room. Will must really be pissed; the whole house reverberates with heavy bass.

"Ugh," I mutter.

I try my best to ignore the music, busying myself with washing dishes Will left in the sink, dusting in the living room. I also try to call Cassie a few times, but big surprise, she doesn't answer. I attempt to read at one point, but find it impossible with the loud music. So, basically, I end up spending the remainder of the morning trying to ward off a headache that is threatening to bloom.

Thankfully, noon rolls around and Chase comes home.

"Jesus," he yells over the music as he walks into the kitchen. "What the fuck?"

I'm seated at the table, head in my hands. I glance up and say loudly, "Don't worry, you kind of get used to it after a while."

Chase shakes his head. He walks back out through the dining room and into the hall. I get up and follow him.

He yells up the stairs, "Hey, Will, turn that shit down some."

I place my hand on his shoulder.

He turns to me. "I'm gonna kill that kid, I swear."

The music continues, loud as ever, and his eyes meet mine.

I shrug. "Maybe we should check on him?"

"Yeah." Chase scrubs a hand down his face. "Let's go see if he has any eardrums left."

But Will's eardrums are of no concern when we walk into his room. He's not even there.

"Shit." Chase turns off the stereo and rushes over to the open window. A screen from the window sits propped up nearby. I notice that, like in Chase's room, the roof is flat in this section of the house.

"Fuck," Chase grinds out as he leans his head out the window. "Will must have shimmied down one of the porch posts."

When he turns to face me, he looks more worried than mad.

"Where do you think he went? I didn't hear any cars." After a thoughtful pause, I add, "Then again, I couldn't really hear *anything* with all that loud music."

Chase sits down on the side of Will's bed.

"I'm sure my brother knew you couldn't hear anything. He turned the music up high like that on purpose."

I sit down next to Chase, and the bed dips slightly.

"Do you think he walked somewhere?"

"No." He shakes his head. "My guess is that he had Jared pick him up at the end of the driveway."

"I'm sorry, Chase." I feel like I've failed him by not watching Will more closely. I just never expected his brother to sneak out an upstairs window. "I should have checked on him."

"Kay—"

"No, Chase, this is my fault." I cast my eyes downward, but seconds later, Chase is tilting my chin up so I have no choice but to meet his soft gaze.

"Baby girl," he says, "don't say that kind of shit. This was *not* your fault."

I nod into his hand, accepting his words. And then I ask, "If you're going to go out to look for him, can I come with you?"

"Sure," he replies, smiling and trailing his fingers down my neck. "We should leave soon since we have no idea how long he's been gone. He could be anywhere, especially if he's with Jared."

Now seems a good time to mention that Will was on the computer when I first returned home this morning.

"He closed whatever window he had open when I walked over," I say once I've gotten Chase up to speed. "And then he snatched something up from the printer tray. You don't think he had Jared take him to the airport, do you?"

Chase scowls and glances around Will's room. "Nah, he wouldn't leave all his stuff behind."

True, all of Will's belongings appear to be in place.

Chase and I go downstairs, preparing to leave to search for Will, but before we walk out he door, I call Missy to let her know we won't be returning to the school this afternoon.

"Why?" she asks. "Did something bad happen with Chase's brother?"

"Yeah, Missy, something kind of bad did happen. Will took off."

"Oh no," Missy says concernedly.

"Chase and I are going out now to look for him," I continue, "but that means we aren't going to make it back for the rest of the rummage sale."

Missy's tone is filled with nothing but concern and kindness when she replies, "Don't worry about anything, Kay. I've got it covered. I can call my mom. She'll be happy to come in this afternoon and help out. Take as long as you need. Oh, and I'll let Father Maridale know what's going on."

"Thank you, Missy," I breathe out, relieved. "You're a lifesaver." And, really, she is, stepping up to the plate like this.

Before we disconnect, Missy says, "I hope you find Will. I'll say a prayer that he's all right."

I am hoping the same thing as Chase and I drive away from the house in his truck.

Since we're fairly certain Jared picked up Will, we head to his house first, in the wealthy part of town, South of Market.

"How do you know where he lives?" I ask Chase when it's clear he knows exactly where he's going.

"I asked Will for Jared's address a while ago, figured it was something I should know."

I reach over and pat his knee. "Such a good big brother," I say, smiling. "That was very responsible of you."

He grabs my hand and laces our fingers together. "I'm getting better," he replies, sighing. "But I have a long way to go."

I squeeze his hand, for support, comfort, whatever he needs.

Chase slows as we turn onto what I assume is Jared's street. We pull up to the curb and park in front of a perfectly manicured lawn that slopes up to a stately redbrick home, a very large home.

"Jeez, nice house," I utter softly as Chase turns off the ignition. "I see nothing has changed South of Market."

This is still the moneyed part of Harmony Creek, a fact made even more apparent when one of three garage doors opens, revealing a sleek red Jaguar. It's a matching twin to Jared's black Jag. Clearly, the Knox family is loaded.

Chase and I wait for the car to back out, but it never moves. Instead, a very thin teenage girl emerges from the front door and bounces over to the open garage. She's dressed in barely there white shorts and a tiny purple tube top. Her dark hair is pulled up into a high ponytail. She opens the driver's side door of the red Jag and grabs something from the front seat. As she heads back toward the house, Chase and I get out of the truck.

The girl slows to a stop halfway across the front lawn when she notices she has visitors.

"Can I help you with something?" she asks, hand on her hip.

A look off disdain crosses her face as her eyes scan over Chase's work truck. But when her gaze moves to Chase, her expression morphs into something best described as lustful.

With an entirely new attitude, she saunters down to where we're standing.

Speaking solely to my man, she says in a flirtatious voice, "Hey, I know who you are. You're Will's brother." She adjusts her tube top to reveal more cleavage. "I'm Jared's sister, Cheri." She licks her full lips. "What can I do for you?"

I roll my eyes. No doubt this young girl has heard all the stories about bad boy Chase Gartner and would like nothing more than to have the town's most infamous resident do unspeakable things to her.

Not gonna happen, Cheri, I hope my eyes convey as I glare at her.

She ignores me completely. She's too busy shooting lustful eyes at Chase.

Bitch.

I clear my throat and get to the point of why we're here. "We're looking for Will, and we're pretty sure he's with your brother. Have you seen either of them today? Do you know where they went?"

Cheri eyes me warily for a beat and then focuses back on Chase. To his credit, he keeps his eyes solely above her neck when she responds.

"Sorry, I haven't seen your brother. Jared left awhile ago, alone. He didn't say where he was going."

"Well, she was no help," I say to Chase when he and I are back in the truck.

Chase is trying not to smile, and I shoot him a curious look.

"What?"

He reaches over and places his hand on my thigh, right below the hem of the peach-colored sundress I'm wearing today. "You're adorable when you're jealous."

"Shut up," I huff while I pretend to push his hand away.

He just grasps tighter and moves up an inch. "You're the only one I want. You know that, right?"

I nod, because I do know that Chase has eyes for only me. But he's right, nonetheless. I am jealous.

I lean over and kiss along his strong jaw, then trail my lips down his neck.

He mock-shoos me away. "I'm trying to drive here, babe."

I laugh, and he chuckles. I kiss him another minute, but then settle back into the passenger seat. We're both still smiling big, but our happy grins falter when the heaviness of the fact that we have no idea where Will is starts to sink back in.

"Where to now?" I breathe out.

Chase sighs heavily. "I think you know."

I do, but it pains me to say it out loud. "Kyle's?"

Chase doesn't answer, and his lips thin to a tight line.

When we reach Market Street, the main road that cuts through town, Chase rolls to a stop. He glances left and right, and then turns left, a turn that will lead us straight to the seedy part of town.

That's all the answer I need. We are indeed on our way to Kyle Tanner's.

CHAPTER THIRTEEN

CHASE

When we start down the long dirt driveway that leads to Kyle's ramshackle house, I'm rethinking whether I should have brought Kay with me. Perhaps a detour back to the house to drop her off would have been wise, since I don't want my girl anywhere near the kind of debaucheries that occur in this drug den.

But it's too late now, so I content myself with just saying, "Hey, I think it's best if you wait in the car. Are you okay with that?"

"Sure," Kay replies, "yeah."

She doesn't sound put off in any way. Hell, I know she has no real desire to meet Kyle Tanner. I don't blame her, either. I wish I too could avoid an up close and personal with that prick today. But I need to know if my brother's been a-calling.

When we roll up to the dilapidated frame structure, there are no cars out front.

Kay remarks, "Huh, it doesn't look like anyone's here."

I point to a beat-up old Dodge truck, circa early nineties, parked around the far side of the house. "That's Kyle's piece of shit." I jam the gearshift in park. "He's home."

Kay nods. "Oh, okay."

I lean back in my seat and scrub both hands down my face, then turn to Kay. "Listen, I'm leaving the keys here. Just let the truck idle. If there's any trouble, any at all, take off."

Kay unclasps her seat belt and twists toward me. "What kind of trouble are you expecting, Chase?"

"Well," I begin, "Will is clearly not here, but he probably was around earlier. And if that motherfucker admits he sold my kid brother anything even remotely illegal, I'm laying his ass out. I don't want you witnessing shit like that, all right?"

Kay presses her lips together tightly, says, "Okay, but I'm not leaving you here with no way home. If something like that does, uh, occur, then I'll go, but I'll wait for you at the end of the driveway."

I give this woman who's so unconditionally supportive of me a sad smile. "I'm sorry I'm even putting you in a position like this."

"Chase"—she places her hand on mine—"don't."

It's important that I finish what I'm saying, though, so I continue. "I'm trying so hard to be the kind of man you deserve, Kay, I really am. But it seems like this shit from the past keeps popping up and leading me back to the ways I used to solve problems." I lift up my hand, make a fist. "Like through intimidation…or by using force."

An image of Doug Wilson's frightened face pops up in my head. Kay doesn't even know about my little discussion with her ex. I think she believes Doug never contacted her because he chickened out. Well, he did, but only due to me. I should go ahead and confess to Kay right here and now.

And while I'm at it, I should probably tell her about my deal with Kyle, share with her how my hand ended up bloodied.

But I don't say a word. I know how disappointed in me she'll be. I can't bear to watch how her face will surely fall, how her eyes will fill with hurt. So my secrets remain hidden.

In the meantime, while I'm ruminating, Kay is saying, "Do what you have to do, Chase. I'll understand."

Oh, the irony.

I just shake my head. This is not how I envision our future—me not sharing things that she has a right to know, me paying visits to my onetime dealer's house, me making deals with said dealer, all while Kay blindly supports my antics.

"Christ," I sigh under my breath as I step down from the truck.

Up on Kyle's porch, I knock on the metal screen door. I didn't notice on my last visit, but the flimsy door is covered in kick marks. I knock again and the battered thing clangs and shakes.

"Hold the fuck on," someone yells from inside the house.

Three seconds later, Kyle swings open the front door. He wavers on unsteady feet, and says in a slurred voice, "Fuck, Gartner. What—"

His glazed-over eyes slide lazily to my truck. When he spots Kay in the passenger seat, he comes to life.

His lips turn up into a lecherous grin, and I respond in a voice full of warning, "You better wipe that smile right off your fucking face."

"What? I can't appreciate a pretty girl?"

"Not mine."

Kyle wisely shuts the fuck up. But after a few seconds elapse, he asks, "What are you doing here, anyway?"

I get right to the point. "You see my brother or that punk friend of his today?"

"What do I look like, a fucking babysitter?"

I take a step toward Kyle, and he backs up. I'm holding the screen door open and now I'm one step closer to being inside his house.

I nod to the darkened living room, where bottles and drug paraphernalia are strewn all over the floor. "There's no place to run, Kyle. You may as well just answer the question."

He fumbles in the pocket of his flannel shirt for his pack of smokes. He digs out a cigarette and places it between his lips. "You mind?" he mumbles.

"No, go ahead."

Kyle takes a lighter from a pocket of his pants and lights up. He inhales and blows smoke off to the side, then admits, "Yeah, your brother stopped by earlier."

"Was he with Jared?"

Kyle leans his shoulder on the frame of the door and nods.

I raise an eyebrow. "You sell them anything?"

For a minute, I expect him to give me shit for not getting his money from the addict. But I think he sees in my expression that he best not utter one fucking word on that subject today.

Kyle takes another hit of his cigarette, exhales, and then looks away. "I didn't sell either of them any drugs, if that's what you're asking."

I'm surprised he's answering so willingly, but something is off in his tone. I just know he's fucking lying about something.

"So why were they here?" I press.

"Beats me," he replies. "Guess they just wanted to say hi."

This motherfucker is entirely too smug. I know he's hiding something. He may not have sold them any drugs, but some kind of shit went down.

"You expect me to believe they stopped by on some kind of a fucked-up social call?"

Kyle tosses his cigarette out in the direction of the yard. As he watches it arc into the air, he replies, "Maybe they wanted drugs, but then they changed their minds. Who knows with kids these days?"

I've had enough of this asshole. I take a step back and let the screen door fall. Kyle catches it a second before it hits his face. Frankly, I'm impressed his reactions are that good.

I point at him and take another step back. "Listen up, Tanner. If you see my brother or his buddy again today, you make damn sure that you *continue* to not sell them a fucking thing. You got it?"

Kyle puts his hands up, and behind the mesh screen, he kind of looks like he's in jail. How crazy is it that this dickhead has never done any time? Nothing, nada. He just continued with his criminal ways, all while my ass remained incarcerated. I'm no innocent, not by any means, but Kyle Tanner takes criminal behavior to a whole new level. After all, I may have been carrying forty hits of X with the intent to sell, but it was *his* supply that got me busted.

"I got it," Kyle says, "no drugs for little Gartner and his pal."

I don't bother responding. I just turn away and jog back over to the truck.

"I gotta get out of here," I say to Kay as I jump inside and slam the door. "That fucker gets in my head."

I'm clenching and unclenching my hands on the steering wheel when we drive away.

Kay, noticing my anxiety, places her warm little hand over mine. "Hey, you did well, Chase. You didn't hurt Kyle. There was no trouble. And I'm proud of you for that."

Ha, if only she knew that I punched an addict who owed Kyle money and that I intimidated the fuck out of her ex-boyfriend. But I can't dwell on that shit right now.

I lift the hand that Kay is covering and bring her curled fingers to my lips. "I love you so fucking much." I brush my lips over her knuckles.

When I release her hand, she trails a finger over my cheek and jaw, rubbing at the light stubble. She leans over and kisses me. When she settles back into her seat, she says, "So, what did Kyle say? Did he have any info?"

"Yeah, he did, actually." I shoot her a sidelong glance filled with meaning. "Will and Jared were at his house earlier, but he claims they didn't buy any drugs."

Kay's brow furrows. "That doesn't make any sense. I mean, why would they go see him, if not for drugs? What other possible reason would your brother or Jared have for visiting Kyle Tanner?"

"That's the million-dollar question, babe."

"It sure is," Kay says under her breath. "It just doesn't make any sense."

"I agree." I turn out of Kyle's driveway. "But something's going on, I'm sure of that. I just have no idea what that something is."

We're quiet on the short drive into town.

When we hit Market Street, Kay asks, "Where should we go next?"

"I was thinking maybe Pizza House. Will really likes their food. Maybe he and Jared stopped in for lunch or something."

It's wishful thinking, sure, but not out of the realm of possibility. In fact, I'm actually hoping all those two kids did today was grab a pizza. But I'd be lying if I didn't admit the stop at Kyle's is weighing on my mind. It has me concerned, very concerned. I think Kyle sold Jared—or more likely, my brother—*something*.

But what?

I am considering possibilities—and coming up blank— when Kay and I walk into Pizza House. Nick emerges from the back, and when he spots us, it's obvious he's shocked as shit to see Kay. But his shock turns into fawning when he starts to speak to her.

"Hey, Kay," he gushes. "You look fantastic. How've you been?"

"Fine, thank you," she responds.

"You haven't stopped in for a takeout in so long," Nick says, feigning disappointment. "I was starting to worry about you, thought I might have to stop by the church and make sure everything was okay."

What a tool. I guffaw, and Kay entwines her arm with mine in an attempt to calm my ire. She knows me so well.

"Aw, Nick," she says, "I've been fine." She leans into me,

cuddling to a point. I know it's her way to dismiss Nick's flirtation. "It's just that Chase, here, has been volunteering to pick up all our take-out orders lately."

"Yeah, I noticed that," Nick says dryly, nodding curtly to me.

Everyone quiets, Nick wipes at his brow. He's sweating. But I can't figure out whether it's because he's uneasy around me—I mean, he obviously still likes Kay—or if he's unnerved because he's the person who facilitated my meeting with Doug Wilson.

Sorry, dude, but we're in on that one together.

I hope my eyes are conveying that exact message when I shoot Nick a meaningful look. He just ignores me, though. I don't know, maybe something entirely different is weighing on his mind.

Nick shoves his hands in the front pockets of his dark pants and leans back on his heels. Back to business, he asks, "So, what brings you in today? You want to order something to go?"

"No, we're good," I reply. "We just stopped in to ask if you happened to see my brother in here today."

Will has accompanied me to pick up a number of take-out orders, thus Nick knows what he looks like.

Nick shakes his head. "No, sorry, man. I haven't seen him, not today."

I turn to go, mutter, "Okay, thanks."

Kay tightens her hand on mine as we leave Pizza House. "Well, there's strike number three," I say. "Shit, Kay, I'm running out of fucking options here."

She softly says, "Let's just go home, Chase. Maybe Will is back at the house by now."

She has a point. It is after four o'clock.

"Yeah," I agree as we get in my truck, "maybe."

"Hey, we'll find him," Kay says reassuringly. "Even if he's not at the house, we'll find him."

I wish I had her confidence.

I rake my fingers through my hair. "Fuck, let's talk about something else for a while, okay?"

"Sure," Kay replies.

There's a long pause. I pull out of the Pizza House lot and turn in the direction of the house.

Once we're on our way, Kay sighs and says, "So I guess Missy is doing okay with the rummage sale. Her mom must have come through. I haven't received a single panicked call or any frantic texts. If things were going crazy over there, I'm sure Missy would be letting us know by now."

"Yeah, she must have things under control." I chuckle, then add, "By the way, that was really nice of her to help out like she did."

"It was," Kay says. "And I'm glad you two are finally getting along."

Kay sounds like she really means it, so I share with her how Missy's actions surprised me this morning, in a good way, especially how compassionate she was regarding the situation with my brother.

"Yeah," Kay replies, "I think Missy is really trying to turn her life around. She must have truly meant it when she said she wanted to be a better person for her kid."

"Speaking of which"—I tap my fingers on the steering wheel—"has she told Nick's cousin that he's going to be a dad in, like, seven months?"

"No." Kay sighs. "She claims she hasn't talked to Tony yet."

I shake my head, and Kay adds, "She needs to tell Tony soon, I know. He has a right to know he's going to be a dad."

"Yeah, he does," I agree.

Talk of Missy ends, and, out of the blue, Kay asks, "By the way, did it seem like Nick was acting weird back at the restaurant?"

"What do you mean?" I hedge.

She shrugs. "I don't know. He just seemed...off."

I chuckle and toss out, "Maybe he seemed 'off' because he still likes you, baby girl."

Kay glances at me from under her lashes. "I don't think that was it, Chase."

She knows as well as I do, though, that Nick Mercurio wants her more than ever. But I sure as fuck don't care to prolong a discussion focusing on Nick's lust for my fucking girl.

So, I re-focus the subject. "Who knows, maybe Nick was acting weird because Missy told him about Tony."

"No, no way." Kay shakes her head. "If Missy said anything at all, even just a hint that she's pregnant with Tony's baby, Nick would definitely tell him. And Missy, for all her hesitation, wouldn't want Tony to find out that way."

"Then I don't know, babe."

I'm kind of done discussing Missy and Tony and Nick. But as we near the church, Missy's name comes up once more. Up ahead in the distance, her car is nosing out from the church parking lot, edging out onto the main road on which we're traveling.

"Guess the rummage sale wrapped up," I say. "Looks like Missy is leaving."

Kay starts to reply, but just then, a dark car flies up over the crest of the hill beyond the church. The car is in the opposite lane, bearing down at a high rate of speed toward Missy.

The dark car—I think it's black—tries to swerve. But it's too late.

"Oh my God!" Kay screams "Missy, no!"

What follows is a sickly sound, metal on metal impacting.

I screech to a halt several hundred yards away from the scene. I pull off to the side of the road. Kay and I jump out of my truck at the exact same time and start running toward the two wrecked cars. But I'm a lot faster and end up way ahead.

I start to slow down, to wait for Kay to catch up. But just then, I get a clear view of the car that's crashed into Missy's car.

It's black, all right. It's a Jaguar.

Fuck, Jared is the person who's just smashed into Missy.

I hope Missy and Jared are okay, but all I can think is: *Fuck, I hope my brother isn't in that car with Jared.*

"God, no," I yell, running faster.

Just as I reach the Jag, I glance back. Kay has detoured over to Missy's car. She has no idea this black car is Jared's Jaguar. Missy's car, pushed several yards away by the impact, is facing the wrong direction. It's smoking and hissing, and fluids are leaking out onto the road. Strapped into the driver's seat, Missy's head is lolling from side to side.

I hope Missy is okay, but first, I have to know whether my brother is trapped in Jared's car.

The Jag has withstood the impact of the crash much better than Missy's car, but I still hold my breath when I swing open the passenger door.

To my relief, Will is not even in the car.

Thank fuck.

Jared is the only occupant. I glance over to the driver's side and ask him if he's all right. He doesn't hear me, though, as he's too busy opening his own door and stumbling out onto the road.

Suspecting he might be fucked up in some way, I fly around to his side of the car and grab him roughly by his plaid shirt.

When I throw him up against the side of the car, I know I should calm down. But still, I growl, "Where the fuck is my brother?"

"He's home, he's home," Jared cries, clearly startled. "I was coming from your house. I dropped him off, like, ten minutes ago."

A huge surge of relief that Will is truly safe washes over me. I let up on Jared and take a step back. "Were you drinking?"

"No, I swear."

I peer at his eyes, assessing their condition. "Are you fucked up on anything?"

"No!"

Jared's eyes are clear. He seems to be telling the truth.

"Why the fuck were you speeding like that? This isn't a raceway, dude. People are pulling in and out of that church lot all the time."

"I'm sorry," Jared chokes out. He glances over to Missy's mangled car. "Is that lady going to be all right?"

Sirens wail in the distance, and Kay, who is kneeling down by the driver's seat of Missy's car, brushes hair away from Missy's face. I shake my head, since I can't tell whether Missy is still conscious.

Jared asks again, more panicked now, if Missy will be okay.

"I don't know," I say. I'm being honest.

An ambulance arrives, and I turn to Jared.

"They'll be coming over here after they take care of Missy. You sure you don't have anything you need to come clean about?" I arch a brow.

"Like what?" he asks, bewildered. "You still think I'm fucked up?"

"I don't know." I shrug. "Some people are good at hiding it. You tell me."

"I *did* tell you," he huffs. "I'm fine, I swear."

"Where were you and my brother all day? What were you two up to? If you just dropped him off, that means you were with him for hours. Where were you, and what were you two doing all that time?"

"Will and I weren't off doing drugs all day, if that's what you're implying. We drove to the lake, the one just across the state line. We hung out, swam a little, just chilled. Will said he needed to get away and unwind. He was going crazy in that house, worrying about Cassie and shit."

"Okay, fair enough." I accept that the lake is probably where he and my brother went, but I still have to ask. "If drugs weren't in the picture today, then why the fuck did you two stop by Kyle's place this morning?"

Jared glances away quickly, and I know for certain there's more to the visit to Kyle Tanner.

I step closer to Jared and whisper, "Tell me before the paramedics come over. Tell me and I won't be pissed. Did my brother buy any drugs from Tanner?"

"No."

I know I'm being played in some way. My blood starts to boil. "What other possible reason," I grind out, "would you two have for stopping in at that motherfucker's house?"

For this brief second, Jared's eyes meet mine, and I fucking know he's about to spill.

But just as Jared opens his mouth, wouldn't you know it, a paramedic steps over to where we're standing. Reluctantly, I move off to the side.

I glance over at Kay, hoping to get her attention. She's still next to Missy, holding her hand as two paramedics maneuver her battered body onto a stretcher. After Missy is secured, Kay finally notices me. She nods and heads over to where I'm standing.

"Is she going to be okay?" I ask when Kay stops in front of me.

"I don't know," she replies. "I think so, but they're concerned for the baby."

"Jesus, I hope everything is okay."

Nodding once to where the paramedic is talking to Jared, Kay whispers, "I can't believe it was Jared who crashed into Missy."

"I know. It's fucking crazy."

"Will's safe at home, then?" she asks.

"Yes."

Kay bites her lip and glances over at the ambulance.

"Would you mind if I ride in the ambulance with Missy? Her mom's been notified, but Missy is going to be all alone until we get to the hospital. She's really scared, Chase, and I feel bad leaving her."

"Of course, babe, go with her." I lean down and kiss the top of Kay's head. "I'll head back to the house to check on Will. I can always meet you at the hospital later if you need me to."

Kay glances over to where the paramedic is checking Jared's vitals. "Is he messed up?" she asks in a low voice. "Were he and Will out partying?"

I shake my head. "No, he claims they just drove out to the lake in Pennsylvania. He insists they hung out and swam all day."

"No drugs, then?" Kay queries.

"No drugs," I say.

Kay's brow creases. "Okay, then. But why would they stop at Kyle's this morning?"

"I don't know," I say. "But, believe me, I intend to find out."

CHAPTER FOURTEEN
KAY

I stay with Missy, holding her hand until we reach the hospital ER. But, as the paramedics roll Missy into a sterile corridor, I am shooed away by a stern-looking nurse.

"I'm sorry, miss, but you're not family," the nurse declares when I protest and beg to stay. "There's a waiting room right down the hall." She points to the area where we came in. "You're more than welcome to wait in there."

"Okay." I sigh resignedly.

I start toward the waiting room, but stop at a coffee machine. Between Missy and Will, I have a feeling I'm in for a long night and could use some caffeine.

As I'm focused on digging around in my purse for some loose change, I feel a tap on my shoulder. Startled, I spin around and find myself face-to-face with Mrs. Metzger, Missy's sweet, portly mom.

"Oh, Kay, I apologize." She rubs my arm consolingly. "I didn't mean to startle you like that, sweetie."

"I'm fine, Mrs. Metzger." I smile. "Just jumpy, I guess."

"Of course," she replies, nodding and dropping her hand from my arm. "I guess we're all a little on edge after what's happened to my Missy."

"Um," I lower my voice, "how is she doing?"

Missy's mom shakes her head and starts to cry. "The doctors don't know much yet. They're examining her now." Her shoulders slump, but she continues. "This is so terrible, Kay. My poor Missy, she looks so broken. Her face is bruised. Her body is banged up."

When she's finished speaking, she sucks in a labored breath. Her grief is palpable, and I give her a loose hug, hoping she feels a tiny bit better knowing there are people who care.

"Please pray for Missy," Mrs. Metzger pleads, her voice cracking. She hugs me back. "And pray for the baby. The doctors are very worried since it's so early in her pregnancy." She sighs, steps back, and dabs a tissue to her eyes. "Oh, I can't even think about that right now."

"I'll say a prayer for both of them," I assure her. "I promise."

"Kay, one more thing..."

My eyes meet hers, and she says, "It was sweet of you to ride here with Missy in the ambulance. I just wanted to thank you for staying with her."

"Of course," I reply. "I didn't want her to be alone."

Mrs. Metzger glances back to where the exam rooms are.

"You go ahead and get back to Missy. I'll be in the waiting room. Let me know when you know more, okay?"

Mrs. Metzger smiles sadly. "Okay, sweetheart. I'll come out and give you an update as soon as I hear anything, I promise."

I nod and thank her. I then decide to forgo the coffee. I just head into the waiting room.

Time ticks by ever so slowly. I tap my foot, waiting and waiting. There's a TV suspended from the ceiling, and it is blaring. Additionally, two screaming young kids are running amok, smacking each other with magazines. One starts to cry, and I decide it's time for a break.

When I step out of the ER, into the fresh nighttime air, I take the opportunity to check in with Chase.

Following a quick greeting, he asks, "How's Missy?"

"Well, her mom is here. But there's no real news yet. Mrs. Metzger promised to keep me updated, though."

"That's nice of her," Chase says.

"Uh-huh." I pause, then add in a low voice, "How's Will? Is he at the house?"

Chase lets out a breath. "Yeah, he's here."

"Is he okay?"

Chase knows I'm asking if Will is messed up, and he answers accordingly.

"Surprisingly, he's fine."

Now it's my turn to release a stifled breath. "So he and Jared really did go swimming at the lake?"

"I guess so," Chase replies, sighing. "I mean, Will spouted off the same story as Jared, so I suppose it's the truth."

In a very low voice, I ask, "Do you believe him?"

"I do, actually. I think they really did go to the lake. My brother has a tan, so they were definitely outdoors."

Before I can ask why, then, would the boys stop at Kyle Tanner's, Chase says, "Oh, I'm supposed to relay a message to you from Will."

"Okay."

"He said to tell you he's sorry for running out on you this morning, said he needed to get his head straight about Cassie, same as what Jared said about him."

Chase sounds kind of defeated, and I wonder why. What else is going on?

But before I start asking questions, I say, "Well, tell Will it's fine. I'm not mad."

"I'll tell him," he says.

Now, I get to my questions. First, I ask, "What's going on with Cassie? Any updates?"

"None that Will is sharing..." Chase trails off, and I imagine him dragging his fingers through his hair. "I mean, I don't know, Kay. There's nothing new to report as far as I know."

From his clipped tone, I know for sure something is wrong.

"What else is going on, Chase? Did your brother say anything about that stop at Kyle Tanner's house?"

"No, not a word." He sighs. "Actually, I haven't even asked him yet. But I don't think Will's going to tell me anything, babe. And, frankly, I just don't have the energy to get into it with him right now."

"That's probably a good idea," I agree. "You can talk to him about it another day."

"Yeah. It will have to be within the next few days, though," Chase mutters distractedly.

"Wait, what?"

This must be what's bothering Chase, why he sounds kind of off.

Sure enough, he says. "Oh yeah, wait until you hear the latest development."

"Oh no," I say, cringing as I think of what could be going on now. "What happened?"

Chase chuckles, but it's devoid of humor. "Will apparently spoke with our mother this morning, and she gave him the green light to go home early."

I can't believe what I'm hearing. "No way," I gasp. "You're kidding."

"I wish I were," Chase says, sighing. "But, no, it's no joke. Will leaves for Las Vegas on Tuesday."

I'm shocked by this turn of events. Chase's brother must have really pressed his mom to convince her to allow him to come home early.

"She changed his ticket?" I ask.

"Nope, he's not flying. He got a refund for his airline ticket and used that money to buy a bus ticket."

"A bus ticket? This is weird, Chase. Why would Will take a bus back to Vegas?"

I imagine Chase shrugging his shoulders as he says, "I don't know, Kay. Will claims the long ride will give him time to think."

I am still perplexed, as perplexed as Chase sounds. Damn, now I know what Will was up to earlier. He must have been working on his flight ticket refund when I walked into the living room this morning.

And that prompts me to ask, "What'd he do with the extra money? I'm sure that bus ticket cost a hell of a lot less than the full-fare airline ticket he had."

"I don't know, babe," Chase says quietly, clearly unfazed by the money aspect.

He's just going to miss his brother. I hear it in his sad tone.

"Do you think your brother will be okay going back early?" I ask softly.

He clears his throat. "I hope he'll be okay. I mean, he

should be fine. The bus doesn't arrive in Vegas until sometime Thursday. And Mom and Greg arrive home on Friday. That leaves Will only one day alone. I think he can behave himself for twenty-four hours." Chase sighs. "Plus, I'm kind of hoping that long ride really does give Will some time to think. Maybe he'll start seeing things more clearly when it comes to Cassie."

"Yeah, I guess," I concede, but truthfully, I have a feeling Will won't be changing any of his behaviors when it comes to his girlfriend.

A beat passes.

"Do you need me to come to the hospital?" Chase asks, breaking the silence.

"No, you stay with Will," I respond. "I'll be back as soon as I get word that Missy is going to be okay."

Just as I'm saying good-bye and disconnecting with Chase, I spot a familiar face striding purposefully toward the ER doors.

It's Nick Mercurio, and he appears quite distracted. Even when I raise my hand to wave, he rushes past me without a second glance.

"Nick," I call out.

Halfway through the open doors, he turns.

Seeing me, at last, he says, "Shit, Kay. I didn't even notice you standing there." He steps back outside.

"Hey," I say. "Is everything okay?"

I can't imagine why Nick would be racing into the hospital so determinedly, but it can't be good.

"God, Kay, haven't you heard about Missy? She was in a terrible accident."

Wait, Nick is here for Missy?

Confusion sets in, and I respond slowly, "Um, yeah, I know. I rode with her in the ambulance."

What am I missing here? Nick and Missy aren't exactly close friends. They only met the night I introduced them at the Anchor Inn. Of course, Nick got to know Missy rather well that night, and rather quickly, though not as well as his cousin supposedly did.

Nick shoots me a weird look. "Well, have you heard anything? Is Missy going to be okay?"

"Uh, there's no news yet," I reply, still totally thrown as to why Nick is here for Missy.

He interrupts my thoughts when he asks, "Is anyone in there with her? She shouldn't be alone."

"Her mom's with her." I glance at the doors. "In fact, I should get back in there. Mrs. Metzger is supposed to update me when she knows more, and she's expecting me to be in the waiting room."

"Let's get in there, then," Nick says urgently as he cups my elbow and hurries me along.

As we're rushing into the hospital, I still can't imagine why Nick Mercurio feels the need to be here for Missy. Even taking into account the night at the Anchor Inn, it's not like Missy had sex with Nick. At least, she *claimed* not to. In any case, if her claim is true, then Nick is little more than a stranger to her. If I expected anyone to show up for Missy, I'd think it'd be Tony, Nick's cousin.

When we're just outside the waiting room, I slow to a stop.

"What's wrong?" Nick wants to know.

"I'm sorry, Nick, but I just can't figure out why you're here."

223

He appears offended. "What the hell kind of question is that?" he barks.

"I'm sorry, really, and I don't mean to pry, but I just don't understand why *you're* here and Tony isn't."

"Tony?" Nick isn't angry anymore; he's utterly confused. "Why would my cousin come to the hospital for Missy?"

Worried that I may have just blown Missy's secret, I gather my thoughts to formulate a response. But then realization dawns in Nick's deep-brown eyes.

"Oh, I get it," he begins. "You think Tony is the father of the baby, don't you?"

"You know about the baby?" I whisper.

"Of course I know." Nick peers at me like I have two heads.

"Well, then you must know Tony is the father," I state.

Nick shakes his head sadly. "Oh, Kay, you have it all wrong. Tony isn't the father of Missy's baby. I am."

What? "But Missy said—"

"Look," Nick cuts me off, "I don't know what Missy told you about the night at the Anchor Inn, but I was the one who ended up with her. I fucked her. My cousin was there, yeah, but he just, uh, watched."

I have a feeling "watched" means something more like "jacked off," but that's neither here nor there. I'm still processing the fact that Nick is the father. And he's obviously known long enough for him to appear comfortable with his impending role.

But why would Missy lie to me?

"Missy said the father didn't know," I mumble to myself.

Hearing me, Nick touches my arm lightly. "Missy told me over a week ago that she's pregnant. I was mad at first, but then…" He trails off. "It took me a few days, but I came to terms with the idea of being a dad. And now I'm actually kind of excited about the whole thing."

Nick smiles, a genuine smile, and I feel happy for him and happy for Missy. Maybe they'll get to know each other better and end up becoming a family. Crazier things have happened. But even if that doesn't occur, I'm happy for their child that Nick wants to be a part of his or her life.

"You're going to be a great dad," I say to Nick, since it seems like that might be just what he needs to hear right now.

The saddest smile crosses his face, though. "I just hope I have a chance, Kay. I pray the baby is okay."

"Yeah"—I place my hand on his forearm—"me too."

We step into the waiting room, where things have quieted. We find two empty seats, and as I sit down, I suddenly realize something: Missy told me Tony was the father in order to protect my feelings, seeing as I used to date Nick. I just wish she'd figured out that I never would have been mad or upset. Maybe she was hesitant to share the truth due to my reaction when I found out she and Chase had hooked up. But that was so completely different. My feelings for Nick never ran deep like they do for Chase.

Still, as a friend, I will always have fond feelings for Nick.

I glance over at him now and nudge his shoulder with mine. "Hey, you should be back there with Missy."

He's thumbing through a magazine, not really looking at the pages. "You think it'd be okay?"

I take the magazine from his hands. "Yes, of course it's okay. She's carrying your baby. That makes you the baby's family."

The mention of family makes Nick smile. But just as he stands, Mrs. Metzger rushes into the waiting room. Her face is red, and her eyes are bloodshot, like she's been crying—hard.

Nick and I go to her. We support her on either side as she crumples.

"What is it?" I ask. "Oh, God, is Missy…?"

I'm thinking the worst—that Missy has died—but Mrs. Metzger is shaking her head.

"No, no, Missy is fine. She'll recover." Her eyes slide from me, then settle on Nick. "The baby, though," she gasps, "the baby didn't…"

Mrs. Metzger breaks down, and Nick swallows so loudly I can hear it.

"The baby is…" Nick whispers, unable to say the words, just as Mrs. Metzger couldn't.

Missy's mom looks at Nick and just cries harder.

I don't need to hear the words to know Missy has lost her baby.

Suddenly, this overwhelming sense of sadness and loss washes over me, like I'm the one who's lost something. In a way, I guess I did. The thought of a new life growing in Missy had me feeling hopeful. I hadn't really put it into words, but Missy's baby was a reminder to me that life is not just about loss. There are new beginnings, new chances to start over. Missy was starting over herself, turning her life around for her baby. And the baby was already such a part of how I envisioned Missy down the road, she and her child together, two, not one.

I was truly excited to get to know this new little person. But now, I will never, ever have that chance.

I want to go to Missy and comfort her. I long to comfort her mom, too. And Nick sure looks in need of support. But just then, Mrs. Metzger leans more heavily on Nick, their shared grief joining them.

I step away to give them some space. Wrapping my arms around myself, I feel like I could use some comforting as well. But comfort won't be found here. My comfort is at home, where Chase is waiting for me. I can't wait to see him, to have him wrap his arms around me. He finds it hard to believe, but he gives my life meaning and clarity. He makes things right.

I've done so well these past few weeks. The despair and grief that shaded my life for so long—over the death of my sister, Sarah—has lessened due to Chase. He brings me joy and shows me there is beauty in life, like he's told me I do for him. But most important, he *gives* me life.

This sad turn of events is a reminder of how fragile life is, how things can change in an instant. One minute a life exists, growing and flourishing, and in just a second, that life can be extinguished.

Taken away, and gone forever.

CHAPTER FIFTEEN
CHASE

After I finish talking on the phone with Kay, I toss my cell to the kitchen table and go back into the living room, where Will is watching TV.

Turning the volume down, he immediately asks, "Is that Missy girl going to be all right?"

I plop down on the couch next to him. "Not sure," I respond. "Kay's waiting to get word from Missy's mom."

"Is it true she's pregnant?" Will asks quietly.

I look over at him. "How do you know that?"

He holds up his cell phone. "Jared called while you were talking to Kay. He said he overheard the paramedics talking."

I nod once. "Yeah, Will, it's true."

My brother lets out a low whistle. "Shit, bro, now it's even more fucked up that Jared crashed into her."

"Yeah"—I scrub a hand down my face—"seems this whole day is fucked up."

"Glad I wasn't with him," my brother whispers.

"Me too," I whisper back.

While we sit with that thought, letting the gravity of it sink in, I again consider whether I should question Will as to why he and Jared were at Kyle's house earlier. However, like I told Kay, I don't expect to get a straight answer. And I sure as hell have no desire to argue with my brother right now. So, since he's obviously not fucked up in any way, I decide to leave it for another day.

"What're you watching?" I ask Will as I grab for the remote.

"Hey!" He yanks his hand away, maintaining control of the channels. "It's *SportsCenter*."

"Okay, okay," I concede, hands in the air. "We'll watch that."

Will keeps his grip on the remote but lowers his hand back down to rest on his leg. It's then that I notice he's wearing the same pair of jeans he had on the day we started on the mural in the school. I know these are the same jeans because there's this perfectly round drop of cinnamon-brown paint right above his knee. It's the droplet that fell from Will's paintbrush when he stepped back to assess his work. Guess it never washed out.

That day with my brother feels like a million years ago. All the shit that has happened since then—it's crazy. I decide to forgo questioning Will about Kyle Tanner, tomorrow, the next day, whenever. I just want to enjoy the next few days with my little brother before he leaves town.

Will and I sit together awhile longer, commenting on baseball highlights. But when I catch little bro yawning, I nudge him with my elbow and say, "Hey, you should go get some sleep."

"Yeah"—he yawns again—"I think I will."

After Will retires to his room, I watch a little more TV. I expect Kay to walk through the door any minute, but truth be told, I am beat and end up nodding off before she returns.

I awake some time later to find that the TV has been turned off and that Kay is curled up next to me on the couch. She's sleeping, but when I shift my body beneath her, she wakes up.

Sitting upright, she rubs her eyes and mumbles, "I didn't mean to fall asleep, but I didn't want to wake you when I first got in." She smiles over at me. "You looked so peaceful."

Even though she's smiling, her red-rimmed eyes tell me she's been crying.

I quickly straighten from where I'm leaned back in the crook of the couch. "What happened at the hospital? Is Missy okay?"

Kay slowly sits back against the cushions, but her eyes hold mine. "Yeah, Missy will recover."

"That's good," I say.

"It's not all good news, though." Kay bites her bottom lip and lowers her gaze. When she glances up at me, her eyes are filled with not just tears, but profound sadness. "Missy lost the baby, Chase."

"Fuck. That's awful."

"It is," Kay agrees. "It's tragic." She slumps down into the cushions. "I found out something else tonight, too."

I raise an eyebrow and wait for her to continue.

"Nick was the father of Missy's baby, not Tony."

"Wow, no way."

Kay quickly averts her eyes.

"What's wrong?" I inquire. "That doesn't bother you, does it?"

I can't imagine why the paternity of Missy's baby matters to Kay, but typical male insecurity makes my throat tighten in worry.

To my relief, Kay rolls her eyes and says, "No, Chase, I'm not bothered at all. I don't care which Mercurio is the father. I'm just surprised, that's all."

I release a held-in breath with an audible exhale of air. *Shit, thank God.*

"What's bothering you, then?"

The second the words leave my mouth, Kay bursts into tears.

"Oh, Chase," she sobs, "I know it's stupid, but every time I think of Missy losing this baby it just makes me feel so...*bad.*"

"Baby girl..." I reach for her, and she crawls into my lap. As she wraps her arms around my neck, I hold on to her tightly. "What can I do to make you feel better? Just tell me. I'd do anything for you."

"I don't know," she croaks out against my shoulder, while she's grasping my T-shirt in her fist. "I guess Missy's loss reminds me of the losses in my own life."

I know what Kay really means is that she's reminded of one big loss—the loss of her sister, Sarah.

I hold her as she lowers her head to my chest and cries softly.

"It's funny," she sniffles after a minute, "but I realized at the hospital that I was looking forward to Missy having this baby." She shifts so she can look up at me. "Chase, just last week, I was helping her set aside baby clothes." Squeezing her eyes shut and burying her face in my chest again, she adds, "God, all the little outfits were so cute."

I'm really at a loss as to how to soothe my girl, but I try

by saying, "I'm sure Missy will have another chance to be a mom." I cup Kay's chin and urge her to look up at me. When her eyes meet mine, I add, "And you'll have your chance, too."

"I know," she replies, nodding into my grasp. "And, to be honest, I've been thinking about it a lot lately."

"What have you been thinking?" I ask carefully.

"That I can't wait to have a baby with you, Chase."

Suddenly, Kay's mouth snaps shut, like maybe she's said too much. But I'm more on board that train of thought than she may realize. First, though, I need to make sure this is what she really wants.

I press my back into the couch cushions and peer down at her. "You sure you really want to have a baby with me?"

She smacks my arm, and I'm happy I've finally gotten her to smile. "Of course, Chase. I love you."

I grab her up in my arms and kiss her. Then as I press my lips to the soft skin on her neck, I murmur, "I love you, too."

But there's more I want to say.

When my lips still, Kay tenses.

"What?" She leans back.

My eyes flick to hers. "It's nothing bad. I was just wondering when you would want to have this baby of ours."

Her red-rimmed caramels widen. "Um, I don't know." She searches my eyes, like she's looking for guidance, but I'm open to whatever she wants. "Down the road, I guess?"

"Is that a question?" I ask her. "Or your answer?"

She shrugs, and I ask outright, "Kay, would you rather have a baby sooner than, as you say, 'down the road'?"

She whispers, "Chase, what are you saying?"

I don't know how to put into words all the things I feel for this woman. But I've known for quite some time that I want to make a baby with Kay, all the way back to the day she showed me the journals she keeps to remind her of Sarah. I long to make a life with her still, partly to make up for all she's lost. But it's so much more than that. When I dig deep, down into my soul, I know I want this, too. I long to create life with the woman who has shown me living is possible. And not just that it is possible, but that living can be good.

I want this for me, for her—for us. I want this for the baby we can make together and for the love we'd shower on that child.

With all this in mind, in an uncharacteristically shaky voice, I ask Kay, "Would it be so terrible if we didn't wait?"

She presses her lips together, like she's contemplating. "It'd be great, Chase," she says slowly. "But it's not going to happen anytime soon. I got the Depo shot back in June, remember?"

Shit. Who would've ever thought I'd be cursing responsible birth control? Not me. But I am.

Rubbing the back of my neck, I want to know, "When are you supposed to get another shot?"

Kay looks off to the side and, I assume, calculates the weeks. "The end of September," she states after a beat.

I arch a brow. "So…don't get it."

"Chase," she breathes out, "I don't know. I mean, I want to spend my life with you, have kids with you—all of those things. But we're not even married."

Ah, so there's the cause of her hesitation. Hell, I can take care of that shit right now. It may not be ideal, but sometimes you have to grab the opportunity.

Smiling and holding Kay's gaze, I slip down to the floor. She shoots me a concerned look as I position myself on my knees. Then, facing the woman I love with everything I am, I take her hands in mine.

"I know this is half-assed and less than ideal, but…" I trail off, and when I look up, her eyes are tearing. But not from sadness like before. No, these are happy tears.

My own vision blurs a little, but I forge on. "Make me a happy man, Kay Stanton. Be my wife. Let's get married, and then we'll have babies. Or let's have babies, and then we'll get married. However you want to do it, sweet girl, is fine by me."

"You're really asking me to marry you?"

"Yes, I am. I love you, Kay. Say you'll marry me. I'll get you a ring, I promise. And I'll ask you again, do it all fancy like, if that's what you want. But say yes right now. Say you'll marry me. Let me love you forever."

She nods, once, twice. She keeps nodding, even as she's sliding to the floor next to me. She then tells me what I want to hear: "Yes."

I brush her hair back with both of my hands. While my thumbs swipe at the tears on her cheeks, I check to make sure I heard her correctly. "Really? You'll marry me?"

She nods in my hands. "Yes, of course."

"Say it again," I whisper, my lips nearing hers.

"Yes."

"Again," I insist, inching closer.

"Yes, Chase. Yes, yes!"

My lips capture hers, and I kiss her, her lips, her cheeks,

and right down her beautiful neck. I cover her skin with my love. And though there's no chance of making a baby tonight, I insist we should practice.

Kay giggles and agrees. "We should definitely practice a lot." She pulls me to her, whispering against my lips, "And I think we should get started as soon as possible."

"I could not agree more," I say, and then that is exactly what we do.

CHAPTER SIXTEEN

KAY

Maybe all the crazy things that have happened lately have resulted in full-on delirium—for both Chase and me. I don't know, not really. But how else can I explain waking up the morning after discussing love, and marriage, and babies, and suddenly remembering I am now an officially-unofficially engaged woman?

I roll over, smiling, happy. It's barely dawn, and my cohort in delirium is facing my way. But he's still sleeping, backlit by early daylight. I don't want to wake Chase—he looks so peaceful—but the urge to touch him is so strong that I have to reach out, trace the strong line of his jaw.

My touch rouses him. And though his eyes open, we don't say a word. As the minutes pass, Chase's lips curve into a smile. And me, I just stare into beautiful blue.

Another beat, and he rolls me onto my back, his body hovering above mine. Suddenly, he pulls the sheet over us to create a cocoon, allowing light the day has birthed to filter in, tingeing our bare skin with a golden glow.

I giggle and he smiles.

We never dressed last night, we were too busy loving. So when Chase lowers his body, all I feel is his warm skin pressed to mine. My breathing picks up, and so does his.

I'm so ready for what he has to give me that I spread my legs for him. And he's in me in an instant, moving, thrusting, and circling his hips.

This is how we start the morning—engaged, in more ways than one, and so very much in love.

Later, at work, things are slow. I have time to keep reliving, over and over in my head, how Chase knelt down before me and asked me to marry him. It sure wasn't what I expected or how I thought something like that might go, but even so, it was beautiful and felt right.

The sincerity and pure emotion in Chase's eyes as he was gazing up at me touched my soul. I knew right then and there that his impromptu proposal was perfect in its imperfection.

Imperfectly perfect, just like us.

Before we fell asleep, we discussed whether or not we should share the news of our engagement. But Chase insists he wants to wait until he can buy me a ring and propose once again, as he so eloquently put it, "in the right fucking way." He says then it will be completely "official."

Silly man. He has no idea that last night surpassed anything I'd ever dreamed of. Sincerity and truth mean more than showy formalities. However, I can wait to tell the world if Chase wants me to. I will keep our news quiet. I kind of like the idea, for now, of keeping our engagement our own little special secret.

And then there's the other topic we discussed—having a baby. *Wow, just wow.*

The thought of having Chase's baby fills me with an almost indescribable joy, a deep, profound feminine sort of satisfaction. But there's fear there, too. And doubt in myself. I don't know if I'm quite ready to become someone's mother. Not that I don't want to do it now, but, damn, what a huge role to undertake.

What if I'm no good at it? What if I fail at motherhood? I sure feel like I failed in the much less significant role of big sister.

It wasn't your fault, Kay. Chase's words echo through my mind, urging me to cast away my doubt. But despite how far I've come in accepting that I am not to blame for Sarah's death, a part of me will always feel some degree of guilt. That is the part that makes me hesitate to fully embrace the idea of having a child.

Well, I have time, I remind myself as I pull up the church activities calendar on the computer.

I count back the weeks to June. Then I count forward. Just as I thought, and same as I told Chase last night, I'm not due for another Depo shot until late September. That gives me about six more weeks of birth control protection before any decisions have to be made.

Since I have the activities calendar open, I work on it for a while, updating and adding events. I get lost in what I'm doing until a call comes in, a call from Missy's mom. She starts the conversation by informing me that Missy is "physically" well enough to be released from the hospital tomorrow morning.

"Oh, that's great news," I say.

Since Mrs. Metzger chose the word "physically" to describe Missy's wellness, I cautiously ask, "How's Missy doing, like, psychologically."

Mrs. Metzger clears her throat. "Aw, honey, it's going

to take some time. But Missy will be okay. My daughter is a strong young woman."

Strong or not, she could probably use a friend, I think.

"Would it be okay if I stop by to see her tomorrow after work?"

Missy's mom sighs heavily. "Oh, I don't know, sweetie. Another day might be better. Missy told me this morning that she's not quite ready to see anyone just yet."

My heart aches for Missy and the pain she's feeling. "Okay, I understand. Another day, then."

"Personally, Kay," Missy's mom begins after a brief pause, "I think Missy should be around people. She needs to get back to doing the things she likes to do."

The whole time she's speaking, Mrs. Metzger's voice is low and conspiratorial, like maybe she and I can somehow keep Missy busy and that will miraculously lessen the pain of her loss.

I doubt anything but time will heal Missy's emotional wounds, but I don't say a thing.

Mrs. Metzger is still talking, saying, "Just give her a few more days, honey. And then I bet she'll be calling you and wanting to get together and go do whatever it is you girls like to do."

I'm not so sure about that, but I pretend to agree.

After my call with Mrs. Metzger ends, it's back to work for me. Chase is tied up with a project in the school. He tells me this when he texts me to say that he's skipping lunch. I'm not very hungry, so I work through lunch, too.

Then, around three o'clock, I receive another text from Chase.

Just finished up. Heading back to the house early. See you there. Love you, bb.

I know Chase is trying to spend as much time with his brother as he can before he leaves on Tuesday, so I text back: *Enjoy your time with Will. Should I pick something up for dinner on my way home?*

Pizza?

Sure, I'll stop at Pizza House after work.

That works. Chase texts back.

A little while later, when I'm in my car after work, I call the restaurant to place the order. It's stupid, I know, but I'm relieved when someone other than Nick answers the phone. I guess I'm still coming to grips with the fact he was the father of Missy's baby. Like I told Chase, it doesn't bother me in any way, but Missy had me so convinced that Tony was the dad that when I learned Nick was the real father it kind of threw me for a loop. And I guess I'm still reeling.

When I return to the house, the pizza is a hit, as it always seems to be. Dinner is pleasant, with the three of us sitting around the kitchen table and making small talk. Will, I take note, is nothing but cheery. It's like the events of yesterday never even happened.

After dinner, I ask Chase in private if Will has said anything about Cassie—or Paul.

Chase shakes his head. "Nope, not a thing."

Will's overly happy demeanor and lack of discussion regarding the Cassie situation has me worried.

Over the next few days, I watch Will closely, waiting for him to either divulge something or have another meltdown. But every minute, every second of every day, Will behaves perfectly. There's no running off, no drug use, and no more contact with Jared, all of which are choices Will makes without any prompting from his brother.

Since Will remains mum on the subject of Cassie, I decide to reach out to Will's girlfriend in hopes of finding what, if anything, has been happening with Paul. Has he been picked up by the police? Has he stopped bothering Cassie? How is she handling everything? These are just a few of the things I'd like to know.

So, throughout the weekend and into Monday, I leave a slew of messages. Cassie ignores me, until, on Tuesday, out of the blue, I finally hear back from her via a text.

Sorry I haven't gotten back to you sooner, Kay. But don't worry. Everything's fine. I can't wait to see Will in two more days. Thursday can't get here soon enough, ya know?

The message arrives late in the afternoon, just as I'm putting dinner on the table. I've prepared a big send-off meal for Will, since he and Chase have to leave for the bus station in a couple of hours. Will's bus leaves tonight, and as Cassie mentioned in her text, he's due to arrive in Vegas sometime Thursday.

Since tonight's dinner is special, we eat in the dining room. When Will is finished eating, he excuses himself from the big oak table.

"I have a few more things to pack," he explains. He wipes his mouth with a napkin and stands.

My eyes slide to Chase when Will walks out of the room. "Guess he's leaving the cleaning part to us," I say in a teasing tone.

Chase laughs. "Looks that way, babe, looks that way." He starts to gather the dishes on the table, and adds, "Might as well get started now."

Chase and I clear the table and take everything into the kitchen. He washes the dishes while I dry. At one point, I rest my hip against the sink and wait for him to finish washing a big serving platter. Chase runs the water in the right side of the sink and rinses suds off the platter.

"I hope everything is okay," I say, sighing.

"What?" He glances my way. "Do you mean with Will?"

"Yeah."

Holding out the dripping-wet platter, Chase says, "I asked Will last night what's going on back in Vegas, and he said everything is under control."

"Everything is under control?" I echo as I take the plate from Chase.

"Yep, those were his exact words."

After a beat, and a swipe of the dish towel across the serving platter, I wonder out loud, "What does that mean, exactly?"

Chase shrugs. "I don't know. But Will's been great these past few days. Maybe that means Paul quit harassing Cassie. I'm thinking the cops must've picked Paul up on that restraining order violation."

I don't feel so certain, so I say, "It seems like Will would mention that, though."

"Not necessarily," Chase replies. "He is a guy, and we don't always *discuss* everything."

"Isn't that the truth," I interject, eyeing him meaningfully.

"Anyway…" Chase looks away. "Why else would Will remain so calm? You have to admit he's been in an exceptionally good mood lately."

Will *has* been in a great mood the past few days, or so he

wants us to believe. That's what I suspect. But my question is, why would he do that? What could Chase's brother be hiding? I know Chase wants so badly to believe the situation with Cassie and her stepdad has been resolved, but I am not so sure. Will's behavior has been almost too perfect, orchestrated in a way.

In any case, I don't want to prolong the conversation and ruin Chase's last evening with his brother.

We finish up with the dishes, and Chase leans against the side of the sink. He asks me, "Are you sure you don't want to tag along to the bus station."

"No"—I stand on my tiptoes, lean toward him, and place a kiss on his cheek—"you should spend these last couple of hours with your brother, just the two of you."

"Are you sure?"

"Yeah, you two go on without me. I'll say good-bye to Will before he leaves."

An hour later, I am doing exactly that, out on the front porch. Will has his duffel bag slung over one shoulder and holds the handle of a small suitcase in his hand.

When he sets the suitcase on the porch, Chase grabs it up. "You sure this is everything?" he asks Will.

"Yeah, I made sure I packed everything," Will replies.

"I'll meet you at the truck, then, okay?" Chase says. "Take a minute and say good-bye to Kay."

Chase heads down the porch steps, and I turn to Will.

"Have a safe trip back," I say as I give him a big hug. "I'm going to miss having you around."

It's true. I am going to miss Will. He's been some trouble, yeah, but his heart is good, just like his brother's.

Will hugs me back, holding on to me tightly. "I'm so glad

I met you, Kay," he says. "I'm sorry I was an ass at times. But just know I like you. You're perfect for my brother, in so many ways, and I'm glad he found you. You're good for him"—his voice cracks—"and he needs you."

This outpouring of emotion is uncharacteristic of Will, especially on the heels of how calm he's been the past few days.

I pull back and frown. "Will, is something wrong?"

He rocks back on his heels. "Nah, I guess leaving Ohio is just hitting me more than I thought it would."

"But I thought you couldn't wait to go back to Vegas," I softly inquire.

Will's eyes dart away, and he rubs the back of his neck. "Yeah, uh, I do want to go back. I mean, it's just best that I do."

Huh?

When my brow furrows, Will quickly adds, "I mean, with school starting soon and everything."

"School doesn't start for three more weeks, Will."

He laughs, but it's a hollow sound. "Gotta prepare, though, right?"

Nodding, I say hesitantly, "I guess so."

Will hoists his duffel bag higher on his shoulder. "I better get going."

"You can come back to Harmony Creek anytime, you know that, right? Maybe you can even fly out over Christmas break."

"Yeah, maybe," Will replies, his voice heavy and sad. "We'll see."

He sounds so final, his tone completely lacking hope. I want to ask him what's really going on here, since something is clearly not right, but just as I open my mouth to do so, Chase calls out from the truck.

"Come on, little bro, we're gonna be late."

Will shoots me a sad smile fraught with finality. And then he walks away.

As I watch the Gartner brothers drive away, I have a sense of dread that something is terribly wrong.

CHAPTER SEVENTEEN

CHASE

Will's departure from Ohio turns out to be uneventful. Sad as fuck, yes, but there's no over-the-top drama or anything. Though, as I lie awake the morning following his departure, I reconsider. Maybe I'm missing something. After all, my brother's behavior at the bus station has kept me from sleeping soundly.

I can't pinpoint exactly what's wrong, though. I mean, Will was very loving before he boarded the bus. In fact, he was the one who initiated a good-bye hug. God knows that shit sure shocked me. Usually, when it comes to my relationship with my brother, I'm the overly emotional sap.

Not last night, though. Last night, it was Will throwing his arms around me, Will who didn't want to let go.

"You sure you want to go back early?" I jokingly quipped.

I felt him swallow hard, and when he finally pulled back, he wiped at moist eyes.

"Yeah, bro," he said on a sigh chock full of resignation, "I have to."

Something felt off, and I gripped his shoulder. "Hey, talk to me."

He shook his head. "It's nothing, Chase."

And then he walked away.

"Will," I called out. When he turned around, only a few feet away, I smiled and said, "I love you, little bro. Have a safe trip back to Vegas."

"Yeah, yeah," he grumbled. Turning away once again, he resumed walking toward the line of people boarding the bus. "Being a big brother till the end, I see."

"You know it," I retorted.

And then I watched as my little brother boarded the bus with the big nevada placard in the corner of the windshield.

Nevada's so fucking far from Ohio; I hate it. Only twelve hours have elapsed since Will left, but I miss him already.

Feeling bereaved, I snuggle as close as I can to Kay, who is fast-asleep next to me.

The sun is just hitting the horizon, and like always, it bathes the bedroom in a hazy, golden glow. I glance down at Kay. My love is gorgeous in this light, all wrapped up in the crisp, new dark-blue sheets she insisted on putting on my bed. Her pale skin looks dewy and translucent, a play of the combination of bright morning light and the dark hue of the sheets.

I watch her sleep for a few more minutes, but then force myself to get out of bed before she wakes up and thinks I'm a freak for staring at her so intently. Chuckling at how crazy in love I am with this woman, I throw on a pair of gray sweatpants I find on the floor and step out into the hall.

With a slight shiver—it's cooler in the hall than in the bedroom—I start toward the stairs, the hardwood floor creaking beneath my bare feet. I have every intention of going downstairs and making breakfast, but when I reach the room where Will was staying, I stop.

The door is closed, just like it would be if my brother were here. But he's not, of course. Still, I close my eyes and pretend for a minute that he's sleeping on the other side.

Unfortunately, I can't fool myself, as I swear I *feel* the emptiness of my brother's absence.

"Enough of this shit," I murmur. I turn the knob and push open the stupid fucking door.

Why is Will's departure weighing on me like this? It's not like I'll never see him again.

I step into the room, like I may find an answer in here, and the first thing that hits me is how much it smells like Will in here. Even with my kid brother's stuff gone, the whole room still smells of him. Nothing gross, mostly just a clean scent. Well, maybe there's a touch of sweaty teenage boy in there somewhere. But it's all Will, and fuck, it reminds me that I sure do love that kid.

Rolling my eyes at myself, I shake my head and turn to leave. But just as I spin on my heels, something on the nightstand catches my eye.

It's a folded piece of paper on an otherwise empty piece of furniture. Even the lamp that normally rests atop the nightstand has been moved to the floor. It's almost like Will was making sure the folded piece of paper wouldn't be missed.

"What the hell?" I mutter. *Has Will left me some kind of note?*

Before I walk over to the nightstand, I notice that the folded piece of paper looks kind of old. It has a yellowed, slightly tattered appearance.

And that makes me think: *No fucking way, no way is that*

the tree house sketch. No way would my brother leave his hope behind.

But sure enough, when I race over to the nightstand and snatch up the piece of paper, unfold it, my initial fear is confirmed—Will has left behind the sketch I drew him all those years ago.

"Why would you leave it here, buddy?" I whisper.

Peering down at the sketch I drew so long ago, I find there are no answers in the lines, curves, or colors of the drawing. However, there is a Post-it note stuck to the foliage of the tree. It's from Will—to me.

I peel away the note…

Chase, my brother and the one person in this world who I have never doubted cares for me. Yeah, I fought that knowledge for so long (as you are all too well aware), but I'm tired of fighting. I love you, bro. I always fucking have.

Anyway, this sketch belongs with you. No matter what happens to me, just know any hope I ever felt was because of you. You always tried to make things better, even when things were all fucked to hell. And in doing so, you gave me hope. In fact, you gave me your hope a long time ago, with this sketch. Well, now it's my turn to return the favor and give it back to you.

Love, Will

I read my brother's cryptic note again and again. His words hit me deeply. But I can't figure out what he is trying to tell me. Why would he leave this sketch, that note? What does he think is going to happen to him that I need to know how he feels?

I don't know, but I have a bad feeling.

I consider calling him, as I'm sure he has his cell on him. But I know if I call him while he's traveling on a bus with a bunch of strangers, he won't divulge a thing.

Someone, though, may have an answer—the same someone who's been hanging out with my brother for the past couple of weeks, the same someone who made that mystery trip to Kyle Tanner's that I never did get to the bottom of.

Yeah, I think as I carefully place the Post-it note and the sketch back on the nightstand, *a talk with Jared is long overdue*.

I skip breakfast, take a three-minute shower, and bolt out the door before Kay is even up. I'm hoping to catch Jared before I start work. But on my way to his house, Father Maridale calls. He needs me to come to the church as soon as possible; there's a broken pipe in the rectory. Water is everywhere.

Fuck. My. Life.

As it turns out, the broken pipe is a big deal, and I'm stuck working on that fucking mess throughout the entire morning. The only good thing is that Kay comes to work, and is right down the hall from where I'm working.

But she gets tied up, too, and we don't have a chance to connect until lunch.

As we walk down to the diner, Kay glances over at me and says, "Okay, we're not at work anymore. No one's around to hear. What's going on?"

I admit I've wanted to talk to her all morning about what I found in Will's room.

"What'd you find?" she inquires worriedly.

"Not drugs," I preface to ease her mind.

She blows out a breath, relieved. "Thank God."

"Right. So do you remember that tree house sketch I drew for Will?"

"Yes, of course, Chase."

I stop right in the middle of the sidewalk and drag my fingers through my hair. "Do you remember how Will brought that sketch to Ohio with him?"

She turns to face me, and then touches my arm. "I remember."

I start to drag my hand through my hair again, but she reaches up and lowers my hand back down to my side.

"He left it here, Kay," I say urgently. "I found the sketch in his room this morning."

"Maybe he just wants you to have it," she suggests as she laces our fingers together.

"I think there's more to it than that."

When Kay frowns, perplexed, I sigh. And then I tell her about the note that was attached to the sketch.

"That is odd," she agrees, her voice conveying her concern. "I wonder why Will would write a note like that."

"I don't know, but it sounds foreboding. I think I need to talk to Jared. After all, we never did find out why he and Will stopped at Kyle's place. And I have a feeling it has something to do with why Will wrote that note—and left it with his sketch."

"I can go with you, if you want," Kay offers.

Since I'd certainly rather do this with her by my side

than alone, I say, "Absolutely. Let's head over to his house after work."

"Sound good." She smiles up at me reassuringly. "Everything will be all right, Chase. Try not to worry too much. I bet there's a harmless explanation."

I know she's trying to make me feel better, and I appreciate it. A sudden wave of absolute gratitude that Kay is always standing by my fucked-up ass washes over me.

I encircle her in my arms, lower my head, and mumble against her neck, "Thank you for doing this with me. I was on my way over to Jared's this morning, but Father Maridale called about that broken pipe." I sigh. "It's probably better if you're with me when I talk to Jared. You keep me solid." After a pause, I whisper, "What would I do without you, baby?"

"Chase, I'll always be here for you, no matter what." Kay tightens her arms around my waist. "I promise."

I know her words are spoken with truth and love. And I want her with me always, but not if it ever poses a liability for her. I long to let myself go and lean on Kay, and I do a little bit of that right now, but at the same time, I remind myself that I can never put her in any situation that might turn out to be dangerous. Kay's well-being will always top my own emotional needs.

We stand on the sidewalk, holding one another, until a few people pass and give us some odd looks. With a chuckle, I take a step back. We break apart and walk down to the diner.

I feel better already, just knowing I'll (hopefully) have some answers soon.

But when Kay and I return to the church grounds following lunch, I suspect the answers to the questions I have regarding Will may come sooner than expected. Jared's sister's car—the bright-red Jaguar—is parked in the center of the church parking lot, standing out like a beacon.

"Wonder what she's doing here," Kay says, nodding to the flashy Jag.

"I don't know, but Jared's with her." I point to where he's seated in the passenger seat.

"Oh," Kay says, "huh. Wonder what he wants?"

I don't answer. Jared sees me in the parking lot and jumps out of the car. He rushes over, waving me down. "Hey, Chase… Can I talk to you for a minute?"

Fuck, this can't be good. Sure, I want to talk to the kid. But if he's here at Holy Trinity of his own volition, then it can only mean one thing—Will is in some serious trouble.

"We shouldn't stand around out here," Kay whispers two seconds before Jared reaches us. "Maybe we should go in the church or something."

The urgency in her voice lets me know she's as worried as I am about what Jared may have to say.

When Jared reaches us, he nods to Kay, greeting her quickly. He then turns his full attention to me. "I asked my sister to drive me over here, since my car is, uh, out of commission. I hate to bother you at work like this." He glances around. "But it's kind of important that I talk with you."

"Is it about Will?" I ask, even though I'm already certain it is.

"Yeah." Jared nods grimly. "It's about Will."

Kay again suggests we move the conversation to somewhere more private than the middle of the parking lot. I agree, as does Jared, so the four of us head to the church.

As we step into the vestibule, the smell of burning candles and incense permeates the very muggy air. It's a hot day, and inside the vestibule, it feels like it might be topping one hundred degrees.

Kay fans herself with her hand, while Jared swipes at the sweat beading on his brow.

I ignore the fucking heat and get right to the point.

"So what's going on with Will? It must be pretty fucking important for you to make a special trip like this."

"It is important." Jared drops his gaze and stares down at the checkered linoleum floor. He takes a deep breath, like he's calming himself in order to continue. Maybe he is.

"Anyway," he says at last. "There's something I need to tell you about the morning Will and I went to Kyle's house, the day of the car accident."

As if I'd forget that day.

"Okay," I prompt when Jared goes quiet, "what do you need to tell me?"

I guess the tone of my voice is harsh. Kay moves closer to me and rubs her hand up and down my arm. It's meant to be soothing, but nothing can calm me right now. I'm ready to fucking explode, implode, something.

Jared shuffles uncomfortably, and then, in a low voice, he says, "We didn't buy drugs that day. When I told you that, it was the truth. But what I didn't tell you is that Will did buy…something…from Kyle."

My heart races in my chest, and my mouth dries up like the Nevada desert Will is closing in on with every passing minute.

"What did my brother buy from that motherfucker?" I grind out.

Jared's eyes, filled with sorrow and pity, meet mine as he says, "Will bought a gun."

Kay gasps from beside me, and I say nothing. But my mind reels and reels.

Shit, shit, shit. This can't be fucking happening.

There are only two reasons why my brother would buy a gun: to shoot himself or to shoot someone else. Despite his problems, and the fact that he left a sketch that symbolizes his hope here in Harmony Creek, I know for a fact my brother isn't suicidal.

But there is a person I know for certain he'd like to see dead, the same man who has been tormenting his girlfriend.

"Paul," I say out loud.

"Cassie's stepdad," Kay whispers at the same time.

We both know my brother will do *anything* to protect Cassie.

And, suddenly, it all makes sense.

This is why Will was so calm and well behaved for the past few days. He sure as fuck had no desire to alert me that something was up. And this is what he meant when he said everything was "under control." He knew then that he'd purchased an illegal firearm; he knew he planned to take it with him to Vegas. This is also why Will had his plane ticket refunded. He wouldn't be allowed to board a plane with a fucking firearm in tow. But the bus was different. When he was boarding the bus, no one checked a thing. He must have known that'd be the case.

"Fuck," I hiss.

I am so incredibly pissed that I can't stand here and do nothing. And I know what I must do. I walk away briskly, on a mission, leaving Kay and Jared in the wake of my fury—fury directed at the one person who could have prevented all of this from happening, Kyle fucking Tanner.

Ten minutes later, I am pounding on motherfucking Tanner's battered screen door. I am milliseconds from kicking in the fucking door, but then Kyle bellows from inside the house, "Hold on a goddamn minute, okay?"

I chuckle humorlessly. "Yeah, okay."

When Kyle opens the door, his hooded, drug-dilated eyes take me in. "Dude, what the fuck?"

Without preamble, I grab him by the front of his shirt and pull him up close to my face. "I've got a 'what the fuck' for you. What the fuck were you thinking selling my brother a fucking gun?"

Kyle blinks slowly. He's so fucked up that he doesn't even realize I could break his ass in two with one solid hit. And I'm about to.

"Man, he said he wanted it for protection, okay? Said he was going back to Vegas, and that it's a dangerous place."

"Yeah," I say, shoving him away from me, "it's dangerous, all right. Thanks to you."

I consider laying him out, and I almost do. He'd be so easy to break right now. But something inside me urges me to just walk away.

Maybe I am changing.

Whatever the case, I turn away, leaving my former dealer trembling and shaking.

Kyle expected the worst. But it's not worth the effort. Not when I need to direct all of my energy to what really matters now—saving Will.

CHAPTER EIGHTEEN
KAY

Chase takes off from the vestibule, leaving me to stare blankly at Jared. He shrugs, and out in the church parking lot, the sound of a truck roaring to life fills the muggy air. Not five seconds later, tires squeal out of the church parking lot.

"That was Chase," I whisper. "He's gone."

It's already stifling in the vestibule, but the air feels like it has shot up another ten degrees, like the temperature reflects Chase's anger.

"I should have said something sooner," Jared laments.

"Yeah," I agree, "you should have."

But there's no time for regret or blame. Will has done something stupid. He bought a gun and now he's in danger.

"Did Will happen to mention why he wanted a gun?" I ask Jared.

He shakes his head. "Not really. I mean, he was going on and on about Cassie's sicko stepdad, but I don't think…" He trails off.

Just then, Jared's sister, Cheri, honks from out in the parking lot.

"Uh, I should get going," Jared says.

"Yeah, sure."

Will's friend leaves, and I am left wondering where Chase has sped off to in his abrupt departure. But, really, who am I kidding? I know exactly where he went—to Kyle Tanner's house. In fact, Chase is probably kicking drug dealer ass right now. Though I understand, it still pains me to accept that Chase was right. He once said that for every step he takes away from his old life, away his former ways of handling things, fate seems to drive him right back to where he once was.

Isn't that the truth?

I sigh and head back to the rectory, resigning myself to the notion that, for as much as things change, and they do, some things will forever remain the same.

But I can live with that.

A long time ago, when Chase and I first embarked on this journey of our relationship, I told him that I was in this for the long run. He said he was trouble, and I asked him to be my trouble. I still feel the same way.

But for all the things we've faced up to this point, nothing compares to this. Chase's brother may actually try to *kill* someone. He may succeed, too, unless someone stops him, someone like Chase.

But I am not letting him do this by himself. I intend to go to Vegas with him, since surely that is where he'll be heading once he's taken care of Kyle.

Unfortunately, a few hours later, I discover Chase has no intention of taking me with him to Nevada. He's bought an airline ticket, oh yes, but only one.

"Chase, please don't do this alone," I beg. "Let me come with you."

We are in the upstairs bedroom. Chase is packing, haphazardly throwing things into an open suitcase on his bed. And me, I am standing behind him, begging and pleading, trying to get him to reconsider. But to no avail, as I'm finding that, on this, there's no changing this stubborn man's mind.

When I returned home from work, I found Chase in the living room, seated in front of the computer, just like Will the other day. And same as with his kid brother, Chase was on an airline site, booking a flight to Vegas.

I leaned against the doorframe and asked him what happened at Kyle's place, and still typing on the keyboard, he said, "Nothing, really. He was high, and there was no point in beating his ass."

"Oh," I said, surprised, and, to be honest, proud of my man.

For as much as I don't like Kyle Tanner, I was still relieved Chase refrained from harming him.

"That just proves how far you've come," I told him.

Oddly, he rolled his eyes and made a scoffing noise. And then he finished booking his ticket—a red-eye departing at four in the morning, several hours from now. But Chase plans to leave for the airport tonight, so he can sleep for a while in the boarding area. That's why he's rushing around now trying to pack.

I step in front of the bed and block Chase's access to the suitcase.

"Kay," he mutters, scrubbing a hand down his face in frustration, "I know you want to come with me, but this situation is too crazy. I don't know what Will's plans are, not specifically. I have no idea of the kind of people he might try to contact." He sighs. "I just can't drag you into something unknown. I love you too much, and it's safer if you stay here."

Chase is set on intercepting Will before his bus arrives in Vegas sometime tomorrow, which is fine. I wholeheartedly agree that his plan is a good one. But I don't want him doing this alone. What if he gets in some kind of trouble while he's trying to stop Will? The overlap of the time Chase's plane arrives in Vegas and the estimated time Will's bus is due to come in is cutting it close. There's a good chance Chase will miss his brother. And, like Chase mentioned, who knows whom Will may try to contact. Who knows where he'll even go. Maybe Will will just head home, to his mother and Greg's house, but then again, maybe not.

Will might go to Cassie's house, or somewhere else entirely. Lord knows what he'll do if he's that dead set on stopping Paul. And if Will involves some shady people in his quest, Chase may very well need me. I'm often the voice of reason; I can keep him calm. Will may need saving, but Chase has been known to need saving, too.

"Chase," I begin, switching tactics, "I told you just today that I'll always be here for you. And now that you need me more than ever, you're pushing me away."

Chase's expression is pained when he turns to me.

"It's not that I don't want you with me out there. I do, Kay. Trust me, I do." He shakes his head. "But there's a good chance things will turn dangerous." His tortured blues bore into me, like he's trying to sear into my brain how important his next words are. "And, baby girl, I made a promise to myself a while ago that I will *never* let my life choices adversely affect you."

"And you think by my staying here, I'll be safe?"

He nods.

I counter with, "There are no guarantees, Chase. Look at what happened to Missy."

It's a lame argument, but it has some merit.

Chase doesn't buy it, though. "Sure, anything can happen. But you'll be safer here than in Vegas. And that's all that matters."

I raise an eyebrow, much like he often does. "So, where does that leave you?"

Chase's eyes tell me everything he won't say out loud. And, frankly, that terrifies me. Because it's clear Chase doesn't care what happens to him. He would die for his brother.

CHAPTER NINETEEN
CHASE

Kay just doesn't get it. I can't take her to Vegas with me. I want to—God, do I want her by my side—but I foresee nothing but trouble, dangerous trouble, trouble that could quickly turn deadly.

So how can I, in good conscience, turn a blind eye and let Kay walk into that kind of mess?

I mean, let's assess the situation…

We'll have my brother tracking down Paul, toting around an illegally obtained firearm, and possibly using that firearm to keep his girlfriend from harm. And then there's the FUBAR situation these circumstances promise to become when my mother and Greg return on Friday from their comfy little cruise down in Mexico. But most important, Kay can't come with me because who knows what kind of shit I may have to do to keep everyone safe, particularly my mixed-up brother.

So I turn away from Kay and supply the answer to her question regarding my well-being. "My priority is to keep *you* safe. Don't worry about me. I'll be fine."

I may not, but I don't dare voice my suspicion.

I resume throwing clothes into the open suitcase on the

bed, and from behind me, I hear Kay say, "But I do worry, Chase. How can I not?"

When I refuse to turn around, only because I am striving to remain resolute in my decision, she threatens, "Maybe I'll just buy a ticket on my own. I have a credit card, you know?"

"You told me you only use it for emergencies," I snap.

"And this doesn't qualify?" she asks, incredulous.

I stop throwing clothes into the suitcase, pause with a T-shirt in my grasp. Kay is determined, and there's a good chance she'll follow through on what she's proposing to do. It's clear to me that she is not going to back off unless I take drastic action.

Unfortunately, I know what it's going to take to subdue Kay. I don't like it. It's going to require me to do something I absolutely do not want to do—push her away. And there's only one surefire way to accomplish that goal—by divulging the secrets I've been keeping from her for the past few weeks.

Stoic, I remain turned away from Kay. I stare down at the T-shirt in my hand, and say slowly, "What if I told you I've been keeping things from you?"

"I suspected as much," she whispers.

I venture a quick glance over my shoulder. The color has drained from her cheeks, and I fucking hate that I'm the one causing that reaction.

I avert my eyes when she asks, "So, what kinds of things have you been keeping from me?"

"I've wanted to come clean with you for a while now," I reply, avoiding the immediate question as well as her gaze.

"What's been stopping you?"

I drop the shirt onto the bed and turn around completely to face her.

There are tears brimming in her eyes, threatening to overflow. *Shit.*

Undeterred, though, I say, "Maybe I've been fooling myself, Kay, thinking I'm becoming a better person. But what if the man I've been striving to be just isn't me?"

"What are you saying?" she whispers, like that's all she's got now in the volume department.

"I'm saying that I haven't changed all that much. Secrets have always been a part of my life. And nothing is any different. When it comes right down to it, you can believe what you want, but I'm still the same man I've always been, baby."

"I love the man you are, Chase."

Her words slaughter my heart with their raw truthfulness.

She continues, gutting me a little more with each syllable. "And you have changed, a lot, in ways that matter. You're better, you're good, and you're—"

"No," I interrupt sharply.

I can't listen to Kay singing my praises, which are undeserved, especially when I'm trying to push her away.

Still, I soften a bit when my eyes meet hers. "I'm not anything close to good," I whisper.

I take a step toward her, but I make myself stop.

Kay's eyes urge me to keep going. *Don't stop now*, they plead. *Come to me.*

However, I don't move.

If I go to Kay, I will take her in my arms, and my resolve will crumble. I need to stay strong, because staying strong means staying distant. And distance is my goal. I need emotional distance so I can do what I have to do. And I need geographic distance, meaning Kay needs to remain in Harmony Creek while I fly out to deal with the impending shitstorm in Vegas.

With all that in mind, I stand firm. My girl's face falls, and I clear my throat.

"What?" she snaps. "Just tell me and get it over with. Tell me what you've been keeping from me."

She is striving to stay strong, striving to be tough with me. If this situation weren't so heart wrenching, I'd laugh at her fire.

"Okay." I nod. "So...the day I went to Kyle's, when I first warned him to stay away from Will, to quit selling him drugs. Well, that request came with a price."

"What kind of price?" Her voice cracks, and the fire she had thirty seconds ago flickers out.

"He asked me to fuck up some addict who owed him money."

Her eyes widen. "*That's* what happened to your hand that night."

I nod, but I don't tell her that I didn't annihilate the guy. I hit him once, sure, but not in a way that would've resulted in the damage my hand sustained. That shit came from hitting the fucking bricks.

From Kay's expression, though, I know she thinks the worst.

Good, that's what I want.

"That's not all," I add, preparing to reveal my other secret.

"There's more?" she replies, her tone weary.

"There's more," I confirm. "Haven't you even once been curious as to why Doug Wilson never looked you up like he was supposed to?"

"Chase"—tears form in her eyes—"what did you do?"

I take a deep breath, then, with my words, push her away some more.

"That day…" I falter momentarily. Shit, this is hard on me, too. "That day Cassie called about her stepdad, the day Will first flipped out. Remember how you couldn't get a hold of me?"

"Yeah?" she prompts.

"Well, I had a little meet and greet with your ex-boyfriend. That's why I was so late in coming home, that's why you couldn't reach me. I turned off my phone before I left work to go talk with Doug."

"What'd you say to him?" she wants to know.

"I told him he'd better stay away from you—or else." I hold her gaze. "And let's just say, I made sure he got the message loud and clear."

Again, I let her believe the worst-case scenario by not elaborating. Let her think I kicked that preppy motherfucker's ass up and down fucking Market Street. She doesn't need to know I only intimidated him.

To my surprise, though, Kay responds vehemently…to both my indiscretions.

"I don't care what you did to Doug. And I don't care about some junkie getting his ass kicked." She juts out her chin, defiant to the end. "Maybe that makes me more like you than you'd like to admit, Chase Gartner."

"No, baby girl." I shake my head. "You are nothing like me."

And that's the point where she chokes back a sob. "It doesn't matter. None of it matters. I can live with what you did, what you may do in the future, but what's *killing* me is that you kept those things from me. We don't keep secrets, Chase, it's not...*us*."

My chest constricts as I take a deep breath, and then I drive the final nail in the coffin. "Kay, I've been living a lie all along, and you don't even see it. Face it: you're good, and I...am not."

"Stop it," she begs, her voice cracking, tears flowing down her cheeks. "Don't say stuff like that. It's not true."

I am the world's biggest dick right now, but I have to ensure Kay remains out of danger. And that, unfortunately, means she needs to stay the fuck away from me.

"You shouldn't want to be with me," I say matter-of-factly.

"But I do want to be with you," she cries. "That's why I said I'd marry you. That's why we're engaged, Chase. Don't tell me that means nothing."

I raise a questioning eyebrow, and that does it.

Her face falls. "You're an ass," she hisses.

My continued silence is the final straw. She narrows her eyes at me, turns, and stomps out of the bedroom, the slamming door punctuating her disgust with me.

The silence that follows is positively deafening. I've succeeded in pushing Kay away, yeah, but at what cost?

EPILOGUE
Lead in to *Just Let Me Love You* (Judge Me Not #3)

KAY

Chase comes down the steps a few minutes following my angry departure from the bedroom. I'm still pissed at him, which is why I'm standing at the front door, contemplating whether I should leave.

My ire lets up a bit, though, when I see the suitcase in his hand. I lean back against the wall by the door, but my eyes can't meet his.

This is really happening. Chase is really doing this. He's truly leaving without me by his side.

I'm still a little surprised he kept those particular secrets from me, but the initial sting has subsided. I knew he was holding stuff back. I didn't press, just allowed myself to believe he had his reasons. It's my fault as much as his that he kept that stuff buried. I should have made him fess up sooner.

But it doesn't really matter, not anymore. I know the truth now. Or rather, I know what he wants me to think is the truth. I know Chase, though. And there's no way those wounds on his hand were caused from hitting a person. He hit something inanimate that night. Of that, I have no doubt. As for what happened with Doug, all I know is that whatever Chase did, it kept my ex away from me. That makes his actions justified in my eyes. Plus, how can I be angry? I did nothing to discourage him from seeking out Doug. Truthfully, I knew in my heart the day I told Chase of Doug's intentions to apologize to me that he would take action. And he did. So I am as culpable as he.

I have to admit, though, when Chase arched his eyebrow at me, questioningly, at the mention of our engagement, I was shocked and hurt. And I'm still bristling. I mean, what the hell did that arched eyebrow mean? That we're not really engaged, or that being engaged means nothing.

Chase nears where I'm standing. He sets his suitcase on the floor. I glance his way. His eyes hold a million apologies. But I know no matter how sorry he is, he is not going to bend. He's not going to take me to Las Vegas with him.

I glance away, and he says softly, "Kay."

I don't respond, but he's not deterred. He comes to me and wraps his arms around me.

"Don't," I snap, twisting away.

"Come on, baby girl," he soothes. "Don't leave it like this."

I resist meeting his blues, but his fingers find my chin, and I have no choice but to look up at him.

His eyes hold nothing but truth, sincerity, and remorse. "I'm sorry, Kay," he says. "I'm sorry I kept secrets. I'm sorry I hurt you."

I cave a little.

"Did you really beat the junkie?"

"What do you think?" he asks.

"No."

"And Doug?"

"Just talked to him."

"I wouldn't have cared if you beat him, not for his sake. But I'm glad you didn't, for yours."

Chase sighs, lowers his hand from my chin. "I don't want to fight anymore, Kay. I'm sorry I mocked our engagement that way. It was shitty. But you know I love you, right? And, if you'll still have me, I still want us to get married."

"We could get married in Vegas," I say slyly.

"Kay…" Chase sighs. "I have to do this alone. You can't come to Vegas, not under these circumstances."

There's hesitation in his voice now, hesitation that wasn't there when we were arguing upstairs. Maybe Chase is second-guessing his decision to leave me behind. Damn, he knows we're better together than we are apart. And he can keep me safe in Vegas, just like I'll keep him grounded.

But before I can say any of this, Chase mutters, "I better go."

There's a short good-bye kiss, a long hug, and then he's gone.

I can't bring myself to watch him drive away, though. It hurts too much.

After he's gone, I walk around downstairs, aimlessly, from room to room. But the emptiness of the house without Chase in it is too much to handle. I head up to the bedroom, where everything still smells like my guy—fresh, soapy, male.

There's an indentation on the bed where the suitcase was. I erase the reminder that Chase is gone by reaching down and smoothing out the covers. Suddenly, I feel exhausted. I lie down on the bed, and when I press my nose to Chase's pillow, I whisper his name.

I roll to my stomach and look up at the wall. Above me hangs the oil pastel of the Eiffel Tower, the sketch Chase drew for me not so very long ago. The drawing is beautiful, and I can't help but smile when I recall the many times Chase and I have talked, laughed, and loved beneath this little piece of Paris.

Paris…

I'm reminded of the evening Chase brought Paris to me, the night of our rooftop picnic at sunset. Everything was so perfect. We feasted on brie spread over pieces of baguette; we drank pink-tinged Kir that matched the sunset that evening. But, best of all, Chase and I made love for the first time that night.

Chase gave me a memory, a beautiful memory, to hold close to my heart. I knew even then that that memory would soothe me in troubled times such as these.

And it does, that memory soothes me now.

My head starts to clear, and get a hold of my lingering wayward emotions. Time to quit lying around, time to quit moping—it's time to take action.

But I'm not exactly sure what I should do.

Rising up to my knees, I glance around.

My cell is on the nightstand. Usually I handle things by myself, or with Chase, but maybe if I talk with someone else, I'll find the direction I seek.

Heck, it's worth a try.

My first impulse is to call Father Maridale, since he's generally a help when I feel uncertain. But I hesitate. Tonight, I feel like speaking with a woman might be more helpful to me.

Decided, and determined, I reach out and grab my cell

from the nightstand. But then I just stare blankly at it. Who can I call—Missy? No, she's dealing with her own things. Sadly, I don't really have any other female friends.

To be honest, though, I know who I'd *like* to speak with. But I am hesitant to call her.

"Oh, what the hell," I say out loud, resolving to do the one thing I never would have imagined myself doing even just a month ago.

I call my mother.

In some inexplicable, weird way it feels right, like my mother and I have progressed to this point, and it's my turn to reach out. Like Father Maridale counseled, I am giving her an opportunity to be here for me.

She's initiated all contact up to this point; she always calls me. She's been great so far too, keeping up with me, warning me about Doug. But this will mark the first time I've taken it upon myself to get in touch with her.

I breathe in deeply. *Let's see how this goes…*

To my delight, my mom sounds genuinely pleased to hear from me. That kind of touches me deep inside. This is the kind of connection I've longed for ever since Mom turned away. Before then, even. I always wanted a real relationship with my mother. After all, she is my flesh and blood. There's a bond there that transcends hurt feelings and past wrongs, no matter how deep they run.

We talk, just small talk. I keep the conversation light, updating her on what we've been doing, like the fair Chase and I took Will and Jared to, our road trip to Pittsburgh, movies we've seen, that sort of thing.

At one point, Mom asks me how work is going, and I

reply, "Actually, I'm pretty much done with the secretary gig. That was just for the summer."

"School doesn't start till September, though," she remarks.

"That's true," I reply, "but the regular secretary, Connie, returns on Monday from her trip. She and her husband were on a cruise."

"Oh, so you have the next three weeks off?"

"Yeah," I confirm. "Father Maridale told me I can still come in and help Connie if I get bored, but there's really no need. I'm sure I'll find things to do around here."

There's a smile in Mom's voice as she states, "Look on the bright side, honey. Think of how much time you and Chase can spend together these next few weeks. You have the rest of August to do things together before you go back to teaching. These dog days of summer are so nice for young couples, lots of end-of-summer events and activities to enjoy."

"Um…"

Mom, misunderstanding my non-reply, says, "Oh, what am I going on about? I'm sure Chase still has to work the rest of the month. Just never mind me, honey."

Chase would still be working through August, but when Father Maridale was told of the latest troubles with Will, he gave Chase the rest of the month off.

Damn. Mom's words resonate, though. How I would love to be planning fun, end-of-summer activities for Chase and me to partake in. But who knows how much of the next few weeks we'll even end up spending together. Chase might be stuck in Vegas for a while.

When I don't immediately respond to my mom, she says, as only moms can do, "Kay, what's wrong?"

I need to talk to someone, and she really is trying, so I confess to her that Chase is gone.

"He's on his way to the airport right now. Chase is flying out to Las Vegas early tomorrow morning to, uh, help his brother. And I don't know how long he'll be gone."

Mom sighs, then says with much kindness, "I'm sorry, Kay."

That prompts me to spill everything that's really happening. Well, almost everything. I leave out my argument with Chase, and I don't dare mention that Will purchased a gun. I do, however, share with my mother that a misguided Will might run into trouble while trying to protect his girlfriend.

My mom is quiet for a few beats, like maybe she's assessing. I conclude she must be good at assessing when she softly says, "You want to go with Chase, don't you?"

"I do," I admit. Why lie?

"So why aren't you with him right now?" she gently prods.

I stifle a sniffle. "He wants to do this alone, Mom. He thinks I'll get caught up in what he terms *a dangerous situation*." I sigh. "This thing with Will, it's, uh, volatile. Besides, Chase told me he needs to do this on his own."

Even though my responses are vague, I expect my mother to do what she's always done—start up with her judgments.

But she does nothing of the sort. Instead of saying something cutting or biting, like I half expect her to, she says, "Honey, don't ever doubt yourself. And don't let Chase doubt you, either. It sounds to me like he might need you with him more than he realizes."

I consider her words and mumble a "maybe."

"Kay," she continues, "sometimes men underestimate what we, as women, can handle. Chase wants to protect you, sure, and that's noble, but maybe he needs you to show him what you're made of. Show him the strong woman I know you are, honey. Show him how *your* strength can actually strengthen him."

"He knows I'm strong," I say softly. "I mean, I think he does."

"*Show* him you are," Mom responds.

"How?" I whisper.

Her answer is simple, but powerful. "Go to him, Kay."

Sage advice from a woman I thought had given up on me, a woman I almost gave up on myself. I feel elated that I've made this call. It was absolutely the right thing to do.

And since I'm ready to keep making the right decisions, I announce, "I am going to go to him. I'll book a ticket and pack as soon as we finish up here."

I hear a smile in Mom's voice as she says, "Then I'd better let you go, sweetie."

"Okay."

But before we disconnect, my mother adds, "Be safe, Kay. And if there's anything you need, anything at all, just call me, okay?"

"I will," I promise, and then I say, "Oh, and Mom..."

"Yes?"

"Thank you."

Two hours later, I am on the turnpike, heading out of Ohio and into Pennsylvania. Another twenty minutes and

I should be arriving at the airport in Pittsburgh. Surely, my presence will surprise the hell out of Chase. I expect he may resist the idea of me going with him at first, like he did back at the house, but I am *not* changing my mind. No matter what he says or does. Nope, I am going to Las Vegas with Chase Gartner. I'm booked on the same flight, and I was even able to book the seat next to him.

There's no going back now.

"Never doubt me," I whisper to myself as I drive.

It's what I'd say to Chase if he were here. Because what he doesn't realize is that danger doesn't frighten me. I've faced a lot, and I've come through okay. Maybe a little roughed up sometimes, but I keep going.

Besides, when it comes right down to it, I'd walk into the fires of hell for Chase. I love him that much. Though I don't think things will come to *that.*

The situation with Chase's brother is bound to be resolved. I just hope it's in a way that everyone comes out safe.

But no matter what happens, one thing is certain: Chase and I are going to overcome this obstacle in the same way we've faced everything else—together.

What will happen in Las Vegas with Chase,
Kay, Will, and Cassie? Find out in the winter of
2014-2015 (December-January).
The story continues in

JUST LET ME LOVE YOU

the third book of the Judge Me Not series.

ACKNOWLEDGMENTS

Thank you to all the bloggers who support my novels, the readers whom I love dearly, and my family and friends, to which I owe so much.

Thank you also to the individuals involved in preparing this novel for publication. Ashley, Beta Reader A, Beta Reader B, the team at Damonza, and Benjamin. Oh, and a huge thank you to Tom.

On a final note, if you, the reader, like *Never Doubt Me*, please consider leaving a review on Amazon, Barnes & Noble, and/or Goodreads. Small indie authors (like myself) rely on word of mouth to get the word out. Thank you!

AUTHOR BIO

S.R. Grey is the bestselling author of *Harbour Falls, Willow Point*, and *Wickingham Way*, all novels in the A Harbour Falls Mystery trilogy/series. She is also the author of New Adult/Contemporary Romance novels *I Stand Before You* and *Never Doubt Me*, books one and two in the Judge Me Not series.

Ms. Grey resides in western Pennsylvania. She has a Bachelor of Science in Business Administration degree, as well as an MBA. Her background is in business, but her passion lies in writing.

Novels slated for publication in 2014 are a brand new New Adult/Contemporary Romance novel, *Inevitable Detour*, and *Just Let Me Love You* (Judge Me Not #3)

When not writing, Ms. Grey can be found reading, traveling, running, or cheering for her hometown sports teams.

Follow S.R.Grey on Twitter for updates and other fun stuff:
https://twitter.com/AuthorSRGrey

Find updates/blog posts on the S.R. Grey Goodreads
Author page:
http://www.goodreads.com/author/show/6433082.S_R_Grey

S.R.Grey Facebook:
http://www.facebook.com/pages/SR-Grey/361159217278943

Author Website:
http://srgrey.webs.com/

Read the first chapter of

HARBOUR FALLS...

CHAPTER 1

Sitting in the idling car in the deserted and rain-drenched parking lot on tiny Cove Beach in Harbour Falls, I absently turned a business card over and over in my hands. Fingertips over smooth, heavy cardstock, with raised, royal-blue printing on one side...

Harbour Falls Realtors
Northern Maine Coastal Properties
Ami Dubois-Hensley
Agent

With an edge of a fingernail free of polish, I traced the outline of the design. It was meant to be a representation of my destination today: a mass of land out there in the churning waters bearing the ominous name of Fade Island. Heavy fogs, quite common in this tucked-away corner of northern Maine, often swallowed up the island—giving the illusion of it "fading" into the sea.

Suddenly the rain intensified without warning. Sheeting off the windshield in thick bands of water, my view of the ink-colored waves crashing along the beach blurred. I leaned forward to turn the wiper control up a notch and caught my refection in the rearview mirror. Wow, this perpetual dampness was really wreaking havoc on my long hair. I smoothed the unruly strands back into place as best as I could and noticed the California sun-kissed highlights, always so evident in my natural honey-brown shade, were already fading. Just like the island in the fog.

I'd only been back a few days, but life as I knew it felt slippery, like it could get away from me if I let my guard down. I adjusted the mirror; uncertainty warred with determination in the hazel eyes—so like my father's—staring back at me. Questions that had haunted me since I'd first decided to return home washed over me anew. *Why had I really come back to Harbour Falls? Just how dangerous could it end up being? Should I turn around and go back...before it turned out to be too late?*

But it was too late. A white SUV had just pulled to a stop and parked in the space to the right of my car. Ami Dubois—or rather Ami Dubois-*Hensley*—opened the driver's side door. As she began to fumble with one of those oversized golf umbrellas, it was clear, despite her seated position and long raincoat, that she was very pregnant. Guess she and Sean Hensley, friends of mine from the past, had decided it was finally time to start a family. Truthfully, it surprised me they'd waited this long.

Five years had passed since I'd last seen Sean and Ami, having attended their wedding in Harbour Falls. At the time we'd all been twenty-two years old and freshly graduated from college—me from Yale, and Sean and Ami from the University of Maine.

How time flew.

A twinge of sorrow tugged at my heart as I recalled how

their wedding was the first major event I'd attended with Julian, a man with whom I ended up spending six years of my life. Of course we'd just been starting out back then. And now it was all over. Back in May we'd decided to go our separate ways. People change over time, sometimes drifting in different directions without ever realizing it. Until it's too late.

Ami's sudden rap on my driver's side window tore me from my ruminations. I yanked at the belt of the black trench coat I was wearing, tightening it, as the thin material of the wrap dress I wore underneath would offer little respite from the cold and rain.

I opened the car door, and Ami, stepping back, smiled warmly and tilted the umbrella so I could slip underneath it. "Maddy, it's been too long. God, how have you been?"

"Good," I replied. "Just trying to adjust to this weather."

Her pale blue eyes scanned down my form. "Well, you look *amazing*. I was so excited when Mayor Fitch…uh, I mean, your dad called and said you were moving back."

Somehow balancing the umbrella in such a way as to keep us dry, she pulled me in for an awkward one-armed hug. Her swollen tummy pressed against my slender frame for a moment, until she drew away.

"It's great to see you too," I said. "But I'm not moving back permanently, you know. It's just for a few months." To keep the conversation from delving into exactly *why* I was back for such a specific amount of time, I motioned to her stomach. "Congratulations, by the way. My dad didn't say anything about—"

"Oh, Maddy, I am *so* excited," Ami interrupted. "Only one more month."

She rubbed her stomach, her hand gliding over the big, clear buttons on her powder-blue raincoat. Standing there—ash-blond hair cascading down her shoulders in big, bouncy curls and a smile as vibrant as ever—Ami radiated happiness.

I'd forgotten how pretty she was, and pregnancy certainly agreed with her. Truly pleased for my once dear friend, I said, "How's Sean? Thrilled, I bet."

"*Very.*"

"Do you know if you're having a boy or a girl?"

"Um, no." Ami hesitated and pressed her lips together. She took an inordinate amount of time to adjust the umbrella to block the swirling winds that were starting to kick up all around us, and added flatly, "We'd rather be surprised."

"Oh," I said slowly, "OK."

An awkward silence ensued, and we both watched as a fast-food wrapper of some sort blew by us. It adhered to the trunk of my car, and Ami reached to snatch it up. "Nice car," she murmured, crumpling the wrapper in her palm and dragging a finger through the beading raindrops. "Sean would love a BMW."

There was something in her tone, something that made me feel self-conscious. Being a best-selling author of several novels allowed me to enjoy perks, such as my burgundy M6, back in Los Angeles. Flashy sports cars were a dime a dozen in California. But I'd forgotten, the people from this part of my life remembered me best as quiet, unassuming Madeleine Fitch—daughter of beloved and low-key widower, Mayor William V. Fitch.

"Thanks," I mumbled as I shifted away, shivering as icy raindrops began to pelt the back of my head.

Ami stuffed the crumpled wrapper in her raincoat pocket and said, "Uh, we should start over to the ferry. Jennifer is expecting us by two." And just like that, everything was back to normal.

Jennifer Weston and her cousin, Brody, owned the only two passenger ferries that operated out of Cove Beach. During the summer, in addition to the usual service, the Westons offered whale-watching excursions, usually for tourists passing through on the much less-traveled route to Canada. Or sometimes folks would venture up from Bar Harbor to explore this quiet little area, since it was relatively close. Not to mention somewhat infamous. But now that we were well into September, there'd be no whale watchers, no curiosity seekers. The ferries would be used strictly as transportation between Harbour Falls and my destination today, Fade Island.

A rocky and rugged landmass, mostly covered in thick, impenetrable forests, the island was located several miles from the mainland. While the eastern half remained untouched wilderness, the western half had seen its share of development over the years. Long ago a tiny fishing village had sprung up near the docks, and several Cotswold-style cottages were built to house the fishermen and their families.

Over time those early settlers dispersed, and the state had the cottages converted into rental properties. When I was growing up in Harbour Falls, it was not uncommon for families to spend at least a part of their summer vacation over on Fade Island. But I'd never been there. Not once. Eventually, as the residents of Harbour Falls expanded their vacation horizons, fewer and fewer people came to the island, and the cottages soon fell into disrepair.

But all that changed a few years back when the state of Maine sold the island to a private party. Almost immediately money poured in. The little fishing town was renovated, giving it a quirky, art deco uplift. The rental cottages were refurbished and made modern but in such a way as to retain their charm.

And a former resident of Harbour Falls—a man named Adam Ward—had a huge home in the style of Frank Lloyd Wright built overlooking the sea on the northern end of the island. Really it was more like a compound, complete with a private dock, a set of garages, even an airfield. It was hard to believe I'd once gone to school with the guy.

I had searched and searched to see if Adam had been the person who'd bought the island. It made sense, with the fancy home and all. But I came up empty-handed. The real estate transaction I culled from public records listed only a limited liability company with a bogus name as the owner. And the bogus name led me back to Harbour Falls Realtors but not to Adam. So the owner wished to remain anonymous. That was fine with me. I was tired of running around in circles.

One thing I knew for certain: Ami, as an agent of Harbour Falls Realtors, handled the business of renting out the cottages to a now-steady stream of wealthy summer vacationers looking for a private retreat. But Ami had no idea, in my case, she was about to rent to someone with a secret reason for wanting to stay on Fade Island.

It wasn't the peace and solitude touted in the online brochure that I sought. Nor did I have a desire to just hang out in a nicely renovated cottage. Not even that picturesque lighthouse depicted on Ami's business card, and located on the far southeastern tip of the island, held any appeal. Many a painter and photographer had traveled to the island to capture the image of the tall, imposing structure that harkened back to days past. Positioned at the end of a rocky peninsula and standing sentry in the shadow of a curved shelf of steep, jutting cliffs, the lighthouse was an artist's dream, even if it was no longer in use. But I wasn't here for that either.

No, I was much more intrigued by something the brochure failed to mention: the huge, private estate overlooking the sea on the *other* end of the island. To be more precise, I was intrigued by the sole occupant of that estate, the former Harbour Falls resident, Adam Ward. In fact, I'd purposely chosen the cottage closest to his home as the one I wished to view.

My father told Ami I needed a quiet place to work through a bad case of writer's block. But that was far from the truth. Only he—and my agent, Katie—knew the real reason behind my wanting to spend these autumn months on a lonely, isolated island. It had *everything* to do with researching the subject matter for my next book and absolutely nothing to do with some silly, made-up case of writer's block.

And my research had begun before I'd even arrived. For example, I knew there were only four year-round residents on Fade Island, as it was not the most hospitable place once the summer faded into fall. Heavy rains and storms were common throughout most of the year, but things became particularly treacherous during the winter months.

Snowstorms and loss of power were not uncommon. And there was no reliable way to get off the island, except for the ferry. But the ferry didn't run when the weather got too crazy. Nothing did, not even the alternative means of transportation—several boats and a corporate jet—that Mr. Ward often employed. During those times Fade Island lived up to its name in another way; it was as if it faded from civilization.

The rain slowed to a fine mist as we approached the ferry, and Ami lowered the umbrella. "So who can I expect to see once we get over there?" I asked and then added, "Like, who lives out there year-round?"

Obviously I was well aware of the identities of the full-time residents. I thought I was being clever, feigning ignorance for Ami's benefit. The less she knew *I* knew, the more likely she'd not question my cover story. Right? Maybe not.

I took one look at her face and wished I'd kept my mouth shut. "You don't know? You've never heard?" She eyed me skeptically. "Surely, your father told you."

I shook my head and looked away. A slender, pale girl with dark hair was messing with some ropes aboard the ferry, so I pretended to be focused on her.

But when I tried to keep on walking, Ami stopped and grabbed my arm. I couldn't meet her gaze, certain she'd catch on to my deception. "Madeleine! You *have* to know Adam Ward lives on the island. It's no secret he moved out there after…" She lowered her voice. "Well, after what happened."

She was right; it was no secret. Back when Adam lived in Harbour Falls, he had everything, the world at his feet. A brilliant mind, he excelled in all things academic. But software engineering was his specialty. He coded and developed elaborate software systems that had every college and university with a computer engineering program vying for his commitment to study at their institution. And since his academic abilities were rivaled only by his athletic prowess, those schools with a football program offered Adam everything they could without attracting the attention of the NCAA. In the end, though, he gave up football and enrolled at MIT.

All those things were impressive, but what had caught my attention back then were his striking good looks. He was tall and had an amazing body, gorgeous jet-black hair, and stunning blue eyes. Yeah, it had been hard not to notice him. And notice him I did. But, sadly, he never seemed to look my way.

"Maddyyyy! Earth to Maddy." Ami waved her hand in front of my face.

"Oh, sorry. I was just...I was just remembering," I stammered, "um, high school."

Ami had once been one of my best friends, and surely she recalled my unrequited interest in Mr. Ward. As if on cue, she smiled knowingly and said, "In case you were maybe wondering, he *is* still single."

I barked out a nervous laugh. "We're not in high school, Ami. I think my crushing days are behind me. Besides..." I trailed off.

She knew why. After all, everyone had heard the rumors.

"They're just unfounded accusations and idle gossip," Ami said in a hushed voice, her defense of Adam surprisingly fervent. "You know that, right?"

"It's really not that." And it wasn't, but I didn't want to explain myself to Ami. "It's just…" I fumbled for an explanation. "I didn't come here to start something with Adam Ward, OK?" *Small lie.*

Ami cast a doubtful glance my way, but before she could persist in her matchmaking attempt, I pointed to the ferry and said, "It's after two. We'd better get going."

The half-hour ride through the choppy waters to Fade Island was mostly silent, Ami and I lost in our own thoughts. Jennifer Weston, the slender, pale girl who'd been messing with the ropes, didn't say anything more to us than she absolutely had to. A number of times when I glanced over at the ferry pilot's house, I caught her glaring at me. But I had no idea why.

Before today I'd never had contact with her. She'd gone to school at Harbour Falls High but graduated a few years before me. Still, I knew who she was. How could I not? Jennifer had been married for two years to my other best friend back in high school, J.T. O'Brien. I hadn't kept in touch with J.T. after leaving Harbour Falls, but I heard a lot about him from my dad. And what he told me wasn't good.

A few years back, J.T. had gotten into trouble with the law—some kind of drug and alcohol charge. After a stint in rehab, he surprised everyone by marrying Jennifer. She'd always had a thing for J.T., but he'd never shown any interest in her. So when they ran off to Vegas for a quickie wedding, nobody could figure out why. My father said there was speculation that she'd gotten knocked up. But nine months came…and went…with no baby.

All of this occurred during the spring and summer before my final year at Yale. At the time I was interning at a publishing house in New York, so I didn't pay too much attention to the updates from home. When I returned to college that fall, I met Julian. And once we were together, I hardly kept up with the Harbour Falls gossip. Following a quick visit back for Ami and Sean's wedding the following summer, Julian and I moved to Los Angeles. I embarked on my writing career, and soon my life was too busy to worry about people from my past. Except for the occasional, short holiday visit home, this whole area had fallen off my radar completely.

Well, maybe not *completely*.

There was one huge Harbour Falls Mystery—as the press had dubbed it—I could not avoid hearing about. The story even dominated the national news for a time. And inevitably, mostly on book tours and during interviews, I was asked for *my* thoughts regarding the case. I imagined people were curious for two reasons. One, I was from Harbour Falls, a primary location involved in the mystery. And two, I was a crime and mystery novelist, and the facts of the case mirrored the kinds of things I wrote about.

Only my cases were purely fictional, so my standard response had always been the same: *I have no interest in real-life cases*. And that had been true. But it no longer was; things were about to change.

The Harbour Falls Mystery was the real reason I was here. I had every intention of basing my next novel on the facts of the case. I was tired of fiction; I wanted to write a true crime novel. Plus there was a little part of me—the detective that lurks in all of us—that dreamed of *solving* this case.

But nobody knew that this case held more than a professional interest for me. Not because the main locale was Harbour Falls, and not because the mystery involved the disappearance of a local I'd once known. And, truth be told, had once envied. Nor was it the fact that this local, Chelsea Hannigan, had gone missing the night before her wedding. Scandalous, though it was.

What piqued my curiosity was the man Chelsea had been on the verge of marrying—Adam Ward. He was the man at the center of the mystery. He was the man whose life had been altered when Chelsea disappeared, after he was named as the number one suspect.

What role, if any, had he played in her disappearance? Though never formally charged, many believed he was far from innocent.

Well I was here to uncover the truth. There was just one small problem.

Contrary to what I'd told Ami, I *was* interested in Adam Ward. Still. Despite how ridiculous I knew it was, I couldn't wait to run into Adam. Would he even remember me? Maybe not. But I wasn't the shy girl I'd been back then.

Of course I was playing with fire. If he ever suspected I was investigating him in order to research my new novel, he'd hardly be pleased. I might even see firsthand just how supposedly dangerous he could be.

At the thought, a little shudder ran through me. Whether it was due to fear, excitement, or both, I wasn't sure. I knew I should analyze it and get my head straight before I ended up in trouble.

But I'd run out of time. Because the fog began to lift, and in the distance, Fade Island came into view.

Printed in Great Britain
by Amazon.co.uk, Ltd.,
Marston Gate.